Jew Boy

by

SIMON BLUMENFELD

LAWRENCE & WISHART
LONDON

Lawrence & Wishart Ltd
39 Museum Street
London WC1A 1LQ

First published by Jonathan Cape 1935
This edition, with Introduction
by Ken Worpole, 1986

Introduction photoset in North Wales by
Derek Doyle & Associates, Mold, Clwyd
Text set by the Alden Press, Oxford
Printed and bound in Great Britain at
The Camelot Press Ltd, Southampton

Introduction
by Ken Worpole

Simon Blumenfeld's influential novel, *Jew Boy*, first published in 1935, is both distant to the modern reader, yet at the same time extraordinarily close. Its significance belongs to that body of knowledge and experience we might term contemporary history. It describes a world still retrievable through living memory; it therefore belongs to the world in which we live. What separates us from the uncertain world of the novel in which Alec gazes fearfully into the future, is that we know what that future turned out to be: an eventual military victory over fascism – but also political defeat. The Jewish East End hardly exists any more, yet the buildings are still there: the Workers' Circle in Alie Street is now a restaurant; the synagogues are now mosques. Where one generation of immigrants tried to start a new life and build a new world, another generation from another continent, facing the same prejudices and discrimination, tries today to do the same.

The very title was an act of cultural defiance, taking a term of abuse and turning it into a badge of honour. That was one of the many new and radicalising qualities of the novel when it was first published. For although one

Jewish writer from the East End, Ashley Smith, had got into print first in 1934 with a collection of short stories, *Children With Fire*, Simon Blumenfeld's novel became the founding work in what developed into a unique school of fiction, autobiography and drama: the literature of the Jewish East End.

This literature could be said to have emerged out of two contrasting trajectories: the first that of the enormous historical burden of dislocation and loss which was the lot of the incoming Jews fleeing from the pogroms of Poland and Russia, the second being that of the new political doctrine of revolutionary historical inevitability that was the organising cement of successive Socialist and Communist Internationals. Both arrived in the same place and at the same time in Stepney and Whitechapel in the first decades of this century. Hope mixed with despair in equal portions, as they do in this novel.

It is easy to sentimentalise the Jewish East End between the wars, and many subsequent reminiscences have done so. Yet there clearly was an almost unique subterranean culture of libraries, political and musical organisations, billiards halls, cafes and education classes that connected to each other in ways that have seemed almost impossible since. For all of the writers and painters of the Jewish East End – Rosenberg, Gertler, Bomberg, Kossoff, Smith, Blumenfeld, Goldman, Mankowitz, Kops, Wesker, Baron, Litvinoff, Piratin, Jacobs, Lipton, Fishman and Hartog – acknowledge again and again the same radicalising and creative influences of the informal gatherings at the Whitechapel Library, the Workers' Circle, the Yiddish Theatre in Commercial Road, the Young Communist League meetings at the junction of Whitechapel Road and

Vallance Road, and so on. Politics, then, had not separated itself off from everyday life. The joke which Alec and Dave share about the ageing actor Kessler still playing juvenile leads at the Yiddish Theatre in his late fifties is just one of many shared cultural references that pervades Blumenfeld's work, and that of all the other writers too. We have to think about the intensity of the cultural life of Jewish East End in the same way that we think about that of the Harlem Renaissance. (And the two are not entirely without their connections; Alec's desire to travel to Moscow is abetted by his knowledge that Claude McKay and Langston Hughes have already made that journey.)

Jew Boy also suggests different tensions. For Alec, though being drawn towards the Communist Party, is in other respects looking for ways out. What gives the novel much of its emotional tension is the struggle against the stifling repression of adolescent sexuality and the acute personal distress created by a culture preoccupied with early – and respectable – marriage. The accounts of Alec's courtship of Sarah, and his later relationship with Olive, are both fully realised and genuinely affecting. As Alec's father continued to remind him, 'Love is not a potato.' Yet also here we encounter two of the most significant generic conventions of the 'English working-class novel' since its re-emergence in the 1930s: prostitution as the only possibility of working-class women's economic independence, and the dominant fear of unwanted pregnancy in sexual relationships, culminating usually in a traumatic abortion scene, an essential set-piece in the novels of this period.

Alec's trade union involvement is a rather less well

realised strand of the novel, although the portrait of the low-wage labour and seasonal unemployment in the clothing trade is more convincing. By the end of the novel Alec has moved to Hackney – the first step 'out of the ghetto' – and is living with Olive, a 'shiksa'. Alec feels he actually belongs nowhere, comparing himself to Eugene O'Neill's haunted proletarian stoker, the 'Hairy Ape', one of the most influential literary creations of the first half of this century. Belonging, or 'coming home', is finally represented in joining the Communist movement, and *Jew Boy* ends on a note of revolutionary triumphalism, of marching feet and scarlet banners streaming in the wind. Few would now argue that this option is available to the contemporary political writer – or reader for that matter. Possibly the most affirmative writing today is being produced as a result of other cultural imperatives, particularly those of feminism and the struggle for identity in the more recent immigrant communities. *Jew Boy* is in many ways a significant precursor of these more recent radical literary movements.

Simon Blumenfeld went on to write three more novels, *Phineas Kahn* (1937), *Doctor of the Lost* (1938) and *They Won't Let You Live* (1939), none of them having quite the same impact as the influential *Jew Boy*. There were no more novels after this brief and intensive period of writing, and Blumenfeld turned his attention towards journalism and the theatre. He was co-opted for a spell on to the editorial board of *Left Review* and was one of the founders, along with actor André van Gyseghem, of the Rebel Players in Manningtree Street, Gardiner's Corner, in East London. This later became Unity Theatre in King's Cross, for which he wrote *Newsboy* and *Enough of All This*, the latter a play about rent strikes, and where he also worked with Tommy Thomas in the Workers' Theatre Movement. After early war service in the army and later as script editor in the Central Pool of Artists, Blumenfeld went on to editorial jobs on the prestigious Norman Kark publications (*Courier, Bandwagon* and *Today*) and from there to a theatrical magazine, where he continues to work to this day. He is currently writing a biography of his close friend, the singular Stepney Communist Sam Berks, as well as working on his own autobiography.

Jew Boy reminds us of a world that has been lost. Yet it is in the nature of such vibrant – and mostly urban – cultures that they arise under specific historical conditions and cannot sustain themselves for more than one or two generations beyond the conditions of their appearance. Trying to keep alive by artifice a culture or a social movement that has outlived the specific conditions of its formation is only achieved at the expense of overlooking what new cultural formations are struggling to be born elsewhere. Each new generation has to create its own specific geographies of culture, and develop the appropriate new forms. What in *Jew Boy* was envisaged as likely to be a short, but decisive, struggle to change the world, is now more likely to be regarded as a long march. Good writers produce good maps. That is why *Jew Boy* remains important to us today.

April 1986
London

CHAPTER I

His mother stood over him, and shook him. Alec sat up in bed and looked at her sleepily. She was furiously angry.

'Twenty to eight!' she shrieked in his ear. 'Twenty to eight! What time d'you expect to get to the workshop, you lazy swine?'

'Awright . . .' he grumbled, yawning and scratching his head as he unbuttoned his pyjama jacket. 'Right away, ma. I'm getting up right away.'

The door shut behind him. He threw off the bedclothes mechanically and sat on the edge of the bed, his eyes half shut, half dozing, resting his toes on the prickly raffia mat. He stretched out his arms, and lowered himself back on the bed . . . Ah! This was lovely! Lovely! So quiet. Even if he hadn't heard the door slam, he'd have known she was gone. While she was in the room, even if she didn't talk, he had the feeling of being noisily knocked about; now she wasn't there, everything was peaceful and quiet . . . Ah! Just another five minutes . . . Count up to a hundred . . . one . . . two . . . three . . .

There was a sharp banging on the wall.

'Well, are you getting up? . . . can't hear you yet!'

He shook himself, and sat up again. Must get up now. Work. Work. Nearly eight! . . . No joke! I'll have to hurry. Jesus! I've got to look sharp! . . . He threw a shoe heavily on the floor to show he was really out of bed, and hastily dressed himself.

His mother ran down the narrow staircase. He was getting up at last, the lazy swine! Doing the whole world a favour because he went to work. Who could he take after? Not her! She was up every morning regular before seven—and not after Jacob either. A pity Jacob wasn't alive now to see his wonderful son, her breadwinner, still stinking in bed at twenty to eight!

She heard him go into the scullery to wash, and she poured out his tea in the kitchen, shouting violently all the while! The same bloody aggravation every morning! The boy had no life in him at all. Wanted some gunpowder up his backside! Twenty-three! Old enough to have a wife and kids of his own. No responsibility to pull him out of bed. She did all the worrying, and he snored like a pig. If she let him sleep, he'd wake up about twelve. Lucky he had a mother, just to get him to work on time.

Alec didn't trouble much about washing. He'd get filthy anyhow in the workshop. He just rinsed his face, and behind his ears; his hair he combed flat back from his forehead. And she was still screaming. Every morning the same performance. Every morning. If something really terrible happened, she couldn't make a bigger fuss. Say they brought him home dead one day, smashed to pulp by a lorry, what then? She would only scream, kick up exactly the same sort of row. Scream and scream, just like this, when he was a couple of minutes late for work.

He gulped down his tea. Luckily, the workshop was not very far away. Five minutes after leaving the house, he was already putting on the coarse cloth apron that protected the waistband of his trousers.

The boss looked at him, his big shears poised in the air. Then he looked at the clock. It was a few minutes past eight. His glance went back to Alec for a moment, and held his eyes challengingly. Then he bent his head, and gave his attention to the pocket flaps in front of him.

'So the clock's fast again this morning,' he murmured to the flaps.

'Only a few minutes,' said Alec.

'But it's not fast when it's time to knock off, eh?'

He looked up and his little bloodshot eyes rested sarcastically on Alec. He had him there. Alec was always the first to knock off. Round about seven, his eyes were always on the clock, and he grumbled if he had to stay a couple of minutes to finish something off. Well, then, if every minute was so precious, let him come to time in the morning!

Alec almost retorted that the boss wasn't so particular about a few minutes himself. When it came to knocking off, the clock mightn't be there at all, he had a sort of grudge against it. He always had to be reminded. 'Seven o'clock, guvnor. Go now? . . .' And the boss would look up reluctantly. Seven! So it was! He was surprised. He didn't think it could be so late. 'Yes. Yes, of course. Knock off. Knock off.' As if Alec and the whole workshop didn't know that he messed about with the clock sometimes too. He would glance at his watch towards the end of the day, and discover that the clock had gained a few minutes, and put the hands back. But it never gained time in the morning. Never. Alec felt like pointing that out to him, but it was hardly worth while starting a row first thing. Let him get away with it. He'd tell him a thing or two later in the day. He bent down and picked up a coat from the floor, and started work.

There was a short break at ten. Alec sent out the apprentice for a jug of tea and a slice of bread and butter from the Italian's, and when it came, he stopped a few minutes to have his breakfast. The other hands worked on steadily as they ate. A bite, a few stitches, another bite, a few more stitches. They kept looking apprehensively at the clock. The boss didn't encourage lingering over meals.

'After all,' he said once, 'I really don't have to allow you any time at all for breakfast.' He pointed to the yellowy fly-specked 'Board of Trade' poster pasted on the wall. 'From eight till one, and two till seven. Only an hour's break for dinner, that's all I'm supposed to give you. If I allow you a little time for breakfast, it's because I'm not a hard man, but I don't want you to take liberties because I'm a bit easy going. Now I want you to understand that, that's all.'

So, at a quarter past, there had to be no sign of lunch papers, and the way was clear for a straight run, non-stop, until one o'clock. Then, blessed hour, would come sixty minutes for dinner.

A dozen automata bent over the garments, sewing, machining, pressing, at top speed. Speed! Speed!

That was the keynote. No time even to wipe your nose, the coats must be kept flying about the workshop, on the move all the while. Speed! Speed! The quickest worker set the pace.

The machinist ran down a couple of seams and threw them to the presser to be pressed open. The presser soaped the seams, clumped the hot iron over them till they were glued down flat, then threw them at the machinist's feet. Without taking his eyes off the work before him, the machinist leaned sideways, scooped up the garments with his free hand, and put them on the table. Snip, snip. A piece of silesia barbered into shape became a breast pocket. Over to the presser. Over to the tailor to baist in canvas stiffening. Back to the machinist, the presser, the girls, the boss. Round and round, and round again, till Harry, the apprentice, got busy with his bodkin, and pulled out the baistings for the last time.

Then the garments said good-bye to the dusty floor, where they'd been knocked about for days, where they'd been trodden on, spat on, thrown about like rags, and graduated to wooden hangers, from which they were suspended on a shiny rail, high up. High up in a place of honour.

But they wouldn't stay there for long. Telephone calls would come through. The cutters at the other end swore angrily . . . 'Isn't it time that bloody coat was sent in?' . . . 'Customer's leaving town to-night.' . . . 'Call yourself a bloody tailor?' . . .

And the boss would wave his hand at the telephone, and make excuses and say 'Yes, sir . . . yes sir,' abjectly, cringingly, and his face would grow redder and redder, until at last, they'd ring off. Then he'd rush over to the coats, bursting with anger — God help anyone who got in his way — snatch them from the rail, and brush them violently with a coarse bristle brush, tearing out the cotton ends savagely with his teeth.

Then the apprentice would go through it.

'Come on, Harry. Ain't you ready yet? . . . Don't go to sleep on the way, they're waiting for 'em. Here's your fare money, now sharp's the word!'

And the coats were bundled into a big black wrapper, securely pinned in, and hoisted on to Harry's shoulder. The boy was glad to get out of the workshop. He started to whistle the moment he got into the street. He stopped to watch children playing gleefully in the gutters.

Holiday! To Harry this was an eagerly awaited hour's holiday. Half an hour's journey to the smart city shops, half an hour back again to the stinking work-room, with the steam and the sweat and the boss shouting like a madman. He wished now he were back in school again. To go whooping about the playground like a wild Indian, without a care in the world. He'd imagined work was exciting and adventurous from the stories of the older boys, the street corner gallants, and his father had paid ten pounds to have him apprenticed properly to the boss. But how could he ever be expected to learn the trade if he always had to rush off to the city? He wouldn't mind staying in the work-shop if the work were interesting, or the boss took pains to teach him; but it was only swearing and shouting, soaping seams, pulling out baistings and running niggly little errands all day long. So he was glad when he had the chance to escape, if only for an hour. Glad to be sent anywhere so long as it was away from the workshop. Go be apprenticed. Become a tailor. Make coats for gentlemen.

... WE ARE PROUD TO OFFER THESE BEAUTIFUL WORSTEDS TO THE PUBLIC. FIVE AND A HALF GUINEAS THE SUIT. PRODUCED UNDER HYGIENIC CONDITIONS BY SKILLED CRAFTSMEN IN OUR OWN WORKROOMS

Hygienic conditions! Own workrooms! Little Harry could tell the public some stories about that. Hygienic conditions. What ho she bumps!

CHAPTER II

'Why do your eyes burn?
Whence are you fleeing?
Let me go, I may not tarry
On my soul you must believe me . . .'

Janey, the chief tailoress, sang softly in Yiddish. Love songs from the Polish ghettos. Tears glistened in her eyes. Songs of love; only love. They made her feel so funny, soft and mushy inside, and the roots of her nose were stuffed up with tears.

After all, she was no chicken. Thirty-seven; even to herself she refused to admit five more years, and still unmarried. They could keep their sheikhs, their tall handsome heroes. If only a cheap little tailor, even if he were bald, and wore spectacles, and couldn't talk English properly, asked her, she'd say 'Yes'. And jump for joy. And not sing these sloppy sentimental songs any more. A man. A man. Anybody, so long as he got her out of the lousy workshop.

The presser struggled with a coat, cursing silently. At last, unable to make it set right, he tore it from the sleeve board and threw it angrily at Janey's feet.

'I'm a presser,' he growled, 'not a magician. Look at the way you've baisted those armholes!'

Janey picked up the coat and examined it. Disdainfully, she threw it back to the presser.

'It's not my fault,' she said tartly. 'It's the machinist. Notice how the sleeves are sewn in.'

The machine stopped suddenly. Max jumped up, excited from his stool . . . 'What! . . . What!' He pounced on the coat, peering closely at the sleeves, stretching the seam with his long, bony fingers. Then he held the garment at arm's length in front of him.

'These sleeves bad?' he shouted towards the boss. 'What! These sleeves are badly sewn in? Look at the way they hang. I ask you, guv'nor, look at them. Perfect! Perfect!'

The boss was silent. He didn't want to interfere, not if he could help it. He hated rowing between workers, it clogged the run of the work, it was a free entertainment, made the girls drop their jobs and look up to see what was happening; besides, he was the only one he liked to hear shout in the workshop. Max took it that the boss agreed with him. He turned to Janey and flung the coat under her stool.

'There!' he said, 'Don't blame me for your rotten work, you dried up old nanny-goat!'

Janey glared. Dried-up old nanny-goat. Really, that wasn't so bad. She expected worse when Max lost his temper, though he never meant what he said. Nanny-goat, that was nothing, she could forget that, but dried-up *was* an insult. And old! Old! She might be eighty, the way they all carried on. As if it were a crime to be thirty-seven and still single. Maybe she didn't want to get married; maybe she was too sensible; maybe she wanted to have a good time first. If Max and the presser were specimens of men, it wasn't any wonder she preferred to stay as she did . . . But that wasn't true. She didn't really feel that way, and they all knew it and if anything went wrong, that was the sure way to hurt her. But she wouldn't be dumb. Oh, no! She'd answer back, insult for insult.

'I may be a nanny-goat,' she snapped, 'but I do know my work. You should ask the apprentice to sew the sleeves in for you, if you can't do them yourself. Four-eyes! Get another pair of glasses!'

She couldn't bear to throw him back 'old' or 'dried-up'. It hurt her even to think of those terrible words. Max was a wicked swine, he had no pity. She was sorry now that she hadn't called him something stronger.

Max snorted with disgust and went back to the machine. What was the use of wasting time with her! He was piecework, and while he argued he was losing money. Besides, he knew he was in the right, though he hadn't meant to insult her that way. The words slipped out, almost by themselves. One of these days his tongue would get him into trouble . . . but not sewn in straight! As if he were a learner at the machine! Why, the scraggy little whore, if she slept at night instead of prowling round Piccadilly, she might be able to do her work better.

Again the machine jumped forward, roaring angrily, a loud, jerky burr-burr. Janey was forgotten. No time now for private quarrels. He had a wife and four children to feed from this treadle, these bobbins, these jumbled reels of coloured cotton.

The boss went over to Janey and looked closely at

the coat. He put it in her lap, and showed her what to alter. It was the machinist's fault after all, but Janey could put it right with a couple of stitches. Janey. It was always Janey. She was the only reliable one. Max took offence so quickly. He might put on his hat and coat and run off in the middle of the whole damn' rush, and good machinists were hard to find. He whispered soothingly in her ear, and squeezed her arm gently.

Janey looked up at the boss, then shrugged her shoulders grudgingly. Oh, all right! There was still a whole lot she owed Max, but she'd be a lady, she wouldn't say anything. Let him choke, the long skinny bastard!

She fastened on the coat like a dog worrying a dead rabbit. A few sharp tugs, a couple of stitches. There, that was better. That was a sleeve! Over to the presser. Over to the tailor, the buttonhole-hand, the finishers, the apprentice, the boss, the long shining rail. Round and round again — the dip filled in with a gurgle. The work impetus, whole again, rushed along, full circle, strongly, without a break until the clock struck one.

They were back again, nearly all of them, bunched outside the street door, a few minutes before two. Janey and the finishers were discussing a new show. Max and the presser looked over the same *4th Star*. It was a serious problem that was agitating them. What was going to win the big race?

Max kept jabbing his finger at a horse.

'That's the one, I tell you . . . that's the one! Look at his form. Nowhere. Second. First. First. Over the same distance, beat Pomfrey, Galloper Smith, Harcoart. It's easy money, I tell you. He'll walk it!'

The presser shook his head. 'Carrying too much. Top weight.'

He pulled a *News Chronicle* from his pocket. 'Captain Heath naps Somertown. So does the *Sporting Life*, so does the *Evening Standard*. I'm doing Somertown. You do whatever you fancy.' He looked at his watch. 'Well, there ain't much time. Now make up your mind, and give me the money quick!'

Alec came up with the apprentice. Harry was munching an apple. Now the quota was complete. The whole factory was assembled outside, waiting for the dictator of its destiny to finish his lunch. Suddenly the latch grated and the door opened. The boss's broad back disappeared down the passage. Alec waited by the door while the others trickled inside. It was still a minute or so to two. A matter of principle to stay outside to the very last second. The apprentice near him gobbled at his apple. The time came to go back, before he had a chance to look round, but he'd finish his apple anyway before he went in. He rotated the fruit with both hands in front of his mouth pecking at it with sharp little bites, while juice and saliva ran dripping round his jacket.

A steam hooter from the docks gave a sharp hoarse shriek. Two o'clock! Time's up!

Alec passed down the passage taking off his coat as he walked, and the apprentice followed, wiping his sticky fingers on a dirty handkerchief. A few minutes, and everybody had settled down. Loose ends were gathered together. A few indolent turns and the wheels started revolving again at full speed. Now, the most tiring part of the day loomed ahead.

'Where's Alec?' asked the boss.

Nobody answered. Nobody seemed to know.

'Where's Alec?' he asked again, louder, looking round the workshop. 'I haven't seen him for about half an hour. Perhaps the chap's not well . . . ALEC!' he shouted, taking a couple of steps towards the yard.

'Hallo,' came a reply from the lavatory.

The boss grinned and breathed a stage sigh of relief.

'Thank Heaven he's all right. He's only having a rest. I was beginning to think that something had happened to him!'

Alec came into the workshop. The boss, all at once, was busy marking buttons. The others seemed absorbed in work, half suppressing grins, but one of the girls smiled up at him and winked. So that was it! The big joke! The boss had had to call him out of the lavatory. He'd been the butt of the boss's malicious tongue — and in front of all these workers.

His cheeks reddened as he sat on the table. Worse than prison this was. No time even to relieve yourself. If he were piecework, say, like Max, the boss wouldn't mind him spending a few minutes in the closet, but he was a time hand. Fifteen pence an hour, and every minute in that hour sold absolutely to his lord and master for one and three. What a life! What a life!

He crossed his legs and sewed mechanically. Soon it would be summer. Thank heaven for that! Sunday rambles in the open country. Nice girls. Intelligent people to talk to. He was already climbing hills in the Chilterns. Lovely Bucks! He could almost smell the pine cones. A good job the boss couldn't buy his mind in with the rest of his body, but then, tailors shouldn't have minds. Or if they had, they should be provided with minds that could bear the sight of the same coats being baisted in the same way all day long without getting fed up with everything about them. The boss ought to get a set of Epsilons from Huxley's *Brave New World* — they'd suit him down to the ground and he could get them conditioned so that they shouldn't go to the lavatory more than once a day, and then, only in the evenings, after working hours.

The time dragged on. At last it was nearly seven o'clock. Harry came back from the city with a wrapper full of work. The boss looked over the bundles, handling the work tickets. When could he get through this load? He wasn't Buddha. He didn't have ten pairs of hands. What did they expect, these lousy cutters — miracles? They had a bloody cheek, sending down twice the usual amount of work without any warning and expecting it all done to time! Well, well. No use grousing. Best to make the most of the few jobs while they were here. His eyes would be crawling out looking for 'em soon enough. He'd have to buckle down to it. The staff would have to stay on a little longer.

'Alec,' he said, 'I'm afraid you'll have to work overtime to-night. Lot of specials come in. I want you to help me with the fixing.'

'Sorry,' said Alec. 'Can't stay on to-night. Got to go to a meeting. You should have told me dinner time.'

The boss spread his hands in the air, 'How could I tell you dinner time?' he protested. 'I didn't know myself!'

'Well, I'm very sorry,' said Alec. 'I've got to go.'

It had just turned seven. Alec took off his apron and put it in the drawer with his scissors and yardstick. 'Good night!' he said and was gone.

Work overtime! Wasn't ten hours a day enough? In the slack time, there wasn't even ten hours work a week. The boss didn't study him then, why should he worry about the boss now? He wasn't afraid of the bullet, there were plenty of jobs about. Singer's and all the trimming shop windows were full of bills. Tailors. Tailoresses. Baisters. Finishers. Shop-boys. Everybody was wanted just now, everywhere. But no more backyard workshops for Alec. This was the last. He'd had enough of slaving right under the boss's nose. A day's work made him dog-tired. Too tired to read, think, or do anything properly. His mind was ruined. He was left almost like a cripple, a limp, screwed-out rag.

Unconsciously he had turned towards home. He found himself in Gunham Street, before he recalled the meeting. That was in Cross Road, just the opposite direction, but now he was so near home, he'd pop in for a bite and rush off right away. Then he remembered his mother wouldn't be there. She'd said she was going out, too, and wouldn't be back till late. Still, he could manage quite all right without her, scrounge anything for now, and have a real meal when he got back.

He unlocked the street door and walked through the passage towards the kitchen. A chair grated on the floorboards. There were the sounds of hasty movements and a quick startled whispering as he opened the kitchen door; but it was too late to turn back. He stopped by the door, inside the room.

His mother was standing up facing him, her hair disarranged, her face a mottled purple beneath its thick dusting of powder. On a kitchen chair by the table, sat a man of about fifty or so, staring sheepishly at the floor. He was heavily built with a big fat face and drooping moustachios, like a Don Cossack. His brown suit was well tailored, of good material and his trousers were drawn up at the knees to preserve the crease. But Alec, the tailor, noticed other tell-tale creases, on his broad thighs, where the stuff was bunched up and badly wrinkled, as if a heavy weight had been pressing on it for some time. And it *was* a heavy weight too! His mother must weigh fifteen stone at the least. Fancy holding fifteen stone on your lap! Damned funny! Reminded him of the great Joseph Kessler at the old Pavilion. Kessler, who was fifty and looked sixty and always acted juvenile leads ... Kessler's throaty heart-broken whispering, centre stage, full spotlight and soft music. 'Ich liebe dich. Du bist mein ganzes welt' to the heroine, also fat and fifty, as he twiddled his hat and hung his head in youthful embarrassment.

A pity he was dead! He used to be great fun, that

tragedian. And did this fat cossack act the same way with his mother? Did he also whisper sweet flatteries in her ear? They ought to be talking about their grandchildren, this pair of lovebirds. What could they have to say to each other? Could he tell her she was beautiful? Would he say it with one hand on his heart like the great Joseph to his gallery: 'Rosa, ich liebe dich. Du bist mein ganzes welt!' with muted fiddles in the background, sighing *liebestraume*?

No. It was too funny! An exact counterpart of the Pavilion stage. The very same technique! Bravo, Kessler! *Wunderbar! Wunderbar!* He had to laugh. It was his own mother in this ridiculous position, but it was too damned funny. He couldn't help it, really not. He burst out laughing at the top of his voice.

'What's the matter with you, Alec?' asked his mother in a strangely subdued voice — quite unlike her own.

Acting Lady to his Gentleman, thought Alec, wiping his eyes. Romeo and Juliet the other end of the scale.

'I'm sorry,' he said, 'I didn't mean it. Who's this gentleman . . . my new stepfather?'

The cossack looked up, startled. 'Stepfadder! Vot's dis? Vot are you talking about? I gut vun vife already!'

He rose to his feet, so tall, his head nearly scraped the kitchen ceiling. Alec opened his mouth to reply. He wanted to make some jesting remark like, 'You bad old man!' Now the first surprise was dulled and he'd got over the funny side of it, he was quite prepared to accept the cossack as one of the family. After all, his mother wasn't so very old. He couldn't expect her to live the rest of her life without another man. He had a suspicion she didn't anyhow, but he couldn't remember her bringing a man home before. He was quite ready to apologize for intruding, and to make certain he'd never blunder in on them again.

Before he could say anything, his mother butted in angrily. She wasn't going to make any terms with him. There was no restraint now in her voice. It was loud and sharp and bitter as usual. Not now, the bashful discovered trollop, but the righteous mistress in her own house.

'You keep a civil tongue in your head,' she shouted. 'Mr. Greenberg is a very old friend of mine. I suppose I can invite my own friends to my own house?'

'It's oll right,' broke in the cossack. 'I'm going now.'

'No!' she insisted, turning to him. 'You stay here. You are my guest. If my son doesn't like you he can clear out, the lazy good-for-nothing. A fat lot I get from him, just the same. A lodger would pay me more!'

'I dare say he would,' Alec answered, piqued. 'Perhaps Mr. Greenberg would like to live here. It'd save him a lot of trouble.'

'Perhaps he *is* going to live here,' she retorted.

'Well, I wish him luck,' said Alec. 'I'll go and pack my things.'

He turned to go but she called after him.

'Alec! Alec!'

She was sorry now. After all, she was his mother . . . 'Alec!'

He turned back. 'Well?'

She looked at him, the colour gushing to her face again. She didn't feel motherly towards him any more. He was too grown up and independent and she hardly ever saw him now, only in the mornings and meal times. Yet, she couldn't turn him out this way. It wasn't right. A mother couldn't do a thing like that. She stammered. She hardly knew what to say to him.

Alec understood what she was struggling to tell him. She was in an unenviable position. Suddenly, he felt very sorry for her. There was no more animosity, no more bitterness in his voice.

'It's all right, mother,' he said quietly. 'It isn't your fault. I'm old enough. I should have left home a long time ago.'

'But, Alec,' she protested, weakly. 'Where will you go? Who'll look after you?'

'Don't worry about that,' he replied. 'I've got somewhere to go to. I won't get lost.'

He closed the kitchen door behind him and went up to his room. When he was a kid, if anyone had dared mention a word about his mother, he flew at them like a tiger and made them apologize, even if what they said might be true. It was a natural childish quixotry. His father was always the biggest and cleverest man. Bigger than a policeman, he used to tell the boys. And his mother was the finest and purest woman. But now, for the first time, he'd seen something. Actually, with his own eyes, and it made a difference, all the difference. It was a wrench to part with his mother all the same. Not in the physical sense, but abstractly. He'd tried hard to think of 'mother' as embodying the noblest and purest of emotions, but gradually, bit by bit, the ground was cut from under his feet, and now he had to give her up altogether.

Good-bye, mother! No father. Now no mother. He was a double-breasted orphan. He grinned suddenly, as he folded together his poplin pyjamas. One of his father's axioms had flashed across his mind. 'Lubov nye kartoshka.' How rich and poetic that used to sound in his fruity South Russian. He remembered well his father wagging a thick forefinger in front of his nose, admonishing him gravely with a twinkle in his eyes. 'Lubov nye kartoshka, Alecle' — and he, the ragged little schoolboy, wondering what it meant, until one day he'd translated — 'Love is not a potato.' Words like rich music, and all they meant — 'Love is not a potato.' True! True, my father in heaven, love is not a potato — and don't I know it!

CHAPTER III

DAVE was getting impatient. It was a bit of a job to cajole the girl away from the Serpentine. She wanted to sit on the bench and watch the couples passing by. What was the fun in that? If you picked up a jane in Hyde Park, you didn't want to sit under a lamp with her all night, but what could you do, if she wouldn't move?

At last, Dave managed to persuade her to shift. They moved away from the dirty little lake, where a constant stream of nondescript people strolled casually up and down. White faces popping out of the darkness like fireflies in the lampglow, shining for a few seconds with a hollow reflected light, black gaps of mouths opening, and words and laughter, then disappearing back again into the darkness.

They crossed the trodden sand paths, and jumped low rails bordering the grass plots. Dave knew his way about even in the dark. Olive did too. She wasn't a greenhorn. She'd been in London long enough. But it was funny, all the boys she'd met in Hyde Park sorted out this place. 'I know a nice quiet spot,' and sure enough, they'd bring you here.

It was a big field. The ragged tops of the scattered clumps of trees black against the dark sky. No lights. Not even a moon. Not a soul about. Not a sound, only the soft rustle of the long grass as the wind swept over the ground. A paradise for lovers. Right bang in the middle of the happy hunting ground.

'Well, here we are,' said Dave. 'Let's get a couple of chairs.'

They moved towards a tree. The chairs were there. But a man and woman sat on them. They looked up suspiciously as Dave and Olive came near. Without saying anything, they warned them off. We came here first. We're staying. You two go somewhere else.

And the whole field suddenly became peopled. Wherever there were chairs in the deeper tree-darkness – the same story. Here a harsh cough kept them away. A woman's giggle. A man's voice. A match suddenly, startlingly, crackling into flame, throwing up the sheen of cheap silk stockings, a man cupping a cigarette with his hands, a sudden gush of grey smoke, then darkness again. House Full. Boards up everywhere!

'Looks like we'll have to sit on the grass,' Dave observed.

Olive bent down and felt the grass with her finger tips.

'It's still dampish,' she said. 'I don't want to get pneumonia.'

He took off his raincoat and spread it on the grass. 'It'll be O.K. now,' he said.

They sat down behind a tall tree and were quite still. Somehow there was nothing to say. His arm crept slyly about her waist. She shook him off. He sat quietly beside her, but in a few minutes, she felt his arm round her again. This time she let it stay. It didn't matter anyhow. If it made him happy, let him enjoy himself; she didn't get much of a thrill out of that sort of thing any more. All right for little boys and girls who'd just left school.

'What's the time, she asked. 'I can't stay here all night, you know.'

He struck a match and looked at his watch. 'Ten — I make it.'

'Well, we'd best be going soon,' she said. 'I'm working in a new job. Got to be in early to-night. Eleven, the latest.'

'There's tons of time,' he answered.

He put his hands on her shoulders and pressed her down to the ground. She lay passive, looking up at him and he bent over her, stooping till their lips touched and she felt the hot breath from his nostrils on her face.

Olive sat up with a start. There was a sudden sense of desolation about the field. Mechanically her hands went to the back of her head and she tidied her hair with quick, nervous movements. Something told her it was very late. Much later than she expected. She was a fool to forget herself like this. She stood up.

'What's the time?' she asked anxiously.

Dave looked dubiously at his watch. He put it to his ear. 'Still ten! Damn! The blasted thing's stopped hours ago!' At once she started to walk off hurriedly, and Dave collecting his raincoat followed, brushing his trousers as he walked behind her. She felt bad. She was shivering a little. God! She wasn't half in a mess! A new job too, and she'd promised the missus faithfully — no later than eleven!

The park was practically deserted. Dave stopped a man and asked the time. Nearly twelve. He hurried after Olive. Nearly twelve! She almost ran. What would the missus say? Whatever would she say?

They crossed the Marble Arch into Edgware Road. From there it was quite a walk to the house. One of a dark row of fifty identical, dirty little dwellings. The blinds were drawn in the upstairs rooms. No lights were showing. Dave stopped by the door.

'Here we are,' he said.

He was about to go, but Olive pulled him back again. She felt he ought to wait until she was safe inside. After all, it was his fault she was so late. She started trembling again. Something was going to happen. She knew it. She dreaded having to face the missus. What would Mrs. Bonny say?

'Stay here for a while,' said Olive. 'I'm afraid she won't let me in.'

'Don't be silly,' he answered, pooh-poohing her. 'Ridiculous! She can't turn you out in the street. Say you went to some relatives a long way off, and missed the bus.'

'All right,' she said. 'But promise you'll wait.'

He nodded and crossed the road, and stood in a doorway. He saw her go up the worn stone steps and ring the bell. There was no reply. She rang again, keeping her finger on the button. Still no reply. She looked over to Dave. She was glad she'd made him wait. He motioned with his hand. The knocker. Bang on the knocker.

She lifted up the knocker, and brought it down with a crack. Again! Again! Again! But the house was still silent. The knocker winked at her viciously.

She remembered she'd cleaned it that morning with Brasso, taken such pains to make it shine. She grasped it again, tightly. Damn her! The old cow! She wouldn't make out she couldn't hear. She'd force her to open the door, even if she had to knock here all night and wake the neighbours.

BANG! — BANG! BANG! — BANG!

Nobody could sleep through that staccato din. She wasn't going away till someone opened the door, and they wouldn't get any sleep till they did.

A second floor window was flung open with a screech An angry curl-papered head peered out.

'Who's that!' it snapped.

Olive stepped down to the pavement.

'It's me, Mrs. Bonny — Olive.'

'Well — what d'you want, this time of night?'

'I'm sorry, Mrs. Bonny,' she said. 'I went to some relatives and missed the bus.'

Her heart was banging away like the knocker. In the same breath she knew that it was a rotten excuse and Mrs. Bonny wouldn't believe her. Mrs. Bonny! What a name for such a woman. A savage toothless bitch, especially when she scowled like that, looking downwards.

'Last bus! . . . last bus!' Mrs. Bonny yapped angrily. 'Don't tell *me* that yarn! You've been hanging about with some soldier in the park. Well you can go back to your soldier. I won't let you in . . . so there!'

The window shut with a sharp smack. That was that. The argument was finished so far as Mrs. Bonny was concerned. Olive looked up. The light had gone out again. What did Mrs. Bonny think, she'd go away quietly? Well — she'd made a bloody big mistake! She wasn't going to! She was not a bit nervous any more, only angry. She wasn't going to crawl away with her tail between her legs. She ran up the steps, and started on the door again. Not too loudly. A regular, monotonous tapping, the sort of noise that drives people off their heads if they listen long enough.

The light came on again, in the upstairs room. Mrs. Bonny's head popped out again.

'Are you going away?' she asked threateningly.

'Not till you open the door!' Olive replied.

Mrs. Bonny's head disappeared. Dave saw her stoop down and reach for something. 'Look out, Olive!' he shouted.

Olive pressed against the door, and at that moment the contents of a chamber-pot fell splashing over the pavement.

'Now, you slut, are you going away?' Mrs. Bonny howled triumphantly. 'You can have your filthy rags in the morning.'

Tiny sunken eyes gleamed wildly in the ugly canine face. The head withdrew and the window dropped with a crash. Olive felt weak and sick. All her resistance broke down completely. She walked over to Dave. Whatever was she going to do now?

'Fine mess you've got me into,' she said.

She was overwhelmingly miserable. All of a sudden, she wanted to cry. She was so terribly alone. A bit of dirt blown about the gutters. She fumbled in her bag for her handkerchief and blew her nose. It didn't help, tears filled her eyes, and she started to whimper. Dave tried to comfort her. It wasn't so terrible. He'd see her right. Find her somewhere to sleep for the night and in the morning she'd be able to walk straight into another job. There were plenty of places going round Whitechapel. Reluctantly she dried her eyes. They walked back to Edgware Road and waited for a late bus.

CHAPTER IV

ALEC heard a soft tapping on his shutters, but took no notice. It would soon leave off. He turned uneasily in bed, and settled down again . . . There it was once more. The tapping . . . Somebody must be playing a joke on him. Well, it was a bloody fine joke, half-past one in the morning! Whoever it was, they'd get a piece of his mind if he had to get out of bed.

He sat up. This time, beside the steady tapping, he heard his name. He listened intently. Yes, it was 'Alec' all right. Who could it be this time of night? What was so important it couldn't wait?

He got out of bed reluctantly and slung his jacket over his shoulders. He felt very grouchy — who wouldn't — having to leave a warm comfortable bed at this unearthly hour? Visitors at half-past one! Good job Becky was deaf as well as nearly blind. No other landlady in London would stand for this sort of thing and nobody could blame them either. Quietly, he unbolted the street door, and opening it a little, stuck his head outside.

'So it's you,' he grumbled seeing Dave by the door. 'Well — what d'you want?'

'Let me in,' Dave whispered. 'I've got to see you.'

He followed Alec into his room. He knew he was taking damned liberties bringing the girl here, but he'd promised to find her somewhere to sleep. It was impossible to get her into his house, and he had no money for a room. Alec was a sport, he was sure he'd help him out. He explained quickly. Alec was silent. He seemed to be turning it over in his mind.

'But there's nowhere she can sleep,' he said at last. 'Only the armchair.'

Dave breathed a sigh of relief. What was wrong with the armchair? It wasn't as though she were used to the Ritz or the Waldorf, she could kip anywhere for the night.

'O.K.,' he whispered. 'I'll fetch her in.' He patted Alec on the back, clinching it. 'You're a pal, Alec. A real pal.'

Olive came into the room after Dave. He made a date for the morning and slipped out quietly. Alec shot the bolts behind him, and went into his room. Olive was already settling in the old cane-back armchair. She was waiting for something to happen. If this other chap started any monkey-business she'd let him know a thing or two. She'd had quite enough trouble for one night. She looked pale and tired. Alec felt very sorry for her, she was so alone, like himself, but he was a man. A man could do all sorts of things — and she was a girl, helpless — that made it ten times worse. He made up his mind — it was no use. He couldn't lie comfortably in bed while she racked her bones in the old armchair.

He went to the door and took down his overcoat. He felt a bit ashamed of himself for being so sentimental; he was going to let himself in for a first-class backache, but in heaven they'd tot it down to his account. He crossed over to the armchair, holding the overcoat on his arm. 'Here you get into bed,' he said.

She looked up. 'What?' — she didn't understand him.

'Get into bed — you're tired. It isn't very clean, but it's comfortable.' ,

She demurred. 'No thanks. I'm quite all right as I am. Thanks very much, just the same.'

He leaned over her, and pulled her up from the armchair. 'If you kick up a row,' he said roughly. 'I'll break your bloody neck! Now don't be a fool — go to bed and try and get some sleep.'

He settled down in the armchair and covered himself with his overcoat. He watched Olive take off her dress and shoes and stockings and get into bed in her slip. He'd never seen a woman undress before. It wasn't a bit exciting; or maybe he was too tired. Poor devil! His head drooped forward and he slept.

Soon after six, he heard her get out of bed and fumble for her shoes. His eyes opened and he watched her sleepily. She noticed him without any embarrassment.

'Can I have a wash?' she asked.

Rubbing his eyes, he showed her where the soap was and the jug. The water gurgled thickly into the basin; it seemed to make so much noise that he thought Becky must hear. The girl made her toilet quickly, combed her hair and smoothed her dress. Now she was ready for the new day, bright and cheerful with the sun. Alec led her to the door. Cautiously he unbolted it and looked into the street. No one about.

'O.K. You can go now,' he said.

'Thanks!'

She gave him a quick look of gratitude and slipped out into the street. He stumbled back into his room again and stretched himself. He was stiff all over, his bones ached. He'd expected this to happen — still — it wasn't every night — good job, too! Quarter-past six. Might get another hour or so's sleep. His eyes shut, he felt his way to the bed and tumbled in. Ahhh! One good stretch! His joints cracked luxuriously. He turned on his side and covered himself with the sheet and a new strange warmth. Not like his bed at all. New smells. Sharp woman-smells, like stale, sickly-sweet perspiration. His head burrowed into them deliciously hot, his mind spun a hazy jig-saw dream. Legs, arms, underslip, all jumbled together . . .

The alarm went off with a sudden shock. Half-past seven! He poked his legs over the side of the bed and sat up. He felt as if he'd been awake all the time. He had a throbbing headache like a pulse hammering away in his temples. God! What wouldn't he give for another couple of hours' sleep. Real sleep! He felt like after a drunk. He ducked his head in the basin. The cold water sobered him up a little. That was better. To-night he must go to bed early, have a proper night's rest.

Becky brought down his tea. She said nothing. So she hadn't heard. Even Becky would jib at her lodgers entertaining young women in their rooms. She went out and he heard her shuffling about the kitchen.

CHAPTER V

In the street there was an undercurrent of excitement. It was Thursday. The walls were placarded with posters. MEET AT STEPNEY GREEN. The Jews were going to march to Hyde Park.

Alec was surprised to find the shops closed. Even the shopkeepers had shut up as a protest. Even they were going to march. He'd thought a few would close but not every one. What an example of solidarity! What a lesson for the whole world! These bloody Jews, these murderers, these misers, these money-grabbers were sacrificing the best day of the week. Throwing away trade worth tens, perhaps hundreds of thousands of pounds to march to Hyde Park because other Jews were being ill-treated in Germany.

In the workshop he found the boss also in an exalted mood. 'It's a great thing to be a Jew!' he kept on repeating — 'It's a great thing to be a Jew!'

The boss had seen early in the morning that all the shops were shut and noticed the excited groups gathering at the street corners. His Jewishness came home to him and made him swell with pride, but he didn't let that interfere with the run of the work. Business As Usual. The shopkeepers could close down. They catered for Jews; it was right and proper that they should. He applauded them for it with his whole heart, but HE worked for the City. Gentlemen had to have their suits done to time, otherwise how could they go golfing in the week-end? So he would have to stay in the workshop, but in spirit he would be with the marchers. He sighed. It was a great thing to be a Jew. Yes. Yes; a very great thing!

Bugles sounded shrilly in the street. Army calls. The boss was curious. He unbolted the fire exit and stood by the door. A platoon of Jewish Ex-Servicemen with Union Jacks and medals were marching by. The boss beamed on them — like an octogenarian sending boys to a war. With a broad gesture, he invited the staff to look out and they gathered round him by the door, and he stood in the middle of them, a plump beneficent patron.

A lump came into Alec's throat as he watched them. They looked like heroes as they marched past. With their grim determined faces, they looked as though they were really going to another war, and they felt like it, and were ready to fight. And ready to die, too — but for the wrong thing. Oh, the pity of it, Iago! The pity of it! That one bitter lesson shouldn't be enough!

'Well, now,' said the boss kindly, as the flags disappeared into Whitechapel Road. 'Back to work!' He waved the staff back into their places and bent down to bolt the fire exit. It did his heart good to see all these old soldiers march by. Made him feel strong, too, like a fighter. By God! We'll show these German bastards! They'll find out they're starting with the wrong customers! He drew himself up. He felt as though he'd heard the ram's horn blast on Yom-Kippur night, when the fast was out. A new man, with all last year's sins washed away. Purged and purified. And now, back to work! Time was getting on. A lot of specials were waiting to be sent out.

There was a knock at the back door. The boss bent down and unbolted it again. Old Joseph, a neighbour, also a master tailor, stood outside.

'Aren't you going to Stepney Green?' asked the old man, 'All my people have left. I'm going, too.'

The boss shook his head. 'I wish I *could* go,' he sighed, 'but I've got a load of specials to see to. You're a lucky man, Joseph. Believe me, I'd give anything to be able to go with you.'

He bolted up the fire exit and walked moodily to his table. It was a pity, a great pity, he couldn't go along, too, but he was a responsible man. He was a servant of the public; like an actor, he had to have no feelings, no emotions, outside his job. Laugh, clown, laugh — the show goes on!

He was working up a pathetic little scene in his head. Come to think of it, his was the noblest part, standing chained to the table, while the others were demonstrating on the streets. But in Germany they were worse off. My poor, persecuted brothers! Tears gathered in his eyes. He blinked and looked up for a moment.

Alec opposite him, was taking off his apron. He watched him put it away in his drawer with his other tools.

'What's this?' he asked, looking at him like an astonished owl, 'where are you off to?'

'Stepney Green,' said Alec.

'B-B-but the work! What's going to happen to the work?'

'Pickle it!' said Alec. 'D'you think I'm going to stay here when every workshop in the East End is closed? I'm marching with the others!'

'And since when have you become such a good Jew?' asked the boss angrily.

'Never mind about that,' interrupted Max. The machinist rose from his stool. 'Alec's right for once. How can we sit here quietly and work, when all that excitement's going on outside?'

The boss turned to him.

'But the work . . . the specials!'

The telephone bell whirred angrily. 'There you are!' The boss danced like a cat on hot bricks in his desperation. One finger pointed at the 'phone. He raised his voice above the metallic clamour.

'There you are! I told you. They're ringing up already. What can I say to them?—What excuse can I give them?'

'You don't have to find excuses,' said Alec. 'Tell the truth. Say we're marching to Hyde Park. Say all the East End's demonstrating. Don't be afraid. They ought to respect you for it. Let 'em see we're also men, not a lot of bloody worms.'

The telephone buzzed insistently. There was nothing for it, the boss had to go over. His hands were oozing sweat. He felt terribly hot and cold at the same time. His throat was parched. A drink. Just now he could do with a drink. Lord knows what they were going to say to him . . .

'Hallo,' he said in a husky voice. 'Yes, sir. Yes, sir . . .' He stared stupidly at the telephone while the metallic voice rasped in his ear. He couldn't hear what they were saying — not a word. He was all mixed up. He wanted to tell them about the demonstration, but somehow the words wouldn't come out, they seemed to stick in his throat. The rasping voice ceased. He heard himself say, 'All right.' There was a click the other end. Now he found his tongue. He wanted to shout about the demonstration. The demonstration! But it was too late; the line was cleared. He looked at the earpiece for a couple of seconds, as if he didn't know where it belonged, then he banged it down on the hook.

'You see,' he shouted at Max, 'they must have the coats at once. You can't leave the workshop now, Max. You can't!'

'Can't I?' said Max. He threw on his jacket and walked towards the door. 'Can't I?'

The presser, after a moment, joined him, standing with Alec by the door. The girls got up irresolutely and reached for their coats. It was useless going on without the key men. Besides, if everyone was marching, why shouldn't they? The boss stood in the middle of the workshop, pleading, cajoling, threatening. He spread out his arms despairingly.

'What shall I tell the shops?' he howled plaintively. 'What can I tell the shops?'

'Tell 'em to go to hell!' said Max, 'and to take their darned work with 'em!'

He followed Alec into the yard, and through the passage to the street. The boss's wife heard the tramping of many feet past her kitchen. Something must be wrong. It sounded as though the whole workshop were leaving. She took off her apron when it became quiet, and rushed into the yard.

Through the open door, she saw the boss standing forlornly in the centre of an empty room. A strike? It couldn't be that, or he'd have told her. What else? Some new madness! These workers were always getting fits into their heads. Wasn't as if they were bound to the workshop at all. They were the whole bosses these days. They called the tune. When she was a girl, a workman was a workman and knew his place. Before they let an apprentice hold a needle, he had to run errands, and milk the goats, and do odd jobs for a few years. Then they grew up to appreciate a job. Now every little stinker was treated like a lord; no wonder they got such ideas in their heads. She approached the boss.

'What's wrong?' she asked, alarmed.

'Nothing.' He sat down heavily on a stool. 'Nothing, only they've suddenly become patriots. They're all "froom" Jews, even Janey's gone along. They're going to march to Hyde Park — and who do you think started it all? — Alec!'

'The dirty swine,' she ejaculated, her eyes blazing. 'I told you to get rid of him a long time ago — the dirty, stinking, Bolshevik!'

'Well, he won't play any more of his tricks around here,' said the boss vindictively. 'The minute things slacken up, out he goes. On his bloody neck!'

He banged his podgy fist on the table, so hard that yardstick, scissors and a couple of cotton reels did a little jig in the air, and fell flat with a clatter. He was boiling. He could wring some of their necks, here and now. The telephone rang peremptorily. At once his anger evaporated. He came to earth with a bang. He felt himself sweating again.

'There you are!' he whined to his wife. 'They're after those specials. He waved his arms helplessly at the heaped coats on the floor. 'What am I going to do about all this work?' he muttered thickly.

He dragged his feet to the 'phone. He was fed right up. He couldn't stand any more. If the cutters started on him now, they'd get everything he had on his chest. After all, he was only human, he could stand a lot, but this was too much. He just felt like a row. Let 'em start, that's all! He snatched at the receiver, and clapped it to his ear.

'Hello!' he snapped angrily. 'Hello!'

'Hello!' came a surprised reply from the other end. It was the head cutter. The head cutter himself! Just the right fellow to rub up the wrong way. There was plenty he could say to him, too, but not now. He had his bread and butter to consider. He'd save this up as well; store it all up for the time he'd be able to let go properly – and when he did let go – ! . . . 'Yes, sir,' he answered meekly, 'yes, sir . . .'

He spoke very softly, his meek tone apologizing for the first rude Hello. The cutter at the other end strained his ears. What had come over the man? He'd heard him well enough at first, what was this mumbling supposed to be? 'Speak up, man!' he shouted angrily. 'What's wrong with you? Lost your bloody voice?'

CHAPTER VI

STEPNEY GREEN was packed with people. The main body of the demonstrators lined up six abreast. Onlookers filled up the width of the road and overflowed on to the pavement. The black caps of mounted police bobbed about at the head of the procession.

The Chief Marshal, a little man wearing a straw hat, clambered up the railings — he held a megaphone in one hand, with the other he clung to the railings like a monkey. He held up his megaphone for silence. What a crowd! He was an old market man, he worked with crowds every Sunday in the 'Lane' but he'd never had such an audience in his life before, and he'd never have another like it again. What a mob! What a mob!

'Friends,' he bawled. 'This must be an orderly procession. No singing. No shouting. Just walk along quietly. The police have orders to take in charge anybody attempting to create a disturbance.'

He sank below a surge of heads. Camera-men were busy photographing the organizers, the *Jewish Chronicle* was scribbling shorthand interviews. Marshals dashed about excitedly.

The banner bearers formed up first, immediately behind them, the ex-service men. Marshals went over them suspiciously. Any man who looked like a Communist was challenged. If he admitted his crime, he was cast from the ranks. This was a Jewish March — they didn't want any bloody Communists. But the

Communists were Jews too — they insisted on marching. They formed their own contingents and marched behind the main body.

It took an hour and a quarter to reach Spitalfields, less than a mile away. The pavements were choked with spectators. People stuck out shiny, excited faces from windows overlooking the route, the walls were alive and coloured. Men and women from the pavement hailed friends and relatives, and the ranks were constantly augmented.

The midday sun dodged from the darkish clouds; misty at first, the veil lifted and the sun glared straight down and soon it became uncomfortably hot. Hats came off, jackets, pullovers, and waistcoats. Navvies repairing the tramway, unscrewed a turncock in the road and passed tin tea-mugs of cool water to the perspiring marchers. B———d if they'd like to march on a day like this. Girls too! And old women! They had some spunk in 'em, these sheenies . . . 'Good luck, mates!' they shouted after them, waving them on. 'That's the stuff!'

Straight through Clerkenwell the demonstration crawled, halting every quarter of an hour or so, to let the traffic pass. It seemed as though the East End had emptied itself. Every time a contingent dragged by, the onlookers thought there, that's the lot — but a few minutes later more banners came in sight, a never-ending ribbon of people.

. . . 'Goodness! Who'd have thought there were so many Jews in London?' . . . 'Look at those medals — wouldn't dream they were Jews, would you?' . . .

And mean, tight-lipped whispers. Dark, nodding heads, vicious glances. Alec could guess what *they* were saying, 'Serves 'em bloody well right! We ought to do the same thing here' — Working people too. Like us. Our own proletarian flesh and blood. Why should they hate us so? What have we done to them? We eat, sleep, drink, work like they do, yet that hatred is always underneath, ready at any moment to flare up in that bitter gibe — 'JEW! JEW! BLOODY JEW!' The priests and parsons and Imperialists had done their work well. It would be a tough job reasoning out of their heads, as adults, the lies that had been hammered into them from the cradle.

Alec marched along with the last contingent, with the reds. Pariahs! Double outcasts! Jews and Communists. The rich said 'Damn Jews! They're all Communists, reds — revolutionaries!' and the ignorant befuddled poor said, 'Bloody Jews! They're all rich — they're all millionaires'. So between the two — smacked in the face and kicked in the backside at the same time.

But all that bigotry would crumble away when workers ruled the land. Jews wouldn't be lumped together as financiers and bolsheviks. Nor would they be pointed out like tame zoological specimens by tolerantly superior Anglo-Saxons, 'See here — these are our Jews. They've got black hair, dark skins and long noses, but they're quite harmless. They're different, but they can't help it.' Under the rule of the proletariat Jews would have the same rights as other workers. In Russia, anti-Semitism was a crime. If a wife quarrelled with her husband she called him an anti-Semite, like saying he was a brute or a barbarian.

> Then raise the scarlet standard high;
> Within its shade, we'll live and die . . .

A scandalized marshal came up. 'Don't sing that,' he begged. 'They'll think we're all communists. We don't mind you marching with us so long as you're quiet.'

They pushed the marshal aside contemptuously. They knew what THEY were marching for. Always consistent; their aim was the brotherhood of man. The rich Jews would soon find a compromise with Fascism. So long as their profits were safe, they didn't mind who was in the saddle, but when their fat bellies were hurt, they squeaked, they marched, they shouted; in a year, two years, they'd raise some other red herring. Last time, the Arabs were the villains; now the Germans. But this contingent wasn't being fooled. Their quarrel was not with the German workers or the Arab workers. Their enemies were the bosses, whatever their religion, whatever their language. So they marched along steadily, lifting up their voices, singing more lustily than before:

> 'Though cowards flinch and traitors sneer
> We'll keep the red flag flying here!'

CHAPTER VII

At last, after four and a half hours, Hyde Park. Another thirty thousand Jews waiting there to greet them. Half a dozen platforms were already spouting resolutions. Everywhere, dark, perspiring faces, flaming arguments in English and Yiddish. The Jews had captured Hyde Park; the shield of David might have fluttered from the Marble Arch.

Alec was tired; it had been a gruelling walk, half round London. If it had been an Empire Day parade, or a Lord Mayor's show, a road would have been cleared for their march straight through the City; as it was, the police had given them plenty of exercise. Some of the constables were grumbling themselves. The mounted cops were all right, their horses did all the work, but they had to march beside the demonstration, mile for mile.

'That's the worst of you bloody reds,' complained one policeman, mopping his brow. 'You walk too much!'

Alec elbowed his way to the fringe of the crowd and sat on the grass. He didn't want to listen to the speakers. He knew all the arguments, for and against. Useless to try and get a cup of tea at Lyons with all this mob about. Tea wasn't a white man's drink anyway — so he'd heard a quack doctor say once, in the street — but maybe he wasn't a white man. An oriental. That explained it. Ah! But a nice hot, strong cup of tea!

The sky became slowly overcast as the sun's brightness faded. People moved before him — three-dimensional silhouettes. Foreshortened, tiny bodies on huge legs. Excited cheers from the meetings. All round him, the steady murmur of conversation. Such earnest, weighty probings into insignificant trifles; laughable things. How could grown people waste their minds on such rubbish, when if they looked, they could see the whole structure of civilization tottering about them?

What did it matter if she *did* break off the engagement after all? Or if she wasn't going to have a big wedding? If padded shoulders weren't really smart, or dog-traps didn't work fairly? Who cared? Who the hell cared? Worrying about these absurdities when they trembled on the edge of a volcano. Jews, convenient scapegoats, ready to be sacrificed the moment it was necessary for blood to be spilt . . . *Vuhyoimer ailov, Avrohom! Avrohom! Vuhyoimer, hinneni* . . . And God tempted Abraham and said to him, 'Abraham, Abraham!' and he said, 'Behold, here I am'. And He said, 'Take now thy son, thine only son Isaac, and get thee into the land of Moriah and offer him there for a burnt offering upon one of the mountains which I shall tell thee of . . .' And here were not one, but a sixty thousand Isaacs. A sixty thousand potential burnt offerings!

A pair of grey pinhead trousers stood over him. Tan shoes, square toed, and grey and black chequered socks. A shoe prodded him gently. Alec looked up. An American. He could tell by the cut of the suit. A big fellow, dark, flat nose like a negro, thick lips, curly hair. Yet the face was familiar.

The American smiled. Sam! Sam, of all people! Alec got to his feet and clasped him warmly by the hand.

'When did you come home?' he asked. 'Why didn't you write me? I'd have met you at the station, or the docks!'

'I wanted to surprise you,' said Sam, 'but I came to the Park on the off-chance — I didn't expect to find you, though I guessed you'd be here.'

He hadn't changed very much in the seven years he had been away. The New York sun had tanned his face to bronze, and made him look more than ever 'High Yaller'. The boys always used to chaff him about his negroid features in the old days, and he'd say his mother must have paid a visit to Africa before he was born. Now, with his dark-gold skin, it looked very much like it. His suit was ready-made — a Hart-Schaffner-Marx. Only his suit and his dark skin and the nasal drawl were American. The rest was the old Sam. Perhaps a bit fatter.

'Well,' said Alec, 'what makes a Jew?'

'What should a Jew make?'

They both laughed. 'And how's America?' asked Alec.

'Lousy,' said Sam.

'Bad as that?'

'Worse!'

'Why didn't you come home sooner?'

'Well,' said Sam, 'I figured it out this way. Things were pretty tough in New York, but from what I read in the papers, they weren't too good here either. But they kept getting worse and worse over the other side, till I thought we'd reached bedrock. But we hadn't, they started falling under the bed. Then I quit. I figured that sooner than starve amongst strangers, I'd come home and starve in good company amongst my old pals.'

They walked towards the Serpentine, the dark masses of people thinning out behind them. Only odd couples strolled about in front. It was hardly believable that this was also Hyde Park, also this particular Thursday afternoon. Coming from the fire and excitement of the East End, it was hard to put the rest of the world in proper perspective. To-morrow in the morning papers there would be one blurred photograph of the demonstration and a small paragraph saying ten thousand Jews had marched to Hyde Park.

Sam looked around him with obvious enjoyment. He felt as though he had never left London. Seven years! That was only a dream. This hour was more real and solid than the whole seven years packed together. The direction of the paths, the position of each garbage bin, the railings, he placed them as though he had walked here yesterday. And the air was so mild. It curled round you pleasantly. In New York, the wind was sharp, like a stepmother, tore lumps out of your flesh. No half measures in New York. If you didn't have a pent-house, or an air-conditioned apartment, you were left to fry in summer and freeze in winter. Good old England! Nothing in the whole world like it, after all.

They sat down on a bench and watched the Serpentine in silence. At last Alec spoke. 'One thing I've always wanted to ask you. How did you manage to get into America? All I know is that one day you disappeared, and then I heard you were in New York.'

'Well,' said Sam, 'it's a long story. This was in April 1926. A week or so before the General Strike, I got a boat for Canada. My brother had a good job in New York. I was to write him from Montreal, and he'd smuggle me across the border into the States. Montreal was a lousy little hole after London. I walked round for hours looking for a place where I could flop, but I couldn't see any "apartment vacant" bills anywhere. At last, I asked somebody and he pointed out little "Maison à Louer" notices tucked away in the windows, stacks of them. I didn't know that in Montreal they spoke as much French as English, maybe more. Anyhow, I got a comfortable little room in an apartment house and sent a letter off to my brother. He wrote telling me to hang on until he'd made all arrangements, and enclosed a ten dollar bill to keep me going.'

He paused and lit a cigarette, and tilting up his chin, puffed a cloud of smoke into the air.

'Well,' he continued, 'I had nothing else to do but mooch round the city all day long. I went to the movies once or twice nearly every day, and shared the rest of the time between cheap cafeterias and park benches. When the parks were closed, there was nothing for it but more movies or bed. I usually went to bed early, but that turned out to be as broad as it was long, because I woke up soon after dawn and couldn't sleep any more, so that there was more time than ever on my hands.

'One day I climbed Mount Royal, and the whole city was spread out before me like a little toy village. I tell you, Alec, that's the one thing about Canada I shall never forget.'

Sam was silent for a moment, as if the picture of Montreal were suspended across his mind again, in all its clear-cut glory.

'Then my dough ran out, and I wrote my brother and he sent me another twenty bucks by registered mail. At that time, the one topic in Montreal was the General Strike in England. I used to hang around the newspaper offices and watch the latest bulletins in the windows. There would be a large white sheet stretched taut across the full width of the window while a machine tapped out the messages in big block letters as they flashed through. I hadn't expected to stay in Montreal more than a few days, but there wasn't any word from my brother, so to make my money last out, I moved to the top floor of the apartment house where I shared a sort of dormitory with four others. I used to lecture them on the strike. "There's working men," I used to say, "Guys with guts! Properly organized, not like you mugs. Able to take the reins in their own hands. I shouldn't be at all surprised," says I seriously, as if I had the inside works, "to see all the trades unions set up a workers' government, and run the country themselves!" You should have seen those old men listening, wrinkling their eyebrows, and shaking their long heads in agreement. "By Gar! The boy's right! The kid knows what he's talking about!" They were certain they had the low-down on the situation; after all, wasn't I hot from London? Then the strike fizzled out, and they had a bit of their own back, and razzed me unmercifully.'

'Served you right!' said Alec. 'It's a wonder you didn't get a hiding as well for your cheek!'

Sam grinned. 'Maybe I did. I can't remember now, but the landlord wouldn't allow any rough stuff in his joint. He was an old Scotchman, a Presbyterian, and very honest. Whenever a registered package came for me I always got it intact, although he knew there was money in it. He used to pass the word to a couple of broken down old pro's who used to visit our house — but I wasn't having any, because I didn't know when I might need a few dollars. Then, it must have been about four weeks later, my brother wrote me to go to Niagara Falls, the Canadian side. A couple of his friends would meet me there, and show me the ropes. They would be in a green Buick tourer, and he gave me the number to watch out for. I checked out, and took my bag, with nothing in it but a change of underclothes, and got the train to Niagara. I waited there for two days, but there was no sign of the green Buick. Somehow I'd missed them, and became disheartened. I was only a youngster, about nineteen then; I thought they'd forgotten me, or maybe hadn't troubled.

'All through the day I hung round by the Falls, near the International Bridge. I had a crazy notion to swim across to the other side. I bought a tough plaited rope. The idea was to fix it to a tree, and pay it out as I progressed, trusting to the current to wash me on to the opposite bank. Reconnoitring one of the deep gorges, looking for a suitable spot to start from, I saw a monument. It was to a Cincinnati youth who'd dived in to save a young couple, but had got drowned along with the other two. That put me off. I wasn't hankering for any monuments of that sort.

'But the idea lingered. I thought maybe it would be a better plan to swim across where the river was wider. I took the train to a one-horse burg a little way off. When I walked through Main Street, all the fifty-odd inhabitants came out to have a peek at the stranger. The St. Lawrence at that point was about a mile and a quarter wide. I put my hand in the water and it was ice-cold. Thinking it over, I realized that battling against those treacherous currents, I'd never have the stamina to last that far. There was a canoe near by. I might have taken a chance and stolen it if there was someone with me, but I funked it all by myself. I decided that the best and sanest thing to do would be to get back to Montreal.'

There came a roar of cheering from the distance, as if a host of unseen listeners were ironically applauding.

'The landlord welcomed me back without any surprise, and believe me, that flop-joint seemed like home. I sat down straight away and wrote a letter to my brother, a real scorcher, and asked for more money. The reply he sent made my ears tingle. He called me all the who's-its you can imagine, and then some! His friends had arrived, but owing to some delay had got to Niagara a day late, and just missed me. It was my own fault. I shouldn't have been so impatient. He felt like washing his hands of me, and telling me to get the hell back to England; but a brother's a brother after all, he sent me fifteen bucks as well, and told me to wait, and not be in such a damned hurry, and not to make any mistakes next time, because it was my last chance.

'Two weeks later I got the tip to meet the Buick again. This time it came off as arranged. One of my brother's friends gave me his bridge pass, and they both spent a couple of hours putting me through a sort of rehearsal in case the bridge officials asked any questions. I was from Buffalo. I didn't live there, I worked there. I came from Scranton, Pennsylvania. Scranton because that was a long way off, and they weren't likely to know anything much about that place. If they asked what were the last letters of the alphabet (a favourite trick), I was to say X-Y-ZEE, not X-Y-ZED. I learned it all pat. They gave me forty dollars and wished me luck.

'I stepped on to the bridge and walked towards the United States. I was stopped at the turnstiles. The officials could have smelt I was an emigrant. I was a raw boy, obviously English from my clothes, and very East-Londonish at that. In fact, I took my cap off when I approached them, and rested it on the ledge by the turnstiles when I stopped, with the lining upwards, and there, right in the middle was a white label with ZISSMAN, WHITECHAPEL in bold black lettering! I covered the label with my fist, and pulled myself together. I had enough sense not to try and put on a Yankee accent because I knew that I'd only forget myself in the excitement, and start jawing my usual cockney.

' "Bridge pass?" '

'I fumbled in my pockets, and brought out as if by mistake the Buffalo trolley-car return ticket the boys had given me. I took care the official had a good look at it before I put it back and got out the pass. I hoped that would convince him that I was from Buffalo.'

'But wait a minute,' Alec interjected. 'If your brother's friend gave you his bridge pass, how would he be able to get back himself?'

'Easy!' Sam replied. 'He'd say he lost it. Besides, the car had an American registration number, and in any case, they could see he was a Yank with their eyes shut . . . By this time, about half a dozen other officials had gathered round. There were no automobiles waiting, and I was the only pedestrian. They had nothing else to do, and scented some sport. I couldn't have chosen a worse time to cross.

' "Where you from?" one fired at me.

' "Buffalo."

' "Live there?"

' "No. Work there."

' "What's your home town?"

' "Scranton, Pennsylvania."

' "From the diamond mines, huh?"

'I grinned. "Yeh. Black diamonds!" I still remembered enough geography to know that Pennsylvania was famous for its coal mines. I thanked my lucky stars I'd taken old Goaty's lessons seriously in school, and been an attentive kid.

' "Y'know Latzo?" said one of the officials with a wink to the others.

' "Sure I know Latzo," I answered, "I used to box with him at the club!"

'It was a remarkable coincidence. When the boys told me to mention Scranton, they didn't dream the Bridge officials would link up the name with Pete Latzo, the boxer. He was a Scranton miner and had fought the championship contender only the other day, in Buffalo, and being a bit of a fight fan myself, and having nothing much else to do, I'd read about a dozen different accounts of the fight while I was waiting for the Buick. So when they mentioned Latzo, I felt as if they'd named an old pal. It came out so naturally they didn't know what to say, and in my excitement I elbowed my way past them and they didn't even try to stop me.

'I strolled down the bridge, not daring to look back, expecting any minute a tap on the shoulder and one of those huskies saying "This way, sonny!" But nothing happened. I got to the end of the bridge safely and took the first turning to the right, like the boys told me, and almost fell into a drug store. I bought a pick-me-up, and sat down for a while, and after that I felt lots better.

Later, when I was on the New York train, I learned they'd caught eleven emigrants that same day, and why I didn't make twelve I still can't understand. I must have had a brace of angels hanging on to each arm, but whatever it was, that sure was my lucky day!'

Sam gestured with his open hands. 'Well! Now you've got it. That's how I crossed the border. — And a fat lot of good it did me, after all!'

Then Sam shot questions in his turn. What had happened to Joe, and Morry, and Tony, and Harry? All those old school friends, boys from the same street? Some were married, a couple had moved, one had been drowned in a row-boat accident at the seaside. But things didn't alter much in the East End. In seven years, he'd seen three different buildings put up on the same site in New York. Nobody cared to live too long in one place, but here in London, his father still lived in the house where his children were born. The streets ran as crooked as ever. The same old dirty buildings, camouflaged at the bottom with shiny black and chromium shop fronts, but from the second story up he could recognize the familiar dilapidated brickwork. He had gone away a boy and come back a man. Seven years ago, he had believed in the *Log Cabin to White House* bunk. Seven years in America had knocked all that nonsense out of him. Government of the People, by the People, for the People! Government where dead men voted three times, and citizens were beaten up if they didn't obey the Ward boss. What did he have to travel three thousand miles for? A worker was a worker all over the capitalist world. Fodder for garbage bins. He worked hard, earned profits for the boss, got fired, and had to stand in bread lines.

Alec was surprised to find Sam talking like this. Sam, who had always been so sure of himself, sure that he only had to work hard to make wads of dollars. America had certainly done one thing for him, taught him where he belonged; now he spoke the same language as Alec, looked at things the proper way. This was going to be good! Now he'd have a real companion. Someone with whom he could go places. Lectures, concerts, meetings, whenever anything was doing in town. Good. He'd waited a long time for someone like that.

It was dark and they were still talking. It might have been the tropics. One minute they sat down on the bench, and the next it was dark; at least so it seemed to them. And there were still so many things to talk about. At last they stopped through sheer physical weariness, and sat back mentally exhausted and stared silently at the oily splotches of light on the surface of the water. Alec was parched. And he suddenly remembered he must be tired and hungry too. He looked at his watch. Gone nine! Surely it couldn't be *so* late? But Sam made it that, too, five minutes past nine, and he'd promised to be home early, his first night back.

They got up from the bench. Alec grimaced. He was so stiff, it was painful, putting one leg before the other. What a day it had been! Two hours' sleep, a row with the boss, an eight-mile jaunt, and now Sam back in London. Something to remember for his grandchildren!

They stopped by the Marble Arch tube and Sam left him for a few minutes to visit the closet. Someone bumped into him, going towards the Park. The man turned, made as if to speak and then laughed. It was Dave.

'So it's you,' said Dave, 'and I was just going to apologize. Waiting for a jane?'

'No. Guess what? Sam's back from America!'

Dave whistled. 'Gee! I'd like to see Sammy again, but I've got no time now. I've got a date for nine and it's a quarter past now!'

'The girl from last night?'

Dave shook his head. 'No! This is a jane I met a couple of days ago . . . a beauty!' he grabbed Alec's lapel excitedly, 'and you'll never believe what's happened to Olive — the girl from last night!'

Alec looked at him. Whatever could have happened? He shook his head slowly. He hadn't the faintest idea.

'What?'

'Great news! Our 'daily' broke a leg or something, yesterday. I suppose she was out on the booze, and she sent word she couldn't come. And my old lady was fed up with her just the same, so she put out a bill for a girl, sleep in — and Olive's got the job. Sleep in! What do you think of that, you old atheist, isn't there a good God after all?'

Alec nodded. There was no need to answer. Dave seemed to be able to get away with anything, but one of these days, he'd go just a little too far and get it in the neck.

'Well — so long!' said Dave. 'Can't wait for Sammy. I hope this jane's turned up. A beauty! I tell you. A pair of whatsanames like this!' He curved his hands in front of his chest. His eyes glistened — give him big women every time. Another Oriental. Tea and fat women. He had the harem, all he wanted was the palace, to keep them in. He winked, slapped Alec on the back and rushed into the park to look for his beautiful jane.

CHAPTER VIII

Olive liked her new job very much. She had never before tasted such rich, well-cooked food in her life. She put on weight. She was contented.

There wasn't too much work; just cleaning the shop in the morning, running a couple of errands during the day, making the beds and helping Mrs. Bercovitch keep the rooms tidy.

Dave's mother was a plump, rosy-faced middle-aged woman, very naive and good-tempered. She had never had a daughter so she rather enjoyed having Olive about the house. She treated her as a companion, someone to talk to; asked her advice and discussed almost everything that cropped up, with her.

At first, Mrs. Bercovitch had been worried about Dave. He was the only child and not used to strange women and she didn't want him to get into trouble, especially with a 'shiksah'. But Dave took not the slightest notice of Olive. When his mother was about, he wouldn't even look at her. Mrs. Bercovitch was reassured.

Mr. Bercovitch was a dear. He reminded Olive of fat, bald-headed little Spilliken of the 'Dot and Carrie' strip; the same tubby figure, black eyebrows and wisp of a moustache. He was easy to handle. The first two days she answered 'Yes, sir,' promptly when he called, but she soon took her cue from the missus, and learned to bully him in an amiable, motherly way. Mr. Bercovitch didn't mind. So long as they let him alone, outside with his groceries, the women could do what they liked in the house, providing his meals were done to time.

That morning, Olive and Mrs. Bercovitch had got up at six. They had scrubbed the shutters till there was not a fleck of dust on them, cleaned the windows, whitened the doorstep, and heaped the gas stove with pots full of savoury food. They were busy as ants all day long, getting ready for the crown of the year, the eve of the Black Fast. Olive wondered how Mr. Bercovitch would manage all day without his food. At sundown they had eaten an enormous meal and gone to the synagogue. It was 'Kol Nidrei' night, explained Mrs. Bercovitch. Jews were forbidden to eat or drink anything from that hour until sundown the following day.

This Black Fast business gave her a queer feeling, frightened her a little. She couldn't explain it, really, but it seemed as though things were happening up in the heavens. With millions and millions of Jews praying and fasting this same night, all over the world, something was bound to be going on. . . .

She even felt religious herself. Sorry she'd missed mass on Sunday, and the Sunday before that. She'd go more regularly in future. After all, she wasn't worse than the Jews. She also had her duty to God and the Virgin Mary. She crossed herself surreptitiously. There was such a peculiar holy atmosphere about the place, as though the sacrament of the wine and the wafers were going on all the time, in a deeper, intenser form, like a much more incomprehensible mystery.

She was up very early the next morning, although there was nothing to do. The house was spotless. The scullery looked like the inside of a kitchen cabinet, newly painted with white enamel. All the food was outside in the safe. She recalled her instructions. When the sun was down low at the end of the day, she had to put the soup on the stove, the roast in the oven. On the table, the decanter of spirit and kummel, one Dutch and one pickled herring, green olives, bread and the horse-radish sauce. Yes, she had it all pat. She knew where everything had to go.

She heard them stirring upstairs. They'd soon be down. She hurried to put on the kettle for tea. Then she remembered; they wouldn't drink anything. She turned out the light. Somehow she didn't feel like having any breakfast herself. It seemed sacrilege to eat on a day like this in a Jewish house. She felt, if she did, the food would choke her.

She heard Mr. Bercovitch coming down the stairs, his comical heavy wide tread, and behind, the softer footsteps of the missus. They were dressed all ready for going out. Mr. Bercovitch wore his frock coat and high hat, Mrs. Bercovitch her new black satin coat trimmed with ermine; it looked very nice finished. Olive had been with her to the tailor's for fitting. Both carried prayer books, and Mr. Bercovitch hugged under his arm an embroidered velvet bag in which was his silken praying shawl.

They stood in the kitchen ready to leave for the synagogue, waiting for Dave to come down. Mr. Bercovitch fidgeted impatiently and looked at the clock.

Time didn't stand still. He went to the foot of the stairs and poked his chin in the air. 'Davey! Davey! Come on — it's getting late.'

There was no reply. At once Mrs. Bercovitch became alarmed. Mrs. Bercovitch always expected the worst.

'P-perhaps there's something wrong,' she stammered. 'I'll go up and see.'

She ran up the stairs straight into Dave's room. He was in bed, lying quite still, his eyes open. Her heart thumping from the climb, beat more violently. He 'taki' looked ill, the boy! She half-fell across the foot of the bed, and stared anxiously in his eyes. 'What's the matter, Davey, boy?' she whispered huskily, reaching for his hand to feel the pulse.

He sat up and passed his free hand wearily across his brow.

'I'm all right, Ma,' he said. 'Just a headache. I feel a bit weakish.'

'Shall I get a doctor?'

She stood up, panting, ready to fly, to shout, to cry; she felt feverishly strong and heroic, she could tear walls down with her fingers. She bent over him again, so he could almost hear the tumult in her breast.

'Well?' she asked anxiously.

He gave her a reassuring smile and patted her hand.

'It isn't as bad as that,' he said. 'I'll be all right in an hour or so. I'll come to "shool" in the afternoon.'

'Are you sure?' she replied. 'Sure you'll be all right?'

'Sure, Ma. Sure. It's only a bit of a headache, really. I'll be feeling first class in the afternoon.'

Mr. Bercovitch was shouting again. She'd gone up

to fetch Dave down, and now she'd got lost herself. Women were a funny lot! What was she doing up there all this while? At this rate, they'd get to 'shool' in time to go home. It wasn't nice for a man in his position to be late on Yom Kippur. 'Hy! Come on, up there!' he bawled.

At last Dave persuaded her to leave the room. She went out reluctantly, feeling as though she were betraying him, a load on her heart. As soon as the door shut, Dave settled down to sleep again.

He woke up at half-past ten and stretched himself lazily. He felt very much at ease. No one could deny he was much better off in bed than cooped up in a stuffy synagogue. He'd have something to eat, and then he'd manage to fast comfortably till the evening.

'Olive!' he shouted. 'Olive!'

The girl came running up the stairs. She'd been warned he wasn't too well, maybe he was feeling queer again. She burst into the room.

'Yes,' she answered breathlessly.

'Fetch me up a cup of tea,' he said.

She stopped, breathing heavily, and stared at him in bewilderment. She couldn't believe he'd said tea. He looked all right, not delirious or anything. . . .

'Tea?' she said.

He nodded, 'That's right.'

'But you mustn't have tea!'

'All right — cocoa, coffee — anything you've got.'

'But, Dave, don't you know what day it is, to-day? It's the Black Fast!'

'I know all about that,' he said impatiently, 'but I

want my cup of tea. Besides,' he grinned slyly, 'I'm an invalid.'

Invalid! She glared at him angrily. It was disgusting. He was no more an invalid than she was . . . and make him tea! To-day! The Black Fast! She had quite enough sins on her conscience already.

'Well?'

'*Must* you have tea this morning?' she asked, fidgeting uneasily.

He answered sharply; he was losing his temper. 'Yes. I must.'

'Then make it yourself,' she retorted angrily. 'I won't!' She slammed the door behind her and went down to the kitchen. Dave jumped out of bed and threw on his clothes hurriedly. What the hell was she wriggling about for? What difference would a cup of tea make to her? For the life of him he couldn't understand what was going on in her mind. He followed her downstairs into the kitchen. She had her back to him and refused to say a word. He lit the stove himself, and waited for the kettle to boil.

The tea went down extra well. The old people were praying all day, in any case — they'd have to put in a word or two for him. Olive had been pottering about in the yard. She had no particular tasks, but she wanted to keep out of his way. She came into the kitchen for a moment and put the pail in the corner.

Dave fixed his eyes on her. She was getting more attractive than ever. Her figure was filling out; she was blossoming. Even under the stiff, gaily flowered cretonne overall, he could appreciate the full soft curves. It was the chance of a lifetime! Apart from himself and Olive, there was not a soul in the house. Not very often that both his parents went out and left him alone with her.

Olive turned round to go to the door. She guessed what he was thinking by the way he stared at her. She turned red. This would just about put the lid on! Any other time she didn't mind, but she couldn't bear to let him touch her to-day. The idea was revolting — made her feel sick!

She hurried towards the yard, but he jumped up, blocking the doorway, and caught her wrists. He smiled at her.

'Where's the fire?' he said.

She turned her head away, refusing to answer. He pulled her closer to him and put one arm round her waist, and bent over her, to kiss her. With her free hand she smacked his face. Some invalid! His grin broadened. He pressed his face against her cheek and kissed her lustfully.

'Let me go!'

He laughed. This was funny! Playing religious! She'd never made a fuss before. Coquetry! Some new stunt to work him up. . . . The girl squirmed in his arms. She was terrified. Sixteen million Jews, praying and fasting. Looking on angrily. . . . To-day! . . . Why to-day? . . . Her head whirled. Everything went black before her eyes. She gripped Dave tightly, trying to keep him off, but she felt herself growing weaker while he seemed to tower over her like a laughing giant, covering her face and neck with hot, wet kisses. . . .

CHAPTER IX

UP in the women's gallery, Mrs. Bercovitch cried softly. She kept making her way to the rails and looking over, but the seat next her husband was vacant. Always vacant. She had nothing to say to the women this morning; she even wished she had been taught Hebrew so she'd be able to read the prayers. She would have prayed and prayed and prayed. Almighty Jehovah in His loving-kindness would have been bound to incline an ear to her supplications in His own holy tongue.

For the fifth time she looked down into the body of the synagogue. Through a greyish fog, she saw the tinkling golden ornaments on the scroll of the law. Before the ark, the richly embroidered veil presented by the Ladies' Society. The cantor in his white robes on the raised dais and the male congregation swaying on the floor all round him. Bobbing skull caps, the constant movement of praying shawls fluttering like striped flags. Someone going out, someone coming in, never still, like ripples on the sea.

The beadle slapped his open palm on the prayer book three times. A hushed silence. Then the cantor's sweet nasal tenor rose upwards, pianissimo, with all the tiddly-bits, trilling fancy cadenzas like an overpaid opera-star. His last note hung in the air, till it was cut short by a roar of responses. The thin ragged contraltos of the choir-boys struggled through the noise with the first verse of a psalm, and the congregation joined in, the throbbing basses of the men chanting mournful incantations.

Everything, everything as it was every year, but no Dave. She couldn't bear it any longer. He might be lying in agony, crying for her, and she was selfishly standing here. The Almighty would forgive her if she didn't stay this once. She put on her coat and went down into the street. The clean air hit her in the face. For a moment she felt weak and faint. She leaned against the wall and someone passed her smelling salts. She sniffed and felt a little better. She started to walk sharply to escape the little nagging demon in her brain. Why hadn't she gone before? She should have left the synagogue an hour ago. Maybe it was too late; Oh, God! No! NO! NO! The suspense was twisting her mind. She never knew it was such a distance to the house. Her lips moved all the while, but no sound came from them. She was praying silently.

'... Preserve him, O Lord. Preserve my Davey. Make him well again, O Lord. If someone must suffer, let me suffer for him. Let me be ill for him. Good God! Dear God ...!'

The side door was open. A bad sign. It made her break into a cold sweat. There was something strange about the house. She'd felt that way before, the day she'd come home to find her father dead. And the side door had been open too. She burst into the kitchen almost demented, making straight for the stairs. She stopped. She must be seeing things. Dave! Out of bed? Dressed? It couldn't be! Yet it was so. And he was bending over Olive . . . what was happening here? What was going on? . . .

Her head swam, she felt giddy. She clutched the dresser to save herself from falling. What was going on here? . . . Olive was crying bitterly in the corner. Her overall lay on the floor. One shoulder strap from her slip had been torn off and hung down loosely. There were red marks like scratches across her chest. Now Mrs. Bercovitch understood. The young whore! They were all alike, these servant girls. She'd trusted her, cherished her, treated her like her own daughter, and now she did this. Servants! They were ruination in a house!

'Olive,' she said, 'what's this?'

The girl raised a moist flushed face. 'But, Mrs. Bercovitch . . . !' she exclaimed piteously.

Mrs. Bercovitch silenced her with a look. 'I'll speak to you later,' she said. She moved to the door. Dave ran after her and plucked at her sleeve. 'But listen, Mother . . . Mother,' he begged.

'Don't call me Mother', she snapped at him.

She was in a white rage. She had never been so near hating him before. She almost felt she could whip the life out of him. That was what he deserved, the miserable little cheat. His touch contaminated her. And on such a holy day — Ach! — she shook herself free and rushed outside.

Dave hurried to the synagogue. He'd try and get the old man in a good mood. He wouldn't budge from his side all day. And perhaps his mother wouldn't tell; he'd have to get round her somehow. Pacify her. He kept glancing up at the gallery, hoping she'd look down like she always did, but she only came to the rail once, and as soon as she saw he was there, she went back to her seat and sat there like a statue.

She sat still, biting her lips, growing hot and cold as she thought of what had happened. She paid no more attention to the service. She scarcely heard a word of the sustained chattering all round her. She hardly knew what to do about it. Olive would have to go, of course, but what could she do about Dave? Disgraceful! Disgraceful! And on Yom Kippur too! Her cheeks burned as she thought of the shameful scene.

'Tekeeooh,' sung the cantor.

The ram's horn squeezed out a piercing howl, 'EE-ee-ee-e!'

'Tekeeooh!'

EE-ee-ee-e! EE-ee-ee-e!

'Tekeeooh Gedaile!'

A last triumphant screech and the fast was over. Sundown, already! She was not at all grateful. She got up from her seat, kissed her neighbours, wished them long life and a prosperous year, listened half-heartedly to their greetings and pushed her way to the stairs.

Her husband and Dave were waiting for her in the street. She stared coldly at Dave, but he turned his head hastily to avoid her eyes. Mr. Bercovitch first shook her hand, then kissed her effusively. He was beaming. He stroked his stomach gently, patting it lovingly in anticipation. There were rumblings down in the emptiness, but he enjoyed the discomfort.

He walked home at a more leisured pace than usual,

stretching out the time, so that when he did get to the house, the food would be still more welcome. First he'd have a good long wash and rinse his mouth. Then a schnapps. Then a couple of olives and some herring, then a plate of steaming hot soup. Then he'd have a little rest, and after that the roast chicken, and the stewed fruit and finish up with a couple of glasses of lemon tea.

By the time he reached the door, he was famished. The wash and rinse could wait. Now, his tongue was hanging out for a schnapps. Just the tiniest drop of spirit and kummel to save his life, and maybe while he was about it, an olive and a piece of herring. Only he'd have to do it on the sly. His wife hated to see him picking from the plates. He rolled the saliva on his tongue, and swallowed it, moistening his throat. Smiling happily, he walked straight into the dining-room.

It was empty. His face dropped. He looked round. No one in the room, nothing on the table. He couldn't understand it; had she gone off her head, the girl? Not a drop of kummel, no herring, no hot soup, nothing to eat at all, and here he was starving. Absolutely starving! It was his wife's fault. This was her lovely management; and for twenty-four hours he'd looked forward to this moment. It was an outrage! He had to slave to keep a family week after week, year after year, to be treated like this! It was enough to make a man burst! He turned to his wife for an explanation, his fat baby face swollen with anger, so vexed he could hardly speak, the tears starting out of his eyes.

CHAPTER X

'AND that's exactly how it happened,' said Dave. 'She just disappeared. That's the God's truth.'

Alec went to the window and looked out into the street. 'And you don't even know where she's got to?' he asked.

'Search me!' Dave answered. 'If I'd have known that Olive would take it so bad, I'd never have started with her. Then there wouldn't have been that row with the old man, and now I wouldn't be a homeless orphan.'

Dave grinned, and made himself more comfortable in Alec's armchair. It didn't seem to worry him a great deal. Alec dropped the dirty piece of muslin curtaining, stuck his hands in his trousers, and turned, pacing across the little room. He hadn't seen very much of Dave lately, he had been going about a lot with Sam. And when Dave came rushing round like this, he knew even before he'd said a word, that he was in some sort of trouble. The girl was only half the story. He wanted something. In a minute he'd cough it up. Probably money. Well, he could spare five bob, but if he wanted more, he'd come to the wrong loan office!

' . . . so what?' said Alec.

'I want you to give me a hand.'

Nearly — nearly — it was coming out.

'Well, what? If I can I will, but don't expect much. I'm on the rocks myself.'

Dave got up from the armchair. 'It isn't money.

I wouldn't come to you for that. I want you to let me sleep here — not for long. Only till I can get a room of my own. I can share your bed — it's plenty big enough for both of us . . . Well, what d'you say?'

'You know, Dave, you've got some bloody cheek!' Alec answered.

He turned away from him, very angry. What did Dave think he was, an old carpet? He'd let Dave tread on him so often, that now he took everything for granted. Coming with demands — the bed's big enough for both of us! — Cheek! He wasn't his father. Why should he always have to clean up Dave's mess?

'But, Alec' — Dave caught his sleeve reproachfully — 'I was relying on you.'

'Well, you shouldn't — besides even if I did let you stay, Becky would be bound to find out — then there'd be the hell of a row. No thanks, I'm too comfortable here. Nothing doing, Dave!'

'But surely Becky won't mind?'

'Won't mind! You don't know Becky!'

Dave knitted his brows, and flopped back in the armchair. Alec squirmed. Another half hour of Dave and he could say good-bye to the chair. And if he fell on the bed like that, the mattress wouldn't hold out for a week. Suddenly, Dave slapped his fist triumphantly on his palm. Got it! He sat up with a jerk. The armchair creaked ominously.

'Tell you what!' he said. 'You pay seven and six a week, don't you? Well, offer her ten bob for the two of us, and we'll split fifty-fifty. It'll be good for me, cheaper for you, and a half-crown extra for her! She'll jump at it!'

'No doubt,' Alec answered drily. He didn't sound very enthusiastic. No doubt Becky would be very agreeable, but he also had something to say about it. He'd sooner pay the extra half-crown and have the bed to himself.

'... Well?'

Alec shook his head. 'Can't you go somewhere else?'

'Nowhere,' said Dave glumly. He could see Alec was weakening. He'd let him stay all right — he knew Alec.

'... Well, I'll see,' Alec said.

Dave grinned. He went close up to Alec and grinned in his face. It was infectious — Alec had to smile. It was impossible to be ratty with Dave for long, he was so irresponsible, a baby in long trousers. Besides, half a crown was half a crown. A week's supply of fags. Dave watched him closely. He hugged Alec cheerfully, the moment he noticed the half smile. Good enough! Now it was all over, bar shouting.

'So it's a bet,' he said. 'I'll move in to-night. Talk to Becky — so long!'

He waved cheerily, and the door shut behind him. No need to stay. Alec would fix it all up. He knew just when to go.

Alec thought it over. He wasn't very keen on the idea of them both squeezing together in one bed, but the half-crown would help him out a lot, and anyway he'd get used to it. Man was an adaptable animal after all. He looked at himself full length in the cheap wardrobe mirror. He was going out. He had to stand at an angle to miss the blemish in the glass. A shortish, slim figure in a blue serge suit. He didn't take much notice of clothes, but navy blue always had suited him, and it was nicely tailored. If it wasn't exactly a West-End fit, that didn't matter, it was well made and would last. He'd seen to that. He looked neat, not showy, not overdressed, just right.

There was a tap on the window and he heard Sam's low whistle. 'All right,' he shouted. 'Be out in a tick!' He brushed his coat hurriedly, locked his room, and went out to Sam. It was quite early, the concert wouldn't begin for another hour. They could walk comfortably to the 'Workers' Circle', have a cup of tea and a game of chess, and even then there would be time to spare.

The 'Circle' was tucked away near Aldgate in a turning just off Leman Street, the street of the Co-operative buildings. Like every Sunday evening, the club room was crowded. The air was thick with the steam from the urn and a bluey-grey fog of tobacco smoke. Someone had lit a cigar and its aroma came to the nostrils first, stood out arrogantly, like a rich man at a wedding.

They managed to get a couple of seats at a small table. All the chessmen were in use. Their neighbours were playing dominoes. As Sam sat down, the man next to him raised his hand triumphantly, and brought the stone down with a smack. Then he repeated the performance again, and again. Double three — smack! Three-five, smack! Five-two, smack! He brought his hand high up in the air before he played each stone, as though dropping rocks on an adversary's grave, making quite sure he was buried and wouldn't come up again. He went off at right angles to complete the pattern. Double-two, smack! Two-six, smack! Double-six, and GAME! He turned to Sam. 'Well, what did you think of that?' he shouted enthusiastically. 'Left with the double-six, the double-three, and four others, and running off with the game!'

'Wonderful,' Sam agreed, 'wonderful!'

The domino player ruffled the pattern on the table. 'How many points, Julius?'

'Eight.'

He grinned, licked a pencil, and scrawled a thick eight on the margin of a newspaper.

'Looks like you'll owe me two teas soon,' he said to Julius.

Alec got up. 'I think I'll get something to eat — want anything, Sam?'

'No. Just a lemon-tea.'

Alec went over to the bar, and ordered himself a portion of chopped herring, brown bread and butter, a couple of tomatoes, and a milk-tea. That would be his tea and supper combined. He rejoined Sam and the steward brought along the food. Sam looked round the clubroom. He hadn't been here before, but Alec was a member. At the table back of him, he saw a quiet little man with a short grey beard, reading *Freiheit*, the Jewish Anarchist paper. One of the old guard. Quite a few of the very old members had been nihilists in Russia. Probably more than one had thrown bombs at

Czars or had been sent to Siberia for their convictions. And whenever Emma Goldman was in town, she was always certain of an enthusiastic welcome at the 'Circle'. Alec came back to his seat.

'Who's that queer-looking guy?' asked Sam.

He pointed to a tall man, with longish black hair and a cadaverous face with dark ringed deep-set eyes. He wore a loose-fitting black suit, a dirty grey flannel shirt too big at the neck, and a carelessly knotted black tie. He was talking excitedly to a stout man who took not the slightest notice of him. The stout man was leaning comfortably against the wall, and nodding repeatedly, agreeing all the time, but he kept turning his head, his eyes roving round the room, searching for a chance of escape.

Alec looked round. 'Oh, that's Kossoff!' he said. 'He's a photographer, a bloody nuisance, if ever there was one. He's always in trouble. If he isn't, he manages to invent some shemozzle to cry about.'

The stout man by the wall broke away. Firmly, he released Kossoff's grip, and went to a table the other end of the room, deliberately sitting with his back to the photographer.

Kossoff stood forlornly by himself. An actor without an audience. He noticed Alec and Sam looking at him. He smiled. Good! Someone else he knew, and even if not, it didn't matter, all Jews were brothers and shared each other's misfortunes. Besides, in the whole world was there another so plagued as he? An artist, a prince among photographers, and he had to spend half his life suffering from the pinpricks of fate.

Alec was a good chap, he was never rude to him, like some of these boors. He'd ask his advice, he might be able to help. He moved towards their table.

'Gosh!' Alec groaned. 'Now you've done it! We won't be able to get rid of him.'

'Excuse me,' said Kossoff leaning over the table, 'but per-apps you ken help me. I vant to ask yoor advice. . . .'

He spoke rapidly in his broken English, moving his delicate hands first one, then the other, in abrupt mechanical gestures. His landlord was putting the rent up. He had no right to do it. Business was shocking as it was. No repairs, the roof was leaking. He'd stop the rent. Bloody landlords! Had it all their own way. It was the Government, a fat landlords' government — said pay the rent or clear out! Clear out, when he'd worked up a fifteen-year connection! What could he do about it! What could be done? . . .

Alec ate his herring stolidly. Kossoff didn't mind if he wasn't listening, so long as he was unburdening his heart out loud. But Sam didn't know him. He was more sympathetic. 'I should go to the Town Hall,' he said.

'The Town Hall,' cried Kossoff. 'Good! The Town Hall!' A wild light leapt to his eyes. Fancy telling him, Kossoff, to go to the Town Hall, as if he were a greenhorn, as if he didn't know that himself. Everyone had told him to go to the Town Hall, but what sort of advice was that, that everybody knew? No, that wasn't what he wanted, and what advice he did want he didn't know, but he'd recognize it all right the moment he heard it.

'. . . So! You say the Town Hall. Good! Good! Tank-you-very-much!'

Kossoff moved away. Alec looked up. This was strange, why had they got rid of him so quickly? Then he saw the photographer holding a pale little man tightly by the arm, firing away at him already. Davis was just Kossoff's meat; the sort of man who never said 'no'; so long as Kossoff spoke he would be prepared to listen, and if ever his attention wandered he would apologize humbly. Alec could almost read the photographer's lips. 'So I vant to ask yoor advice' . . . Kossoff had found his audience.

An electric bell rang shrilly in the clubroom. It was nearly eight o'clock. The concert in the hall downstairs was due to commence in a few minutes. Sam was surprised when Alec got up from the table.

'Is it really going to start on time?' he asked.

Alec laughed. Sam knew his *yiddlech* all right. If a concert was billed to commence at eight, they came at a quarter to nine, and were upset if it had started without them. But this wouldn't be a yiddishe 8 o'clock. If it was billed for eight, it would begin at eight, prompt.

They sat at the back of the hall – it could accommodate about two hundred people and was fairly full already. More people drifted inside in ones and twos. Mostly East-enders. Here and there were a few strangers. It was not their clothes which betrayed them, nor their faces, but an unconscious air of frigid aloofness. Either in search of good music or new thrills. The novelty of watching a proletarian audience lapping up Brahms and Beethoven.

Sam nudged his companion. Four chairs away was a strikingly beautiful young woman, a blonde, in an expensive tailor-made costume. She was absorbed in the programme notes, apparently paying no attention to what was going on around her.

The strings tuned up back-stage. Little pizzicato notes and the longer low throb of the 'cello. The lights went out and the bottle-green plush curtains swung up, gracefully gathered together in mid-air. The quartette filed on to the stage. They faced the audience, bowed diffidently, and sat down. They fidgeted with their music stands, tightened screws, played a few scrappy notes, and were ready, braced for the signal from the first violin.

With a nod the fiddler drew down his bow and his colleagues, at exactly the same moment, fastened on the opening chord . . . Alec's head nodded to the sparkling, vivacious menueto. All round him bright eager eyes were concentrated on the stage. A miracle this audience, created from nothing by a couple of musical enthusiasts. The older 'Circle' members shook their heads. 'The youngsters don't want music,' they said, 'give them dances and light concerts,' but the enthusiasts persisted. 'No, let them hear good stuff and they will learn to appreciate it!' And it was so; in three years, the concerts had gathered a solid band of loyal supporters.

Alec looked at the blonde. Her face stood out in profile, very pale in the reflected light from the stage. Her eyes were shut. A soft grey face — long lashes, short straight nose, full lips, a firm chin. Not real at all, an idealized face, shaped from silver granite. He couldn't keep his eyes from her. He felt he could sit like this all night, and stare at her face without a word.

Suddenly there was a burst of applause. The quartette was over and he'd missed at least half. Too busy looking at her. Shame, when he'd come specially to hear papa Haydn. But he wouldn't miss the lieder. Songs were his first love in music; they'd shown him the road. From Schubert's 'Serenade' and Toselli, to the Old Vic operas and the touring B.N.O.C. Then symphonies, then chamber music, then back again to lieder.

The singer fingered the string of imitation pearls around her neck. She moistened her full red lips and inclined her head to the accompanist. Her bosom heaved, she seemed bursting with life. The piano gave out the introduction and she opened her mouth, and suddenly seemed to grow, to swell out and fill the hall with song.

> 'Er, der Herrlichste von allen,
> Wie so milde, wie so gut!
> Holde Lippen, klares Auge,
> Heller Sinn und fester Muth.
> So wie dort in blauer Tiefe,
> Hell und herrlich jener Stern,
> Also er an meinen Himmel,
> Hell und herrlich, heh und fern.'

German! So easy for a Jew to understand. A wife, singing about her husband. Clear-eyed, handsome, ever-smiling. He, more knightly than the noblest; so mild, so good, so kind. But only a happily-married Schumann could write such songs. Songs which made the heart ache with yearning. He was short of something like that. He shot a quick glance at the blonde. Her eyes were fixed on the singer, but she seemed to be looking through her. The music meant something else to her. She was smiling gently. Complete! She was complete. She had none of those aches or yearnings, that part of her was complete.

At the interval they went up to the clubroom, to the bar. The flushed attendants were busy pouring out teas, coffees and minerals, and as fast as they handed them out, others clamoured to be served. 'Tea please — coffee and cheese cake — chopped herring — two teas and a cheese roll — Hurry up, Mrs. What's-a-name, I've been waiting nearly half an hour.'

'Half an hour! You mean half a minute — don't crush — vot's de hurry? You'll all get served. Vy all dis excitement?'

Alec ordered two teas from a steward. He'd get them quickest that way. He sat on the edge of one of the little tables, chatting to Sam, but back of his mind was the blonde, all the time. And why not? He was nearly twenty-four, old enough to get married, or, if not married, at least to live with a woman. But she'd have to be intelligent, say, like the blonde, she was sure to be intelligent. And as beautiful? Well, that didn't matter so much, but he wouldn't object if she were pretty, too. A pity the blonde didn't know all this. She'd jump at such a catch. A penniless, skinny little Jew tailor.

'Yes . . .' said Sam, 'the long and short of it is, that a wife is cheaper than a vice.'

Alec looked at him. How did they come to be talking about wives? Surely he hadn't been thinking out loud. But Sam had his own problems. His father had married again — Sam had moved out of the house. He was fed up with living in digs. He wanted to get married, but it was so hard to find a nice girl who could cook. Whenever he had something to eat or drink out, he thought of a wife, a scullery, and a kitchen of his own.

'After all,' Sam continued, 'not only we two, but all of us, are living like barbarians. I hold that the first necessity of a civilized community is two square meals per day per person. That statue of Liberty in New York Harbour wouldn't be such a joke if, instead of a torch, the old lady held an aluminium frying-pan in her hand, with a couple of eggs in it, for ever french-frying.'

Alec smiled and nodded in agreement. Yes, Sam was right. Hunger and Love. Those were the two important problems. Alec sipped his tea thoughtfully. . . . 'Nu, Alec, what's going to be?'

A skeleton had come up to him and was talking. A skull with a long, straggly grey moustache, and a domed bald head. The dark Angel wouldn't have much of a job with Sherman. Just a little puff. Pfooh! But he'd have the laugh on the worms. Take a good look, Alec. Sherman, a presser, a wage earner for fifty years. Emaciated, worked out, slung on the scrap heap! Take a good look, Alec — this'll be you in thirty years time, if you last that long! Walking about, waiting to die. How could anyone think of life or love, or be hopeful about anything when there was this corpse always on the scene, like a live skeleton at the feast. Pointing with his gnarled, dead fingers and his hopeless query . . . Nu, what's going to be?

Alec shrugged his shoulders. 'What'll be, will be. What'll happen to everyone else will happen to us.'

He turned away. The old man made him feel depressed. He was too real. He had plenty of time in which to be reminded of what was waiting for him, but he was going to forget that to-night. To-night was for music. For Haydn, and Schumann, and Beethoven, and to hell with everything else.

He noticed the blonde standing by the bar. She looked a little bewildered as she stood there, waiting to be served. Such a commotion! Such shouting! On the boil, bubbling noisily all the time. What a peculiar set of people. Didn't they have any restraint at all? Why such passion about ordering a cup of tea, or playing a game of dominoes, or a game of chess? So much warm life, flowing over, wasted on nothing. This was an experience all right, but it gave her a headache. They were too intense, even when they were listening. She had felt it in the Hall, a warm out-flowing to the artiste and it had made her uncomfortable. She wasn't used to it. She didn't take her music that way. She missed the calm, quiet, detached atmosphere of the Wigmore or the Aeolian. The pleasant soft voices and the correct clipped English. . . .

It looked very much as though she wouldn't get

served to-night. She stood only a little way from the bar, but someone was always pushing in front of her. She stared at them, but they didn't seem to understand and pushed their way back again just as unceremoniously, without a 'by your leave' or a 'pardon me'. Very well, she wasn't going to scramble, she could do without tea.

'Excuse me,' said a voice behind her. 'Can I help you? Is there anything you want?'

She turned. 'Well, I would like a cup of tea if you can get one for me.'

Alec led her to a table and she sat down. He went back to the bar and returned in a few minutes with the tea. She smiled gratefully.

'How much?'

'Er — well — er — nothing! I'd like to treat you if you don't mind.'

She smiled again. 'Thanks!' What an extraordinary fellow. Blushing like a schoolboy. She was sorry now she'd accepted. If she had to put up with him for the rest of the evening, it would be a very expensive cup of tea. He'd probably bore her to distraction. To her surprise, he excused himself and walked away. Well, that was very nice of him! At least, he hadn't tried to force himself on her. Thank heaven the interval was nearly over. She'd stick it for another half-hour or so, then they wouldn't see her heels for dust.

When they took their seats, Alec had a plan of campaign all mapped out. After the concert, he'd ask her whether she lived a long way off, and if she didn't object, he'd see her home. Maybe she'd go to some concert with him, or a ramble one Sunday. There'd be no beating about the bush with her. After he knew her for a little while, he'd tell her straight out that he'd like to get married, but he could hardly keep himself. She was bound to understand. Perhaps they would live together or something like that. Anyhow, he'd have a shot if she only gave him the chance.

He glanced over to her. She sat near the gangway, the marvellous creature, and she actually smiled as she met his eyes. Good! . . . Good! He could even see that wild dream of his coming off after all. His heart jumped as he turned his attention back to the stage. The singer waited with clasped hands for the applause to die down before she gave an encore — another German *lied*.

'Du meine Seele, du mein Herz,
Du meine Wonn', o du mein Schmerz,
Du meine Welt, in der ich lebe;
Mein Himmel du, darin ich schwebe.
O Du mein Grab, in das hinab,
Ich ewig meinen Kummer gab.

'Du bist die Ruh', du bist der Frieden,
Du bist von Himmel mir beschieden.
Dass du mich liebst, macht mich mir werth,
Dein Blick hat mich vor mir verklärt,
Du herbst dich liebend über mich,
Mein guter Geist, mein besseres Ich!'

The audience clapped wildly. They liked these songs and she sung them well. The soprano was a good-natured woman. She obliged again, with one of the 'dichterliebe'

> 'Im wunderschönen Monat Mai
> Als alle Knospen sprangen,
> Da ist in meinem Herzen
> Die Liebe aufgegangen. . . .'

Alec was excited. This might have been written for him, the way he felt now. His face was red, his eyes danced with fire. He was enjoying himself. He clapped and clapped with the rest.

The singer appeared on the platform before the curtain, and excused herself. She was sorry, but she had brought no more music. Perhaps — another time. They gave her a last long round of applause and the concert ended. The lights came on with the scraping of dozens of chairs. Alec rose to his feet. The first thing he noticed was that the blonde had disappeared. He turned to Sam, motioning to the empty chair.

'Did you see her go?'

'Yes — must be about ten minutes. Why? Was she supposed to wait for you.'

'No,' said Alec quietly.

Suddenly everything inside him was empty. His excitement turned cold. The flame was extinguished like a match fizzling out in a gutter puddle. But it served him damned well right! He should have remembered who he was and who she was. This was life — not *Poppy's Paper*. Served him damned well right! Now, what was going to be?

CHAPTER XI

Two suits. Two hats. One light overcoat. One mack. Four pairs of socks. Shirts . . . Dave ticked them off, made a pile of his belongings, and gave a last look inside the wardrobe. No. No more. That's the lot. He closed the wardrobe door — the damned thing never would shut properly — and turned to Alec.

'Well, you've got rid of me at last. After to-night, you'll be a bachelor again.'

'About time, too,' said Alec. But he was sorry now Dave was going. His few days had turned into a few months, and he'd got used to sleeping with him. And then there was the money. The slack time was coming along and he knew he wouldn't be kept on at the workshop. The boss was always complaining about his work. Paving the way. A couple were marked down for the sack, and he'd be one of the first to go. Lucky for him he had a few pounds saved up to hold out till the next season. But every penny would count, and here was half a crown being lopped off his income right away. Still, that couldn't be helped; after the walk-out, he'd expected something like this to happen. The boss never took anything lying down. Maybe something would turn up. Perhaps the Messiah would come. If Dave could get himself engaged to a nice respectable girl and settle down, then it was time the Messiah did come. He lay back on the bed, watching Dave.

'So you're almost engaged to be married, eh? And when's the happy day?'

Dave looked up from the pile of clothes. 'What do you mean?'

'I mean when's the engagement?'

'Oh — that. To-morrow!'

'Doing it in style? Diamond ring and everything?'

'I should say so.' Dave straightened himself. He was indignant. 'How can you get engaged without a ring? — And what a ring! You should see the stone. A splonker! Cost two hundred and fifty quid!'

Alec whistled. Two hundred and fifty pounds for a ring! And he'd have to work, say at two-ten a week, that was a hundred and twenty-five pounds a year, two hundred and fifty, two years; work in the factory ten hours a day, fifty-two weeks a year for two years before he got that much as wages. And how many starving families could have bread, babies milk, kiddies boots, with two hundred and fifty pounds? Why, it was a criminal offence to waste the equivalent of so much labour-power. They deserved at least six months apiece — he for giving and she for receiving. And another thing struck him. Where did Dave pick up two hundred and fifty pounds? He was always broke.

'How did you get all that money for a ring?' he asked, puzzled.

'I didn't!' Dave grinned. 'She bought it herself.'

That was different. It also explained things. She must have tons of money. If she could spend two hundred and fifty pounds on a ring, Dave was in for plenty more. He didn't blame him for taking the easiest way. Dave had no principles anyhow. The prodigal son was going home to his parents with a humble and a contrite heart, and they'd prepared for him the fatted cow. He'd get married, become a prosperous business man, raise a strictly orthodox family, and probably finish up as president of the local synagogue.

Dave packed away his things in two large portmanteaux — that was one job done. He stretched himself, this bending gave him the cramp. Must be getting old. He'd be finished with bending now. No more 'Shave, sir?' 'Haircut, sir?' — no more tuppenny tips. He was going to be his own boss. David Bercovitch, Furs and Skins. It would look nice in neon lights, in bold block letters.

'Well, that's that!' he said, wiping his hands. 'Now I'm going out to celebrate. Going to take a nice long 'bus ride to Purley.'

'Purley? With your fiancée? Alec asked casually. He'd lost all interest now in Dave. He really didn't want to know.

'Fiancée! Not on your life,' Dave retorted. 'I'm going to sow my last oats. And if you saw my jane, you'd understand why. Legs like tree-trunks and the same shape too!'

Alec nodded. Yes, he understood that. And if he told the rest, a face covered with black-heads and she was probably just a few years younger than his mother. But Dave was going into it with his eyes open. He should have known by this time that nobody gave anything away for nothing. He was taking a chance, betting on a docile wife. Above all things, Dave wouldn't like to let married life interfere with his little pleasures, especially his women. But if he caught a Tartar, he'd go through the hoop. These old maids could be nice and easy-going while they were courting. Wouldn't eat a lot. Never said no — ingratiating, accommodating. But they weren't married long before they started to lay down the law. Showed who wore the pants. She might not be that sort, but if she was, he didn't envy Dave, not if she bought herself a ring worth ten times two hundred and fifty.

He locked his room and went out. The streets were half-empty as usual on a Saturday. A nice day too. Dave would enjoy himself at Purley; find a deserted field a little way out. Dave knew how to work the oracle. He had a way with the girls. He would pick up anybody in skirts. The chap was irresponsible, a social bandit, but that sort seemed to enjoy themselves most. At times he almost wished he could be like Dave, but it was no use. He didn't see life higgledy-piggledy, didn't snatch and run. He had to be steadfast, a class-conscious proletarian, but it was hard. This woman business was getting him down. How could any young man be expected to lead a normal healthy life without some satisfactory sexual relationship? It was so necessary. He was top heavy without it, but that was an old, old story; he'd come to that conclusion a long time ago. And the only way to restore the balance was a mistress, that was also ancient history, though here economics came in. Always in the way. Another major defect of the damned system!

He went up to Sam's digs. Sam didn't feel like going out. He didn't go to concerts much now. He'd stuck quite a few for Alec's sake, but he wouldn't go to any more. He had to admit they bored him. And when he didn't go to the movies, he spent his time in billiard saloons. He'd learnt the pool-parlour habit in New York, and was slipping back to that sort of life again. True, most of the billiard hall boys were roughnecks, but they were honest blackguards without any pretensions. They didn't pose as anything else, and Sam accepted them for what they were and got along hunky-dory. And they had a real thirst for knowledge, some of them. Often, they'd hold up a snooker or crap game while Sam would get up on a chair, and give a snappy lecture on the political situation, or else he'd warn them to take proper precautions when they went out with any dames. Always to have potassium permanganate and calomel ointment handy. They could play around as much as they pleased, but there was no sense in getting a dose. They respected Sam and looked up to him and Sam enjoyed himself in his own fashion, surrounded by racing touts and sneak thieves and other hoodlums.

No. Sam didn't want to go out. He was going to get something to eat, and then for an all-night session at the saloon. Then he'd go home, have a wash and a couple of hours sleep and play solo all day Sunday. Alec was on the right track, he admitted that, but he got more kick out of life this way. Every man his own salvation! When the revolution came, he'd take a hand with a rifle at the barricades, but the revolution was a long way off. Meanwhile, he'd spend his time educating flash crooks and potting the red.

Alec wasn't very disappointed. He'd seen this coming a long time now. Anyway, that let Sam out; another pal gone west. He walked to Aldgate and got the Charing Cross bus. There were long queues outside most of the theatres and cinemas. It was a wonder there were still enough people willing to pay to see these shows. Cramming the theatres and cinemas every night. Barnum was right after all. But really, there was nothing for him to see. In the whole of London, the capital of the world, not one film or play that an intelligent man could sit through without leaving his intelligence outside.

There used to be the German films, but they'd dried up when the brains were kicked out of the industry. A few weeks back, there'd been a Réné Clair film and 'Poil de Carotte' and 'La Maternelle' but he'd seen all those. 'Thunder over Mexico' was cut to pieces, so it didn't look a bit like Eisenstein, and the other Russian films were banned except for private societies, but who had guineas for membership and three and sixes for seats? No, there was nothing for it, but the News Theatre. The last standby. Sevenpenn'orth, with Mickey Mouse and a Silly Symphony thrown in for full measure.

He took a short cut through the back to Shaftesbury Avenue. A couple of women eyed him as he passed by. A potential customer. One of them walked in front of him a little way, showing off her figure, ready to bargain. She turned and faced him, smiled and caught his arm familiarly, and pressed it against her soft body. The blood rushed to his head — he flushed crimson. There she stood before him, peddling her sex. Why didn't she go away, the bloody woman? He felt horribly embarrassed and a bit frightened. Her full breasts swayed loosely with her seductive movements — a challenge and an advertisement, stuck out in front of her — Hey boys — look what I've got! Why the hell didn't she wear a brassière? Like walking about naked in the street! At that moment he trembled with excitement. He felt like grabbing hold of her breasts with both hands, right here, in the middle of the pavement. Damn it all! Why shouldn't I go home with her — why not?

But he wavered too long, the old cautious demon possessed him again. She might be diseased, you never could tell with these women. He looked at her, his mouth opened, he tried to speak. The words choked in his throat. He dropped his eyes, turned away, and walked off quietly, and heard her angrily uttering filthy swear words after him. He cursed himself for a coward. He wasn't a man — couldn't be, to behave like this. But one of these days he'd do it. If he couldn't get a woman any other way, he'd get blind drunk and pick up the first that came along. It wasn't as if he were insensible to the desire for women, then, there might be an excuse for turning his back on them, but this longing was eating him up. It was terrible to feel like this. Like having liquid fire imprisoned inside him, boiling up without an outlet. St. Francis, when he felt the fleshly lust come over him, would throw himself on some prickly bushes. But *he* wasn't a monk, so why should he scourge his body? It was a natural impulse after all. It was Life. Something to accept, not dodge. He'd sooner throw himself on a nice-looking jane. Theoretically, of course. He'd bolt for his life, he thought bitterly, if some nice-looking jane actually did invite him to throw himself on her.

He came out opposite the neon signs of the News Theatre. Thank God for that! He'd get rid of this overwhelming desire. Canalize it. Tuck it away for the time being. But something was very wrong. He couldn't keep on running away for ever. It was a problem that would have to be faced and solved, and it looked very much as though prostitutes were the only solution. He paid sevenpence and took his seat. An end to sweet futile dreams of a strong mutual passion; in future he'd be prepared to buy his love like his entertainment. Cash on the counter!

And even inside, surrounded by darkness, there was no escape. Women sat on either side of him, and he found himself glancing surreptitiously at their soft white hands and pale faces, looking down to see whether their skirts weren't caught up above their knees. He even imagined their legs were brushing against his, when it was only his own nervous fidgeting. And there seemed to him something suggestive about Minnie Mouse on the screen, about the long legs in the thick high-heeled shoes and the absurd little lace-trimmed drawers.

And the travel film. That was just as bad. He was in a fever. Close-up's of natives with bare breasts and protruding bellies. The explorer's slow wise-cracks, flowed over him without even denting his consciousness. His eyes were fixed all the time on the female torsos. He hated himself for it, but he hoped they'd show some more shots like those. More! . . . More! He remembered how disgusted he had been when a friend of his who ran a bookshop, had pointed out to him a shabby old man passing by, who was prepared to pay as much as thirty shillings for a set of obscene postcards. He groaned shamefacedly. He was just as bad as that filthy old degenerate. God! What a state to be in!

He walked home and undressed in the dark. It was gone twelve. He felt tired, washed out. No sign of Dave. But he was used to his little expeditions. He'd come in about three, switch on the light, throw his shoes on the floor, cough, blow his nose, stumble over the chamber pot and move about so noisily that he'd have to wake him up. Then he'd apologize, turn off the light, and creep into bed to fall asleep soundly in a moment, while *he'd* toss about for at least another couple of hours before he settled down for the night.

Dave had all the breaks! He tried not to think of him, but he tossed from side to side and couldn't sleep . . . Dave! . . . Girls! . . . Purley . . . Big twin black breasts. Soft flesh rubbing up against him . . . He was getting hot again. His body was on fire. Burning. This was torture. Women. Women. Out of perspective altogether, obliterating everything. Couldn't he think of something else? . . . Now get this straight, Alec. It isn't so terrible. You're a bit neurotic. Go to sleep, and in the morning you'll be normal again . . . Sleep! It was all right to say sleep . . . But would he be normal in the morning? Was he normal and Dave abnormal, or was it the other way about? . . . He'd go off his rocker if he kept on like this. He must make his mind a blank. Think, say, of a flag fluttering gently . . . or count up to a thousand . . . Oh, What was the use of his trying to fool himself. Back of his brain was Women. Women. Women! All the while, women. God! Did everyone have to go through this at one time or another? . . .

He bit his lips, and turned his face to the wall and screwed up his eyes. Sleep! Damn you, sleep! He heard someone fumbling with the latch outside. That would be Dave. He'd better not let him see he was awake. Dave would only begin gloating over all the details and the bloody business would start all over again. He heard him come into the room, and switch on the light. Involuntarily his eyes closed tighter to shut out the glare. Dave sat on the edge of the bed. Alec heard the mattress creak and felt Dave bending over him, his body blotting out the light.

'Alec! – Alec! You asleep?'

Alec made no movement or sound. Dave shook him gently. 'Alec! Alec!'

He lay quite still. He didn't want to hear anything about it. Bad enough as it was. Dave wasn't even attempting to undress. Why the Hell didn't he go to sleep and leave him alone? . . . Dave shook him again. He seemed determined to wake him up. Well, he couldn't pretend to be asleep much longer, but Dave wouldn't half get a piece of his mind! He'd shut him up, damned quick, too! Wouldn't listen to a word he said. He turned round, stretched himself, and leaned on one elbow, shading his eyes.

'Well, what the bloody hell d'you want now?' he growled.

'Have you got a late paper?'

'A late paper?' he said, yawning. 'I think so. Have a look in my jacket. I believe there's one in the pocket.'

A paper! Only that. Funny thing to wake him up for. Anyway, that was better than having to listen to his yarns about the girl in Purley. He hoped Dave would be satisfied now. He turned on his side, and pulled the bedclothes over his head. The electric light burned through the thin coverlet. He could hear Dave pacing up and down. He had never known him to behave this way before. Suddenly his request for a paper struck him as peculiar. A late paper! What the hell would he want a late paper for! There was something fishy about this. He sat up.

'Found what you're looking for?' he asked.

'No. It's not in here.' Dave seemed very agitated. 'When did you buy this?'

'Nine o'clock. It's the last edition. Have you seen the *Star* or the *News*? Maybe you'll get it in one of those.'

'No. It's not there. I've looked. I've even bought a *Sunday Referee*. Not a word!'

'Now look here, Dave,' Alec said, 'what's all this mystery? Spit it out, for Christ's sake!'

Dave sat on the bed. Now he was close to him, Alec

could see how pale he was. Looked really ill. He was shivering a little too. A bad cold. Maybe the 'flu. Pity there wasn't any whisky in the place. He ought to take a stiff dose, and sweat it out. Dangerous to neglect these colds. But he hoped Dave wouldn't pass it on. He'd have to dose himself with quinine in the morning. Suddenly he heard Dave muttering. At first he thought he was talking to himself. Jabbering a lot of nonsense. Queer disconnected sentences; he couldn't make head or tail of his words. Maybe he was delirious. Alec put his hand on Dave's forehead to see whether he had a temperature. Dave brushed it off impatiently.

'I'm not ill,' he said. 'And I'm not mad. I tell you it happened exactly like that. Just the way I've been telling you. I didn't mean to hurt her. Just tugged her scarf. She kept on chaffing me. Leading me up the garden. "What the hell did you bring me out here for?" I says, and she keeps on laughing in my face. Well, it got my goat, same as it would anyone. All right you little mare, I'll give you something to laugh at! And then she went limp all of a sudden, she flopped on top of me with all her weight. No life left in her at all. Gosh! Lucky there was no one about!'

Dave took out a handkerchief and wiped the sweat from his forehead. He couldn't bear to sit still, like this. He jumped up and started pacing about again. He felt terribly cold. Had the jim-jams bad. At any moment the door might open and a couple of big splits would walk in and they'd say 'Are you David Bercovitch?' and he'd have to say 'Yes, I am'. He'd tell them he did it, right away; he only hoped they'd come soon and get it over. But how would they know where to find him? Hundreds of people had been to Purley that day, hundreds of people had come back. They couldn't trace him. Impossible. Unless . . . unless her people had said something. He'd been to her house once or twice, but they didn't know where he lived. They *could* give his description. Five foot eight. Dark skin. Small black moustache. Aw! There were half a million they could pick up like that in London. They'd never catch him! Never! What the hell was he sweating about? Might even be a couple of days before they found her in any case. . . .

Alec threw off the bedclothes and sat on the bed in his pyjamas. He couldn't believe it. Dave must be raving!

'You mean you killed . . . murdered . . . ?'

Dave turned on Alec fiercely, took a couple of steps towards his friend, and bent over him.

'Shut your bloody row!' he whispered savagely. 'D'you want the whole street to hear? Why don't you open the bloody window and shout out loud?'

'I'm sorry,' said Alec. 'I'll talk quietly if you like. But no one can hear us just the same. There's only Becky in the house, and you know she's as deaf as a door post . . . Now take it easy. Sit down.'

Dave sat beside him on the bed. So it had happened at last. Alec knew his luck couldn't last for ever, but he'd never expected him to come a cropper like this. It was too bad. He didn't even feel like saying 'I told you so'. Murder! Terrible! Terrible! He was sorry for Dave and more than sorry for the other poor kid, whoever she was. But she was dead. That episode was finished, done with, what was the best thing to do now?

Dave buried his head in his hands and started to cry. He sobbed bitterly shaking his body from side to side.

'Good God!' he moaned. 'What a bloody fool! What a bloody idiot!' He lifted his tear-stained face and looked at Alec piteously, and caught hold of his pyjamas jacket, gripping him tightly. 'God! what can I do now?'

Alec loosened Dave's fingers. His knuckles were pressing uncomfortably against his bare chest. It was no use being hysterical. No good rushing into a panic. He should have thought of these things before. It was all over now. Now, it had to be faced in a rational manner.

'What were you thinking of doing?' Alec asked quietly.

Dave got up again. 'God knows! There's nothing I *can* do. I killed her and stuck her away in a ditch, and they'll catch me and I'll swing for it. That's all.'

'They haven't caught you yet,' Alec said.

'But they will. It's only a matter of time. Damned if I'm going to shave my whiskers off and hide somewhere, and shiver and shake every time anyone stops to ask me for a light! It's been bad enough the last couple of hours, God knows! It isn't worth it, Alec, I tell you, I'm going to give myself up! – Yes! I'll give myself up!'

His eyes shone wildly, he moved towards the door. Alec caught him by the shoulder.

'Now look here,' he said gently. 'You've done something terrible. You lost your head and choked someone. You must have been mad when you did it, but you're not mad now, and you want to give yourself up to the police. They'll only take you and choke you in revenge. But *they'll* do it in cold blood . . . I don't know which crime is worse!'

'That's all very well,' said Dave irritably. It was easy for Alec to talk. 'But how can I expect to get away with it?'

'I'd take a chance!' Alec answered. 'If we were civilized, I'd advise you to give yourself up. Perhaps you'd be sent to a mental home for a few years, or some sort of school. But we live like savages — head-hunters. As it is, if you give yourself up, you're throwing your life away. It's useless to expect them to treat you like a human being.'

'But it's no better than the way I treated her,' Dave answered dully. 'I deserve to be hanged!'

Alec gripped his arm angrily. 'Talk sense man, for God's sake!'

Dave shook his head.

'I deserve to be hanged!' he repeated.

'Oh, you're a bloody fool!' Alec shouted, losing patience with him. He lowered his voice to a whisper. 'I'm doing my best to help you and you keep telling me you want to get hanged. Well get hanged! If you do it'll be nobody's fault but your own!'

He got back into bed, shifted up to the wall, and pulled the coverlet over his ears. He'd finished arguing with that lunatic.

'Now turn out the bloody light,' he said testily. 'If you don't want to get to sleep to-night, I do!'

Dave switched off. Alec heard him pacing about in the darkness. He was sorry for him, but he couldn't help because of his pig-headedness. It was ten to one on him getting away if he wanted to, but he wasn't trying at all. It was a shame to let him throw his life away like this. He was still young, there might be a lot of good in him yet. Maybe to-night would be the lesson of a lifetime. He'd have one more go at knocking some sense into him. He sat up again. He spoke quietly, pleading . . . 'Dave! Listen, Dave.' . . .

'Aw, leave me alone!' the other shouted hysterically. 'Can't you bloody well leave me alone? Ain't I got enough trouble without you nagging? God! I do'no, I do'no . . .' he wailed despairingly.

On a sudden impulse he rushed out of the room and Alec heard the street door slam. There was a draught running through the passage into the room. Dave had left the door open and the wind blew in from the yard. He felt too lazy to get out of bed again, but the night was chilly and he hated draughts. He put it off as long as possible, but he couldn't feel comfortable with the wind flapping the curtains over the windows. He got out of bed, closed the door, and snuggled back beneath the coverlet.

What a night! First that tart in Shaftesbury Avenue, then those tantalizing visions, then Dave. He wouldn't like to be in his boots. What was he up to now? he wondered, rushing off like a madman . . . He could feel himself going off to sleep. He was empty, all washed up, the reaction from the night's excitement. Sleep! . . . sleep! . . . Good job, too! He needed a rest. He drifted into a dreamless darkness. . . .

Not very long afterwards, Dave came back. It was just beginning to dawn. The grey light from the street straggled in through the two inverted heart-shaped holes in the shutters. He went straight over to the bed, and bent over Alec, calling his name.

Alec opened his eyes, saw Dave's face, and sat up with a start. Back already! His head was throbbing. He was in a muddle. He shook himself. They must be after him. Get him away! Maybe through the back. The yard door was open. He could climb over the wall to the next street. . . .

Dave was laughing hysterically. There was a big bruise down the side of his face, and one eye was puffed up and almost completely closed. So he'd got into a scuffle with the cops! There was no time to waste. Alec's head was singing, but he thought quickly. Out of here! Get him out of here. Out of the way!

Dave kept laughing in his face. He'd never get away in that condition. He must pull him together somehow. He jumped out of bed, grabbed a glass of water from the washstand, and dashed it over his face. Dave threw himself on the bed and stretched himself out, his arms at right angles to his body, the palms outward, as if he were being crucified and the water trickled from his head over the coverlet.

Alec was alarmed. He bent over Dave, caught his

shoulders in a tight grip and shook him fiercely till the bed rattled. This was getting serious, but Dave still didn't seem to understand. His mind must have cracked under the strain. He laughed more immoderately than before. Alec straightened himself, looked at Dave for a moment, then gave him a sharp smack across the face with his open hand.

'Now stop it, Dave,' he said urgently. 'Snap out of it for God's sake! You've still got a chance.'

Dave slowly brought his hand to his face, gingerly feeling the bruises and sat up shakily. He looked haggard. 'It's all right,' he said with a sickly grin, '. . . she's not dead!'

Alec looked at him. 'What?'

'Yes. She's all right, the little mare! I don't know what made me go round to where she lived, but the old man must have seen me hanging round by the door, and her brother came out in his nightshirt and they both set about me, while she egged 'em on from the window. God! I don't think I've got one whole bone in my body! But it's worth it. I'll say it's worth it!'

'. . . Oh! . . .'

Alec felt a sudden sense of disappointment. It was a mean impulse, but it had flashed spontaneously through his brain. All this shemozzle for nothing! He really should be glad for Dave's sake, that it had turned out this way, but he only felt angry, sort of frustrated. Maybe that was because he was still half-asleep. Lucky it was Sunday. He'd lay-in a bit later, and make up for what sleep he'd lost. Thank heaven he was getting rid of Dave now, for good and all, though he felt sure that as soon as he had any more trouble, with his wife or anyone else, he'd come running round as usual.

He got into bed without a word. The sheets were damp, as if he'd wetted himself. Ugh! The blasted swine!

Dave kicked off his shoes. He groaned painfully as he sat down, yet he managed to sound quite cheerful, like a successful athlete after a gruelling run. After all, what were a few broken bones, compared with what might have happened? He felt like singing a hymn of praise.

'Shift up,' he said.

'I can't get through the wall,' Alec answered without moving.

'All right then – I'll let you off this time . . . but don't rub up against me, for God's sake. I'm black and blue!'

'Serves you bloody-well right!' Alec growled. He felt hard done by. All his brilliant schemes wasted. 'I hope it teaches you a lesson; you won't forget this in a hurry!'

'You're right!' Dave answered, as he lay down carefully beside him. 'If I take any more janes out, you won't catch me going round their houses first. No sir!'

He laughed. It was a lucky get-out and no mistake. And he was supposed to be getting engaged to-morrow. He'd have to invent a motor car accident or something and put it off until he looked more respectable. He yawned deeply and grimaced, as his ribs seemed to catch fire from his breathing. He felt as if his bones were prodding through the flesh. He stifled a second yawn, they were too painful luxuries, and in a few moments he was fast asleep.

CHAPTER XII

It was a quick engagement and a quick wedding. Her folks, shrewd business people, didn't like these affairs to drag on for months and months; she'd been on their hands quite long enough, and if they didn't snap up old Bercovitch's boy, it might be years before they found another 'chosan', or else, God forbid, she might be left on the shelf altogether. It was certainly time they had a few grandchildren!

Alec came to the synagogue early. He wanted to be in at the death. He had known Dave so long, he just had to see him get married.

The guests were just beginning to arrive. Big be-ribboned Daimlers drew up outside the gates, disgorged a full load of sweating men in top hats, and drove off again for another lot. The guests, mopping their red faces, snuffed out their cigars as they entered the synagogue and Alec trailed in behind.

The women kept to one side of the synagogue and the men to the other. In the centre, raised up a few steps, just in front of the arc of the Law, stood a purple plush canopy, glittering with Hebrew letters, picked out in gold embroidery.

The beadle, a faded, wrinkled old man, in a blue serge suit and a frayed top hat, twiddled fussily beneath the canopy, tightening screws, seeing that all four supports stuck up exactly at right angles. Then he ran about, looking for the best place to put the bottle of ceremonial wine, and the silver goblet. He finally decided to rest them on the pulpit steps, which were conveniently placed. In all his thirty years at the synagogue, he had never put the wine and the goblet anywhere else, but he always rushed about like this, making himself conspicuous. If the guests noticed him they would remember when they went out. 'Ah!' they'd say, 'the poor old man works hard', and they would be generous with their tips.

The women were jabbering to each other. What a marvellous frock the bride wore, and how well she looked (What bride didn't on her wedding day?) and those marvellous bouquets . . . and where did you buy that lovely hat? . . . and who made you that beautiful frock? . . . and he's very good . . . I never go anywhere else for a 'perm' . . . and I hear he doesn't live with her any more. It must be her fault . . . if you want to eat garlic you can't expect you breath to smell sweet . . . Gallstones. I've been to three hospitals, and they all say the same thing . . . Births, deaths, bad husbands. The things such women talk about, wherever they happen to get together, especially after a few ports and cherry brandies; busy as bees with their tongues.

And the men on the other side were discussing business and religion. They always felt religious at marriages, deaths, and circumcisions. Some grey-beard could always be trusted to trot out what Rabbi Akiba said on such and such an occasion, and be countered by another old man with what Rabbi Gamaliel said about the same thing somewhere else. And the middle-aged men followed these dialectics with keen enjoyment, while the youngsters discussed boxing and dogs and horse racing.

And above the throbbing dynamo of conversation rose the subdued reedy tones of the organ. The organist, despairing of ever getting a hearing, had given up a Bach fugue, and meandered casually along a piece by Handel, playing it very softly and very badly. He didn't know why he had to play, nobody was listening anyhow. It was all the same to them whether he played or not, but he got a few shillings for doing it and he had to carry on. It wasn't as if he'd get good tips, either, like the cantor or the beadle. Push Bach and Handel down their gullets, and the porter outside, who opened the doors of the Daimlers, even the lousy porter, would finish up with three times as much as him.

Suddenly there was a hush. The bridegroom had arrived. Dave took his seat in a special box just below the raised central dais, in between his father and his father-in-law. All three wore cut-away coats and striped trousers, cravats, and top hats.

Then the cantor came in, attended by his 'shammash'. The old beadle distributed the prayer books and thumped a reading-desk heavily for silence. Mincha — the afternoon service — commenced. Everybody carried on talking, just as before, except the very old men.

At the conclusion of the short service, Dave took his stand beneath the canopy. The beadle came rushing down the central gangway, very excited. The bride had come in. He gave a signal to the organist, and the organ belched forth the arch-anti-Semites march from

Lohengrin and the bride appeared, walking slowly towards the canopy, resting on her father's arm.

Alec could not see her very well. He sat at the back, and all the relatives stood up in front of him, and craned their necks to observe the procession with its bridesmaids, and page-boys. Alec didn't think it worth while making any effort to look the bride over. He would take her on trust. It was Dave's funeral anyhow. All he could see was a tallish figure in white satin, veiled — and carrying a huge bunch of lilies, standing modestly at Dave's side beneath the canopy. The cantor started to sing in a high nasal tenor. He made a prayer over the wine, and the bride and groom each had a sip. Then, word by word, he intoned in Hebrew, 'Hurray — udd — mikoodashes — lee.'

'Hurray — udd — mikoodashes — lee,' Dave repeated after him, and at a sign from the cantor, slipped the ring on her finger.

. . . 'Hurray — udd — mikoodashes — lee' — in Alec's head ran a couplet

'Hurray udd mikoodashes lee,
You son of a gun, you belong to me.'

His father once had an old gramophone record of a couple of American music-hall comics, singing a funny song with that refrain. Coupling the sonorous Hebrew with ribald Americanisms, like the Viennese he'd told him about who loved singing bawdy songs to solemn old Italian tunes, like 'Santa Lucia'.

Nach yahre einig,
Hat sie etwas kleinig,
Fahlt nur der papa,
Santa Lucia.'

The cantor read over the wedding contract in Hebrew. Then he turned the parchment on the reverse side and read the English translation, in a monotonous sing-song, lisping slightly.

'Abstract of the Kesubah. On the third day of the week, on the fourteenth day of the month Ab, in the year five-six-nine-three, corresponding to the twenty-fifth of July, nineteen-thirty-three, the holy covenant of marriage was entered into in London, between the bridegroom David Bercovitch and his bride, Anita Brenner. The said bridegroom made the following declaration to his bride:

' "Be thou my wife according to the Law of Moses and of Israel. I will honour and cherish thee. I will work for thee. I will protect and support thee. I will provide all that is necessary for thy due sustenance, even as it beseemeth a Jewish husband to do. I also take upon myself all such further obligations for thy maintenance during thy lifetime, as are prescribed by our religious statutes."

'And the said bride has plighted her troth unto him in affection and sincerity and has thus taken upon herself the fulfilment of all the duties incumbent upon a Jewish wife.

'This covenant of marriage was duly executed and witnessed this day according to the usage of Israel.'

He paused to catch his breath, raised another incantation over the wine, and passed the goblet to the bride and groom. Then he nodded to the bridegroom, and Dave trod hard on a wine glass lying on a tray at his feet.

He smashed it to pieces and as the glass crunched, the guests shouted greetings, wishing them the best of luck.

'Mozeltov! Mozeltov!'

The cantor raised his hands above their heads and intoned the final blessing,

'May the Lord bless you and keep you. May the Lord lift up his countenance upon you and give you peace. Amen.'

Now the ceremony was over. The cantor walked towards the dais and the newly wed couple followed behind him to sign the register. The guests left their seats and invaded the gangway, kissing right and left, almost obliterating Dave and his wife.

The bride's mother pulled her aside and whispered swiftly in her ear. The bride nodded and passed on to another orgy of kissing. At last, they were able to mount the dais. The cantor looked at Dave benevolently, waiting for a tip. Dave took out a half-crown. He'd meant it for the beadle, but two and six should do for the cantor as well, he got quite enough money for the job in any case. He pressed the half-crown into the clergyman's hand. The cantor was surprised and disgusted. He looked down at the coin, turned it over in his palm, and reached up to Dave's light waistcoat with the pearl buttons, and put it back in his pocket.

He patted the pocket gently. There you are! You're a nice little boy, but you might need the money yourself now you're married!

He turned away, full of righteous contempt. A lot of schnorrers! And they expected him to come to the dinner too! Well, in the evening, he was going to stay at home. They could recite the seven nuptial blessings themselves. He was going to have a very bad headache.

Dave's father shook hands with the cantor. A crisp ten-shilling note tickled the clergyman's palm and disappeared into his trousers pocket. He congratulated the bride's father and glimpsed a green one. That also vanished like magic into his trousers. Ah! That was better. Something like a wedding! To-night he'd sing the nuptials with such sweetness that the very angels in Heaven would join in the responses. There would be good pickings and a first-rate dinner on top of it. He hummed a little tune to himself, and stroked his glossy Imperial, beaming all round him.

The witnesses signed their names. Very cordially, the Secretary handed Dave the parchment. More money. Now it was all over, and a damned good job too!

At the foot of the dais, on the bottom step, his bride trod heavily on his toe. He winced, and to make up for it, she gave him a little hug. So those were the mother's whispered instructions. Tread on his foot as you go down, and you'll always have the upper hand. Oh yeah! Very nice and poetic, but a pity she had such whopping feet!

They had to push their way through the gangway

to the porch. Another bridegroom had arrived with a bevy of guests, waiting to be seen to. The beadle smirked at Dave, received his tip, rushed inside, and waved frantically to the organist. Poor chap! They didn't give him time to breathe. One job wasn't properly over, and now he had to tootle again.

The cantor smoothed his robes over his generous paunch, adjusted his praying shawl, and took his stand beneath the canopy, in readiness for the next customer.

In the porch, there was a bedlam of excitement. The guests were all mixed up. Nobody knew who was coming and who was going. The ubiquitous Daimlers stood in a row outside the synagogue and guests kept rushing over to drivers, shouting and gesticulating... 'Are you from the first wedding?' ... 'Are you from the second wedding?' ... The drivers sat stolidly in their seats and shook their heads. What the hell did they know of this business anyway? All Jews looked the same to them!

Half a dozen managers appointed themselves, took charge immediately, and made the muddle still worse. A crowd of people surrounded Dave and his wife and clamoured for cars. The managers rushed all over the place, getting in each other's way, shouting 'Gangway! Gangway!'

At last the Daimlers sorted themselves out. Dave's guests crammed inside and were driven off in relays. Alec walked home. One thing he promised himself, after this, if ever he had to get married, it would be quietly, in a registry office or not at all.

CHAPTER XIII

SOMEHOW or other, Alec and the girl got separated from the rest of the party. They had all kept together as far as Box Hill, but on the way back to Leatherhead, a bridle path near the Hand-in-Hand had struck Alec as being very attractive, and the girl had thought so too. They decided to cut across that way to Headley Common, and link up with the others at the station in Leatherhead.

Now Alec had a good chance to look at her. She was easily the prettiest of the girls in the party, and she was quite intelligent too. About the same height as himself, maybe an inch or so shorter, hair cut close round her small ears, like a boy, a well-developed figure, and nicely shaped muscular legs. He liked her clothes too. They were sensible, without being exaggerated. A hand-knitted fawn jumper over an open-necked lemon shirt; a short suede jacket, and a well-cut brown tweed skirt, ankle socks, and sensible brogues. That was how a girl should dress for the country, not like some of those in the batch they had left behind. Fancy coming on a ramble in silk dresses, and court shoes! No wonder they'd crawled along at about two miles an hour, and sweated like navvies climbing Box Hill.

Come to think of it, it was a miracle they'd got that far without any accidents, but perhaps it was the first time they had ever been out for a long walk in the country. Only used to flat town pavements, and factory floors. It wasn't their fault they didn't know what to wear; or maybe they didn't have anything else. Yes, that was probably more like it. There was a deeper reason for almost everything. You laughed without thinking; on the face of it, their get-up was ridiculous, but when you weighed it all up, it wasn't such a laughing matter after all . . . 'Well, are you satisfied?' the girl asked, stopping. She smiled mischievously, looking straight into his eyes . . . 'Satisfied?' He didn't understand.

'Well,' she said with a grin, 'You've been looking me over for the past ten minutes. I hope I'll do.'

Alec laughed. 'You will. Very well. But I didn't know I was doing it. I'm sorry. I suppose, being a tailor, I'm more interested in clothes than most people.'

She put one hand on her hips, with the other posturing in the air, and turned round slowly, like a mannequin on a pedestal.

'The latest style, modom,' she simpered, '34 bust, 38 hips. Suede jacket, good imitation, twenty-eight shillings, shirt, five shillings; jumper eight ounces wool, six purl three plain; skirt home-made, a yard and a half material at three shillings a yard; ankle socks, one shilling; shoes, eighteen and eleven. I hope modom likes the ong-semble?'

'Very nice,' said Alec, acting up. 'I'll take the whole damn lot! And I could do with some underwear too. Have you anything special to show me in bloomers?'

She laughed. 'You don't know much about underclothes. I can see you haven't got any sisters. Bloomers!

The only girl I know who wears them is my grandmother!'

He grinned. 'Pardon my ignorance. But I'm still young, I can learn. I'm only twenty-four.'

'It's quite all right,' she said. 'I'll forgive you this once. Now let's drop the subject. We'll leave it at the underclothes, eh?'

He nodded. They walked on for a little while in silence, then gradually they warmed to each other, and spoke together easily, as though they'd been friends for a long time.

Her name was Sarah Goodnick. She had no father. She lived at home with her ailing mother and four grown-up brothers, and kept house for them. She had one sister who'd been a mistress at a secondary school, but she had married another teacher, a gentile, and given up her position.

Alec told her all about himself. There really wasn't much to tell. He avoided any mention of his mother, just said he lived in digs; that seemed to be enough. He was glad he'd met her, perhaps she was THE girl for him. From a working-class family, she knew the things he knew, was used to his sort of life; crude things wouldn't shock her, she was used to plain talking. And she was a housekeeper. She could cook, and sew, and darn socks.

Alec thought of Sam. Just the person Sam was looking for, maybe, what he was looking for, too, only he didn't want to get married, not if he could help it. All sorts of pleasant combinations ran through his mind. Sarah going with him to concerts, on rambles, to theatres, lectures. He hoped it would turn out all right. It was about time he had a break.

And Sarah, walking beside him, kicking dead twigs and little stones with her feet, was very sorry for him. Poor boy! Living all by himself. What sort of life could it be? She knew how helpless her big brothers were when she wasn't about. Never had clean handkerchiefs or properly laundered shirts. He looked quite tidy, but she guessed he must find it hard. She felt she'd like to gather him into her family, to mother him.

'You must come round to my place one Sunday for dinner,' she said.

He blushed. It was very nice of her. He only hoped she meant it.

'Thanks very much,' he stammered. 'I'd be glad to, only I don't want to be any trouble.'

'Don't be silly,' she answered. 'It isn't any trouble at all. When you cook for six, you can just as well cook for seven. You don't even notice the extra one.'

She was much more self-possessed than Alec. She wondered what made him so flustered. It was the most natural thing in all the world for her to invite him to dinner.

Alec was silent for a few minutes. He hardly knew what to say now.

'It's very good of you,' he said at last. 'We'll fix it up later.'

She nodded. 'Right!'

He really would like to have dinner at her place. How long was it since he'd had a proper home-cooked meal? They never made things in restaurants like you had them at home. He didn't realize until now how much he missed his mother's cooking. Nobody made chicken soup like she did, and her lockshen pudding! His mouth watered. Yes, he must go round to her house. It certainly was good of her to ask him. But he'd have to go careful. You never could tell. It might be a trap. Baiting the hook with a few dinners ... Well, it wouldn't work; he'd keep his eyes wide open. The moment he caught her making any demands, he'd back out of it. No entanglements! He couldn't afford to get married. That must always be fixed at the back of his mind.

The sun began to sink. The air seemed to grow thicker and sweeter as the dusk crept on. The last red rays of the sun lit up the low, banked clouds with a fringe of ruddy light. They stopped on the crest of a hill, and looked down on the glory of the setting sun. Speechless city dwellers, looking with delight at a diurnal miracle, denied them six days out of seven.

'Like kippers and jam!' she said suddenly, in a low voice.

He laughed. And so it was! The brown banks of mottled cloud like crisply fried kippers, and the deep red radiance of the fiery sun, like smears of jam across the western sky. It was well put, but he thought he'd heard the phrase somewhere before. Still, he couldn't expect her to have the mind of a poet, she was well enough endowed as it was. She was pretty, intelligent, had a nice figure. She could cook, and sew. What more could a man want? — a working man at that?

She turned her face to him, and it shone bright and warm and flushed, like the setting sun. He kissed her, naturally, as if he had to, and she seemed to expect it. He walked the rest of the way to Leatherhead, with one arm round her waist. They didn't talk very much, they understood each other so well, it was warm and comradely to walk along in silence.

The sweet country air filled their lungs, loaded with the soft smell of flowers and wet grass. Through Alec's head ran the Song of Songs. Only music, or poetry, could describe the way he felt now, walking linked to this girl, along the quiet country lanes. His father had beaten him with his leather belt more than once for skipping Hebrew classes, but now he wasn't sorry he had been forced to go. It was worth it, just to be able to repeat in his head the music of those ancient Hebrews. That wonderful pastoral, Shir Hushirim.

. . . Rise up my love, my fair one, and come away. For lo, the winter is past, the rain is over and gone, the flowers appear on the earth; the time of the singing of birds is come, and the voice of the turtle is heard in our land; the fig tree ripeneth her green figs, and the vines are in blossom. They give forth their fragrance. Arise my love, my fair one, and come away . . .

They met the whole, flushed, jolly party at the station. They explained, not very convincingly, that they had tried to explore a sidepath, and missed the road. Nobody believed them. Only couples got lost that way. The men grinned indulgently. Lucky dog! Making whoopee! They only wished they'd had half a chance of losing their way with Sarah.

They all managed to squeeze into two compartments, and Alec and Sarah sat side by side, pressed tightly together. When the train steamed on to the platform at London Bridge they were both sorry. Alec hadn't enjoyed himself so much for a long, long time.

CHAPTER XIV

He went down to her house for dinner the following Sunday. She lived the other side of Whitechapel. Her mother and brothers all seemed pleased to see him. Alec took to them at once. He felt at home immediately. They had bortsch, roast chicken and French potatoes, with stewed apples for dessert.

She cooked as well as his mother. Better! He'd never tasted such bortsch before in all his life. While the women cleared up down below, he went upstairs with the boys into the little parlour, and played two games of chess. They were no match for him. Out of sheer gratitude, he tried hard to lose, but they were too easy, and blundered each time, into simple mates.

Then Sarah came up. She had taken off the overall she had worn at the table, and changed into an oyster satin blouse, and a fawn skirt. She looked scrubbed clean, like a little schoolgirl. Alec would have guessed her age at seventeen, not twenty-two. She sat at the piano, and played little Hebrew melodies, and the brothers hummed in harmony, or sang the words softly.

> Der rabbe hat geheisen froelich sein
> Tra-la-la-la-la-la-la-la-la
> Trinken bromfen, nicht kein wein
> Tra-la-la-la-la-la-la-la-la . . .

One by one the brothers found excuses for leaving

the room, until Alec was alone with her. He wasn't in the least embarrassed. He couldn't even feel suspicious. He sat back, sated, on an armchair, and begged her to play something for him. She protested she couldn't play very well, but she stayed at the piano, and he insisted, so she played for him, with a light, delicate touch, the Brahms Waltz in A. Then, accompanying herself, without any further cajoling from Alec, she sang *Auf dem Wasser zu singen*. Alec joined in. That rippling song of Schubert's was one of his favourites. Then *Röslein auf der Heide*, and *Maytime*, that he knew from Tauber's records, and *Where e'er you walk*, and other songs. He was in luck to-day, and no mistake!

They got to talking of the Workers' Circle concerts. Now it came back to him, that he'd often seen her at Circle House, and she had noticed him as well. Funny, that they should get really friendly for the first time at a ramble. It was a tiny world after all! And before he left, he discovered that her father had worked in a tailor's shop, been a presser, too, like his. Tinier and tinier!

He hated to leave her, but he didn't think it nice to stay too late the first time. He wanted to come again. Walking home, he thought of her all the way. She was just the girl for him. The same background exactly, yet like him, she had managed to grasp at more beautiful things. He had been searching years for someone like her, and here she was all the time, right under his nose. He was happy. He knew for certain she wasn't trying to trap him. She was a wonderful friend. He hummed to himself.

Das tausend schöne Jungfräulein
Tausend schöne Herzelein
Wollte Gott, bin ich heute bei ihr,
Wollte Gott, bin ich heute bei ihr ...

CHAPTER XV

SARAH had promised to visit her sister one Saturday, and she persuaded Alec to go along with her. It was a long ride to Barnes, but the day was fine, and they sat on top of the bus, and all the windows were open. It took the best part of an hour to get there, but they chatted so pleasantly, they were both surprised to find they had reached their destination.

Her sister lived in a clean little semi-detached villa. Five rooms, kitchen and bathroom, and a garden at the back. Just right for a couple with a small family.

Mr. Saunders, the husband, opened the door for them. He was tall, and fair, and timid-looking, wore big spectacles, and stooped slightly. A real novelist's college professor. Alec could just imagine him saying in a thin squeaky voice: 'Now, boys! Now, boys!'

Her sister was in the kitchen. She resembled Sarah, but was darker, more Jewish looking, and wore spectacles like her husband. Through Alec's mind flashed a picture of half a dozen grinning kids in a row, all wearing spectacles, the boys looking like mum, the girls like dad.

Mrs. Saunders kissed Sarah affectionately, and shook Alec's hand. She summed him up at a glance. Not too bad. Clean and respectable, probably intelligent. And didn't look too much like a Jew either. She was glad of that. She didn't want her sister to fetch along any snotty Vitechapel Jews. She didn't want the whole neighbourhood to know she was Jewish. Besides, Ronnie was coming to tea as well. She would hate Miss Ronald to tell all the other mistresses at the old school that she was mixed up with a lot of dirty East End cockneys.

'Now go along to the drawing-room,' she said. 'I won't be a minute. Just dress this salad.'

They hung up their macs, and joined Mr. Saunders in the parlour. Alec sat down quietly in a chair.

'Where's Alice and Ralph?' asked Sarah.

'Oh, they've gone to a friend of theirs who's giving a party,' Mr. Saunders said. He chuckled. 'It's a treat to get the little rascals out of the way for a bit.'

'Oh, but I think they're little darlings!' Sarah protested.

'So would I, if I came to see them once in six months, and found them on their best behaviour. They're a couple of terrors, Sarah, you can take it from me!'

'Personally,' interjected Alec, wondering if he might say something. 'I prefer 'em that way.'

Mr. Saunders grinned.

'Well, tell you the truth,' he said. 'So do I.'

Alec got up and walked round the room. There was a big earthenware vase in one corner, and a bunch of willow catkins stuck out, and made a dab of shadow on the wall. There were two or three bright pictures hanging from the wooden rail that ran round the room like a frieze. Coming close up to them, he saw they were framed L.M.S. posters. A damn good idea! Art for the million! He worked round to the bookshelf. Nothing very interesting. The usual stuff, middle to three-quarter brow. Amongst others, Warwick Deeping, Ethel Mannin, David Garnett, Arthur Symons. Several Shakespeares . . . A Dickens set (probably from the *Daily Mail*) . . . Bernard Shaw . . . H. G. Wells . . . Macaulay . . . Professors Lodge and Jeans . . . A fat Nuttall's dictionary . . . Fowler's *Modern English Usage*.

Just what he might have expected. A catholic taste. Quite conventional middle-class, even to the ready-made guides to the Universe, handy keys to the problems of the eternal whys and wherefores. A whole library of escape. You had only to pick up one of these books, and your mind soared into the vast empyrean, and you forgot there were such mundane things on earth as employment queues for example, and labour colonies, and filthy East End slums. He took down the dictionary, and perched himself on a chair, skimming through the pages.

Mrs. Saunders came bustling in. The salad was done, and the table laid. Tea would be ready just as soon as Ronnie arrived. Sarah's sister felt slightly embarrassed, as though she had to entertain two human beings from a much lower stratum of society, people to whose company she was entirely unaccustomed. She felt it was up to her to make conversation, to get her guests to feel at home. She started on Alec first. He seemed interested in books, that would make a fair opening gambit.

'. . . Er . . . You read a lot?' she asked.

'Fair amount,' he answered. He didn't feel like getting into any arguments.

'I suppose you've other things to do, more important than reading?'

In spite of herself, a rather sarcastic, superior, schoolmistressy tone had crept into her voice. Alec bridled.

'There ARE more important things than reading!' he answered.

He couldn't stand the way she spoke, condescendingly, from some lofty elevation. Damn it all! He wasn't a pupil of hers! Still, perhaps she couldn't help it after all those years in school.

'. . . So there are more important things than reading . . . Such as?'

'Thinking.'

She smiled. Quite good.

'I agree with you,' she said.

There was a strained silence for a few minutes, then she started again. After all, she had her duty as hostess. She had to make him feel at ease. She wished Ronnie would hurry up!

'Do you go in for sport? . . . Do you play any games?' she asked pleasantly.

'No.'

'Football?'

'No.'

'Walking, or swimming, or anything like that?'

'No. I don't like sport.'

'But surely you must do something in your spare time?' she insisted.

'Oh, I play draughts,' he said, 'and go to the pictures.'

Mrs. Saunders was silent. He was a real ninny, this fellow. Whatever made her sister get hold of such a chap? He wanted a thorough shaking, something to wake him up. Bothered if she'd be troubled with him. She looked at her sister, and noticed Sarah was blushing. She was sorry she had made her uncomfortable, but she hadn't really meant to show up her boy friend. His own foolishness had done that, she thought maliciously.

Sarah was very angry. She knew Alec was lying. She could see that her sister's questions had got his back up. Fancy her having the cheek to cross-examine him like that! Why, he had more sense in his little finger than she had in her whole head, although she'd been a teacher at a secondary school for donkeys years.

Mrs. Saunders changed the subject. She dropped Alec. That nincompoop she decided, was not worth bothering about. She turned to Sarah.

'You know, I've been pretty busy lately. Doing some coaching at the prep. school.'

'More coaching? I thought you'd done with that.'

'Well, it's for rather a difficult examination. I didn't want to take on the job, but they pressed me so much I had to oblige them. There are only eight lessons a week in any case. Seven and six an hour. That's three pounds for eight hours' work.'

She looked pleased with herself, preening her feathers like a turkey cock. She expected congratulations. A brilliant woman! Alec could guess she always tried to impress strangers that way. Led up the conversation ... Yes, I've been pretty busy lately ... Coaching for exams you know ... Seven and six an hour ... See what a brain I've got! Admire me, pat me on the back. Am I not wonderful? ...

The bell rang. Mrs. Saunders jumped up, very excited.

'Ah! — That's Ronnie!'

She ran to the door and Alec heard her greeting the woman in the hall. She came into the room a few minutes later with the other woman, her arm round her friend's slim waist.

'This is Ronnie — Miss Ronald,' she said proudly. 'She's on the staff where I used to teach. This is my sister.'

'How-de-do?'

'Her friend.'

'How-de-do?'

Alec got up, gave a little bow, and sat down again.

Miss Ronald was a tall, thin, hungry-looking spinster. She looked as though she had lived all her life in Barnes, or Dulwich, or Balham, and never been anywhere else. And yet she had travelled a good deal. Switzerland, the Black Forest, Italy, Greece, Mallorca, Minorca, Egypt; and for all the impression this had made on her mind or her outlook, she might have stayed in Balham all the time. Here was one incorruptible suburbanite, another bit of for ever Tooting.

Sarah's sister obviously looked up to her, and Mr. Saunders seemed to regard Miss Ronald as an extremely cultured person. He listened respectfully when she spoke her grammatically perfect no-split-infinitive, nicely balanced little sentences. She was extremely delicate with her words, scraping them out with a tooth-pick, carefully selected pearls. Alec put her down as teaching English. He pitied the poor kids in her class.

Most high-school teachers were like Miss Ronald, fond of using emasculated prose. If they ever came across some real English, stuff with guts in it, they would probably hold their noses, or else faint clean away.

He was terribly bored at the tea table. Ronnie's mild, schoolgirlish witticisms were getting on his nerves. Mrs. Saunders was beaming. There's a friend to have! Ronnie was on the top of her form. She was glad she'd invited her down to-day. Sarah would see the type of people she mixed with, and tell them at home. And that little jew-boy was dumb. Didn't have a word to say for himself. At least she had to give him credit for enough brains to remain silent; he'd certainly put his foot in it if he tried to open his mouth.

Sarah glanced across to Alec, and winked. She could guess what was going through his mind. She was sorry she hadn't prepared him for this, but if she'd told him what to expect, he wouldn't have come, and having already promised, she hated coming here by herself. Without the kids, the whole house had lost the feeling of being lived in at all, seemed to her dry, and schoolmarmy. She felt out of place, like a little girl invited down to tea by the headmistress. Minding her p's and q's all the time.

They lit cigarettes, and Ronnie led the way to the drawing-room. She was evidently a frequent visitor here. Mrs. Saunders stayed behind to clear the table, and they heard the clatter of plates in the kitchen. She was back in the parlour a few minutes later. She wasn't going to trouble about washing up now. Alice would help her when she came home in the evening. She was a peculiar child Alice, liked doing things like that, loved dipping her hands in soapy water. Well, she could help if she wanted to, by all means, that gave HER more leisure. She could sit down now, and listen comfortably to Ronnie the whole afternoon without any interruption.

For half an hour Ronnie continued her genteel, well-modulated twaddle. Alec fidgeted in his chair. He couldn't stand this much longer. He kept motioning to Sarah when none of the other's were looking ... Let's get out of here for God's sake! ... But Sarah took no notice of his gestures, and smiled, a little teasingly. Do him good, she thought, a lesson in self-control like this. She wasn't making such a fuss, and after all she was in the same boat herself.

Suddenly Alec had an idea. He thought of the piano. Music wouldn't be so bad; anything would be better than more Ronnie. He waited till there was a slight lull in the recitative, then he jumped in.

'Would you mind, Mrs. Saunders, if we had a little music?'

Ronnie clapped her hands enthusiastically.

'Oh! That's de-lightful! ... Do you play, Mr. ... er ... er?'

'No. I don't, but Sarah does. Very nicely, too.'

Ronnie turned to her with an ingratiating smile.

'Oh, will you pl-ease play something for us, Sarah dear?'

Sarah nodded, and got up, blushing, from the chair, and went over to the piano stool. Alec had wriggled out of it after all. This was his revenge for having to stay here. She ran up a few brittle arpeggios, and swung round on the stool, her hands crossed on her thighs.

'What shall I play?' she asked.

'Do you know that thing from *The Mikado*?' asked Mrs. Saunders quickly. She whistled a few bars.

Sarah nodded. She could play that with the tip of her nose. Her sister had never grown out of Gilbert and Sullivan. She wouldn't spend two shillings on a Symphony concert, but she'd ride ten miles, and wait six hours in a queue to hear 'A wand'ring minstrel I'.

'Very nice,' said Ronnie when Sarah had finished. 'You play extremely well.'

Sarah nodded gravely. Eight marks out of ten.

'I say,' Alec broke in, 'I wish you'd play a couple of those little Hebrew songs I heard at your house the other week.'

Mrs. Saunders' face became flushed. She was terribly embarrassed. She would hate that above all things, yet she couldn't say no. Ronnie seemed interested. She leaned forward.

'Please do,' she begged.

Of course she knew Mrs. Saunders was a Jewess, but she never liked to mention it. She always avoided talking about Jews in her presence. It was tacitly understood that Jews were non-existent as far as Mrs. Saunders was concerned. She really would have liked to know more about that peculiar people, but her friend was so secretive on that subject. She always turned red, and shut up like a clam whenever Jews were mentioned.

Sarah played two little melodies. Ronnie liked them very much. Reminded her of when she was in Egypt. Real Eastern music. Mr. Saunders sat up and took more ,interest. Quaint little things, in the minor key both of them, like negro spirituals. One of them did sound like the tune of 'When Israel was in Egypt's land'. He was a Paul Robeson fan. It was his opinion that Robeson was the greatest natural basso in the world. He went everywhere to hear him sing.

'Don't you think those songs have much in common with negro spirituals?' he threw out tentatively, although he hardly expected an answer.

Alec nodded in agreement.

'True,' he said. 'That's probably because they're both the musical expression of beaten, oppressed races.'

'Oh!' said Mr. Saunders.

He hadn't looked at it that way before. He never spoke to his wife about her religion, or her people, because he had discovered early in their married life that she was touchy about those things. He would like to have a long chat with this young man one day, if he'd care to come round. Very interesting, their old ways and picturesque customs. Very interesting indeed.

'That last one was very nice,' said Mrs. Saunders.

Her tone implied that it should stay the last. She saw Alec was about to speak.

' — er, Do you remember that Mozart minuet you used to play?' she interjected hurriedly.

Sarah nodded. She was here on show, she might just as well take it philosophically. She turned back to the piano, but Alec broke in loudly.

'— That's right!' he exclaimed. 'I've got it now! "Der rebbe hat geheisen froelich sein". That's the one I wanted to hear.'

Mr. Saunders pricked up his ears. German?

'Der rebbe hat . . .?'

Alec explained briefly. It was a chasidic song. The chasidim were a jolly rabbinical sect, and on feast nights the disciples gathered round the rabbi, dancing and clapping their hands, and singing these songs. He translated roughly. The rabbi has commanded that we be merry. To-night we drink brandy. Brandy not wine. Yoshke, Yoshke, harness the sledge, we're going out on a jolly ride.

Mr. Saunders shook his head. Very interesting. He'd look it up in the *Encyclopaedia Britannica*. How would Alec spell Chasidim? . . . C-H-A-S-I-D-I-M . . . Ah! He jotted it down in his little notebook and sat back in his chair, and listened with enjoyment as Alec sang the song in Yiddish, at the top of his voice:

'Der rebbe hat geheisen froelich sein
Tra-la-la-la-la-la-la-la-la . . .'

He enjoyed making himself appear stupid. Sarah's sister must be dying for him to shut up. He imagined what she must be thinking about him. There was a chuckle in his voice.

'Tra la-la-la-la-la-la-la-la. . .'

Mrs. Saunders felt that the lobes of her ears were burning. She hoped the neighbours wouldn't hear anything. If they asked her, she'd say they were German folk songs, the words sounded like German anyway. She wished Sarah would take that imbecile home, he was spoiling her whole afternoon. Whatever could Ronnie be thinking about it all? She couldn't really be enjoying this!

Alec finished. Ronnie and Mr. Saunders clapped enthusiastically.

'Bravo! Bravo!'

'Well we've got to be going now,' said Alec. 'Got to see some friends in the West End.'

Mr. Saunders looked at his watch.

'But it's still quite early. Stay a little longer, do!'

Alec glanced at Mrs. Saunders. She was probably offering up a fervent little prayer for him to say no. She wouldn't be disappointed; he didn't intend to stay any longer. He'd played around with her quite enough, and after all, she WAS Sarah's sister . . . No. They really couldn't stop. He was sorry, but they had to go. They'd stay later another time. He thanked them for a nice tea, and a very pleasant sociable afternoon.

Mr. Saunders shook his hand cordially by the door. He had taken quite a fancy to this young man.

'You really must come again, old chap,' he said. 'I've enjoyed myself immensely.'

'Yes, don't be strangers, the two of you,' his wife said lamely.

She kissed Sarah good-bye, shook Alec's hand, and stood by the door waving, till they passed out of sight down the road. Somehow or other she'd make Sarah understand quite definitely that she didn't want to see that vulgar ignoramus again, not in her place, at any rate.

On the bus Sarah tried to be angry.

'You shouldn't have done it,' she said.

But there was a half-smile on her face. So he was forgiven. Sarah, he was sure, must have felt that way herself. He liked to see a woman like her sister, having the courage of her convictions, leaving her home and her people for the man she loved, marrying a gentile in spite of bitter parental opposition. He admired her for that, that was all to the good, but to throw overboard one set of hidebound prejudices, and take up a whole set of new ones. To masquerade as a hundred per cent Aryan! Why, they only had to look at her nose! She probably had roast joint on Saturday, had it cold on Sunday, and hashed up on Monday, and sent the kids to the Church Army. At least the Jewishness she had discarded, for all its faults, its turbulent excitable people and habits, had life and colour, throbbed with vitality. He couldn't for the life of him understand how any intelligent person could exchange that for the anaemic narrow-minded dreariness of suburbia.

'... I'm sorry,' he said. 'But I really couldn't help it.

She nodded after a while in agreement. He thought she'd forgotten about it, but a few minutes later she spoke again. '... Well, I must admit she asked for it.'

CHAPTER XVI

THEY broke their journey in the West End. They didn't have to meet anyone. That had been invented by Alec on the spur of the moment. Sarah wanted to see a certain show. From the reports she had heard, it was supposed to be extra good.

There were not many people waiting outside the theatre, the play apparently was coming off shortly. That was one point in its favour, the size of the audience was usually in inverse proportion to the quality of the play. Sarah insisted on paying for herself, she refused to go in otherwise.

They had a good seat in the gallery, the fourth row. Gradually it filled up, mostly with women. Alec felt uncomfortable amongst all these females, surrounded by row on row of sweating women. Fat ones, thin ones, loud-mouthed babblers. He saw immediately they had made a mistake coming here. Judging from the appearance of the audience, he could tell what the play would be like.

It was a romantic pastiche of a girl who danced her way to fame in the ballet. She passed from one lover to another, wedded only to her art. The first act ended. They went to the bar to have a drink.

It was horribly smoky in the overcrowded room. Red faces, steaming spectacles, unbuttoned waistcoats. Snatches of conversation . . . 'Isn't she marvellous? . . .

Now isn't she?' . . . 'I just love the way she say's "darling," don't you?' . . . 'He's very, very good. I saw him in *On the Way*, and *Good Evening Albert*, and two or three other shows. I think he's splendid!'

Alec looked appealingly at Sarah. She finished her drink quickly, and they went into the auditorium. Like stepping into a flower garden. Breatheable air. They passed along the gangway to the low iron rail, and looked down on the boiled shirts. Beautiful backless frocks, silver ermines, Lamé coatees. Solomon's concubines in all their glory!

Three fat women were leaning over the rail, spotting celebrities. Their broad behinds rested on the wooden bench, and spread out in massive bulges of fat. Alec wished he were an artist, just to draw in a few bold strokes, a quick impressionist picture of those sprawling buttocks. And he'd call it 'Saturday night at the Theatre'.

The warning bell rang. They took their seats for the second act. More lovers. More soulful speeches about art. Then a ballet. Alec sat up. He recognized Stravinsky. How in the world had the *fire bird* blundered into this cretinous jungle?

The dancers pirouetted like elephants. When they landed on the boards the stage shook. The premier dancer posed like a coquettish chorus girl. He gazed up at the gallery with his cupid's bow mouth and big mascara'd eyes, and kicked off his exits with feminine simperings.

Alec had to shut his eyes. He felt sick. He hoped the music would carry on. That was one small consolation. And this had been running for six months!

And the press had praised it up to the skies! . . . A splendidly constructed piece of work . . . The finest thing the author has given us to date . . . Should run for at least a year . . . The very thing the public wants!

Maybe, he thought, but what the author wants, is a jolly good spanking, and a few more years in school, or better still, a spell in a workshop, or factory. That'd larn him!

The second act ended. The *prima ballerina* had met her mate. She was giving it all up; her career, everything, for Love. She was going to marry the poor composer. The last act would probably find the composer's *magnum opus* snapped up by the Scala, Milan, and she would come out of retirement, bigger and better than ever, the *première danseuse* in her husband's opera. Oh la! la! – Who wouldn't be a *prima ballerina?*

Excited conversation burst out all round them. People got up from their seats to stretch their legs. They all looked shiny and triumphant. The women were all ballet dancers, and the men, noble, unappreciated, composers.

Alec had enough. 'Look here,' he said, 'Let's go. I can't stick any more of this.'

His mood communicated itself to her. Because he couldn't enjoy the play, she was unable to either. Without a word, she picked up her coat, and followed him into the street.

They walked slowly along the Embankment, looking over the parapet at the coloured lights playing on the water, and then cut through Queen Victoria Street, towards home.

He had the same feeling as on that day in the country, when he had first met her. It wasn't Love, he didn't believe in that, but she attracted him physically, and he felt somehow fulfilled and contented when he walked beside her. He hoped they could keep on like this for ever, walking quietly, soothingly, through the deserted city streets.

They sat upstairs in the little parlour. Her mother had gone to bed. As each of the boys came into the house, they went straight to their rooms without disturbing them, just saying 'good night' as they passed. Alec smiled at the way they stepped heavily past the door. Giving Sarah plenty of warning.

It was getting late. All the brothers had gone to bed. They heard them moving about for a little while above them, then the house was silent. Sarah nestled up against him on the couch.

Now the touch of her excited him. The faint smell of her perspiration went to his head. He trembled as he put his hands on her breasts. But this wasn't enough. He knew what he wanted. He must get things straight with her. He could not go on like this, they had to come to an understanding. He was not a kid any more, he was a man; this part of his life was long overdue. He didn't quite know how to tell her, but it had to be done; he had to know exactly where he stood.

'... Sarah, I want to talk seriously to you,' he said.

She sat up pouting. 'Oh, mister, this is so sudden!' She mocked the gravity in his voice.

'But it *is* serious, Sarah. I was never more serious in my life.'

She composed herself.

'Well now, I'm serious, too. Go ahead, Alec.'

He got up. It was more difficult to put into words than he had thought. He tried to hedge.

'. . . Have you been out with any chaps before, Sarah?' he asked in a stumbling, awkward voice.

'Why, of course I have! – Dozens!'

She seemed surprised at the question. What was he trying to tell her?

'Oh, I don't mean like that!' he persisted. 'I don't mean just acquaintances.'

She understood now. So that was it!

'Well, I'm still a virgin,' she said. 'If that's what you're driving at.'

That was straight talking, if you like! It put him a bit off his balance. He had expected to have to say those crude things himself, and was struggling for the best way to put them without offending her. Out of the mouths of babes and sucklings!

He sat down again beside her. This made it still more difficult. It would have been so much easier if she had known other men. And yet, in a way, he was glad she hadn't. Subconsciously, he must still be full of the old prejudices. Well, now was his chance to smash through to a newer, saner life. Now or never! If only she would understand! If only . . . Always that qualifying phrase . . . If only I had a better job . . . If only I had more money . . . If only I had more guts . . . If only she would come away with me. If only! If only! If only! . . .

'Sarah,' he heard himself saying, 'I want you to come

away with me somewhere. For a week-end. We'll stay together . . . What do you say?'

She was silent. Alec talked on eagerly.

'We can't carry on like this, Sarah, at least I can't. Holding hands in the dark, and kissing, and cuddling, and canoodling. It works me up, then leaves me plop in the air, and makes me feel terrible afterwards. It doesn't satisfy me, and it doesn't satisfy you. Tell the truth, now does it?'

Sarah shook her head slowly. He was quite right. She got up and went to the piano, and still standing, picked out a tune softly with one finger. He crossed to the piano, and bent over her.

'It's too long to wait until we're married,' he whispered urgently. 'I can't afford to get married yet, and it might be years before I can. It's idiotic to torture ourselves like this in the meantime. Let's be sensible about it, for Heaven's sake!'

He caught hold of her, and turned her round till she faced him.

'Well?' he demanded.

Sarah was silent. She hardly knew how to answer. She had felt he was going to ask her to marry him, and she had already made up her mind to say 'yes'. But this was something altogether different. She didn't quite know how to take it.

'Will you come away with me?' he persisted.

She turned her head a little, looking towards the window. This was all so cold-blooded, all so matter-of-fact. If he'd have caught her in his arms; if he'd said, 'Sweetheart, darling, I love you, you must come away with me, I can't live without you,' she'd have understood. But Alec wasn't the gushing sort, though in her heart, she was sure that he had felt that way. And she really did like him . . . She would be quite willing to go away as he had suggested, if only she could be certain it would turn out all right. But how could anyone be certain? After her sister had had that terrible time in labour with her little boy, she'd sworn she wasn't going to have any more children, and yet, a year later, she had borne Alice. And her sister was a clever woman, experienced in these things, and she had certainly tried every way she knew to get rid of it.

'. . . I'm frightened,' she said, 'something might go wrong.'

'Don't be childish!' he exclaimed. 'Nothing can go wrong. Accidents are one in a million!'

'. . . And I might just happen to be that one,' she said.

He laughed, and caught her in his arms again, and kissed her wildly. He couldn't talk any more. Couldn't she feel how his body was bursting with desire for her? He pleaded with his eyes . . . Sweetheart! My love! . . .

She wanted to let herself go, too, hot from his heat. She felt his body drawing her to him. Her head was thumping. She must keep cool. At least one of them must stay sane, or they'd both be sorry. She put her hands against his chest, and pushed him away resolutely. He sat down on the couch, and leaned back on the cushions, panting.

'I'm sorry, Sarah,' he said . . . 'I couldn't help it.'

She sat down beside him. She had again that impulse to gather him in her arms, like a child. He looked so miserable, like a little boy hauled over the coals after a forbidden game. His excitement had burned away, leaving him rather bedraggled. He had been punished enough! Sarah felt she owed him something.

'All right,' she said impulsively, like giving the child a penny, anything, so that he wouldn't cry; 'All right. I'll come away with you.'

Alec's eyes danced with excitement . . . At last! At last! . . . Those past few moments, he had almost given up the idea altogether. Wonderful, wonderful, Sarah! He leaned towards her and kissed her hands. She surely didn't realize what she was doing for him!

'You're a pal, Sarah,' he said, gratefully.

The boards on the top landing creaked, and they heard soft footsteps pattering overhead, halting by the stairs.

'. . . Sarah! . . . Sarah!'

It was her mother calling. Sarah went to the door.

'Yes, Mum?'

'It's half-past one, Saritchka.'

'All right, Mum. I'll be coming up now.'

The soft footsteps shuffled away gently, and they heard a door close. Alec got up and put on his mackintosh. Sarah came up to him, and he embraced her tenderly.

'. . . But supposing something did happen . . . Would you marry me?'

She didn't know why she said it. She hadn't meant to. It just came out.

He made an impatient gesture with his hand. He thought she'd forgotten about that.

'Look here, Sarah,' he said. 'We've gone over this thoroughly, haven't we? I've told you I can't get married. I don't earn enough to keep myself in decent food and clothes, and I won't drag anyone else in with me. If you get into trouble, it'll be your own fault, and you mustn't blame me for it. If only you do as I tell you, you've got nothing at all to worry about.'

He kissed her again confidently.

'Well, good night, Saritchka,' he said. 'I'll see you on Wednesday.'

She followed him downstairs. He kissed her once more before he went out, and she bolted the door after him, and ran up to her room.

She liked the way he had called her 'Saritchka', almost like one of the family. And although she'd said 'Yes', she was still undecided what to do. Those little endearments in the parlour weren't enough, she felt that too. They couldn't go on like that much longer, continually keeping themselves in check. But she was afraid. She couldn't get over that blind fear. For all his reassuring talk, the more she thought it over, the more frightened she became . . . And he'd looked at her so hungrily. She could imagine what he was going through. She really ought to do this for him — it would be for herself as well . . . Poor Alec! Poor boy!

CHAPTER XVII

On the Saturday morning he was waiting under the clock at London Bridge. He kept glancing at his watch and comparing it with Findlater's. Five minutes past the half hour, and she'd promised faithfully to be on time. It wasn't like her to keep him waiting, she usually came on the stroke, or a couple of seconds before.

He hitched his rucksack up to a more comfortable position and walked slowly to the station. She'd be bound to come along any minute now, then they would go into the country, over that same route that had first thrown them together, and in the evening they would stop at one of the villages, and sleep together in some farmhouse, or a little inn. He was journeying into a new life. This would be the end of adolescence, after this, he would become a whole man. Then there would be a string of fresh problems to face, but at least, he'd be successfully over this first, terrific stumbling block. Going away with Sarah wouldn't give him a better job, or improve his material position in any way, but he would be able to face up to things with a clear mind; other problems were outside himself, he felt he really had no right to approach them, until his own personal tangle was straightened out.

He glanced casually at the papers on the bookstall, and strolled leisurely back to the clock. Nearly a quarter to, and no sign of her. Perhaps she was walking.

He went slowly across the bridge towards the Monument to meet her, keeping a sharp eye on the buses as they passed.

Back under the clock again, and no Sarah. Nearly ten! He was beginning to feel worried. Perhaps she'd been taken ill suddenly; there wasn't a phone at her place, so there was no way he could find out. Just his luck! To be taken bad to-day, of all days! . . . But she'd been in perfect health on Wednesday, she'd never looked better . . . Maybe she'd changed her mind. That was more like it. She'd funked it at the last moment. He would give her till half-past ten. Perhaps she'd mistaken the hour, although he knew that was practically impossible. She might come along then . . .

Batches of happy ramblers passed continuously. People waited near him for a few moments, then they were joined by friends and off they went, while he stood there alone all the time. He began to feel self-conscious about hanging around, in one place all by himself. People must be looking at him, silently jeering. The newspaper man at the corner, the girl in the tobacco kiosk, the fruit pedlar; they must all be pointing him out, laughing up their sleeves . . . All dressed up, and nowhere to go!

The clock struck the half hour. He wouldn't wait any longer. It was evident she had broken her word. He walked morosely to the station, looking back every few steps, half expecting her to come running up, even now. He stopped by the booking office and waited another few minutes. No! She wouldn't come. He was positive now; he could wait there all day!

Suddenly he felt he couldn't go on. He had no desire to go on that ramble without her, not now, at any rate. He couldn't bear to pass across that same country, bitterly disappointed as he was. He turned back and walked out of the station. He stopped for a few seconds under the clock, idiotic, he knew, there wasn't a chance of her coming now, but he couldn't help himself, the spot drew him like a magnet. At last he tore himself away, and got a bus to the West End. He walked to Oxford Circus, and caught the High Wycombe coach. Bucks was still beautiful, and this wasn't the end of the world, after all!

He struck off right away across country to Hughenden. He remembered there should be a little stream on his right as he cut through the grounds at Hughenden Manor. He looked for it, but it wasn't there, the dry summer had emptied the rivulet. It lay very pathetic, a dry bed scooped out between two low banks. On the bottom were bits of wood, and rusty tins, and brownish stones, and where a merry little waterfall used to trickle, a line of big boulders stuck up, overgrown with moss.

It made him feel very sad. All this seemed to work in with his melancholy mood. It was all Sarah's fault. If she'd have been here with him, the stream would have still been beautiful, parched though it was, not looking like some dark, mysterious symbol, omen of stagnation and decay.

And the little parish church also, was sombre, and dark, quiet and mysterious looking. The church in whose shadow the Jew Lord Beaconsfield lay buried. His banner hung inside the church, above a marble slab set in the wall, inscribed with devoted words of friendship from his queen, Victoria. And all round were evidences of his connection with the church. Illuminated parchments, the family pew, the family prayer books. Benjamin Disraeli, Lord Beaconsfield, Jewish patron saint of the Primrose League of diehard Tories.

From the church, it was a hard climb, uphill all the way to Hazelmere. The inn was open. He bought a glass of beer, and ate his lunch outside, on the wooden form. He pushed on from there to Great Missenden. To keep on walking! That was the great thing. If he walked hard, he'd have no time to think, because if he thought of anything, it would only be saturated with Sarah ... Sarah! ... Sarah! ... Damn the girl! It wasn't fair of her to lead him up the garden like this.

At Kingsash, it was time he turned back. He didn't want to stay out over Sunday; he'd forget more easily in London, here, he only had himself for company, and thoughts of Sarah. An elderly gentleman in a straw hat, faced him on the path.

'Pardon me,' said Alec, 'I want to get back to Hazelmere. Can you show me the quickest way?'

'Yes ... Yes, indeed!' answered the old man.

He started on a complicated string of instructions, jabbing the air with his walking stick. Alec kept nodding politely. He knew he would be completely lost after the second stile, but he didn't like to tell him that, the poor old boy was working so hard. At last he stopped, and wiped the sweat from his forehead with a trembling handkerchief.

'Thanks!' said Alec.

He turned to go, but the old man tapped him lightly on the shoulder with his stick.

'Are you fond of roses?' he asked.

'What?'

'Are you fond of roses?' the old man repeated.

'I am,' said Alec.

But what the hell was the old boy getting at? If he thought he'd be able to sell him some, he'd made a big mistake. Maybe if Sarah were there . . .

'We've a lovely show of roses in the church grounds. Some beautiful specimens!' the old man said enthusiastically.

'I'm sorry,' said Alec. 'I haven't much time. I've got to get back to Hazelmere for the High Wycombe bus, otherwise I'll miss my coach.'

The old man waved his stick disparagingly.

'Oh, it'll take no time at all to get to Hazelmere, if you go the way I showed you. And we've got a fine old church too. Dates back from the twelfth century. But DO look at our roses. Just through those gates there.'

'Thanks,' said Alec.

He was defeated. The old man would make a good tout for the Lane. Alec nodded to him, and went into the churchyard. The old boy was so persistent, he didn't have the heart to say no, although he didn't want to be bothered with flowers just now, he wasn't in the mood to appreciate them . . . And he'd already been inside one church to-day, this would be the second; funny, when he hadn't been near a synagogue for ages.

The roses were really beautiful. He was glad now he'd stopped. All shades of red, and pink, and white, breathing out their exquisite perfume. He felt soothed somehow by the peace of their natural beauty. Again he began to think of Sarah, only without any bitterness. She was also like a rose, like a flower; he hummed to himself . . . *Du bist vie eine blume* . . . Music! Music when soft voices die . . .

The sun was sinking as he walked down the lanes towards Hazelmere. Kippers and Jam! He thought of that time, not so long ago, when he had wandered through the country with her. There wouldn't be any more of those walks, not with her, or anyone else. He could never feel like Shir Hushirim again; something had died inside him. So he went on, shedding bits of himself; there in Bucks, another part of his life was left behind.

A letter was waiting for him at home. His heart began to thump wildly as he saw it. He had been expecting something like that, yet the sight of it gave him a shock.

He tore open the envelope. From her, all right. She couldn't come. (Very nice of her to let him know!) She'd thought it all over. It was too much of a one-sided arrangement. He was safe whatever happened, but if she got into trouble, it wasn't so much for herself she worried, but her mother would never live over it. It would be best to call it a day! . . . And she'd signed herself Saritchka — The cruel bitch!

He tore up the letter, and crumpled the pieces in a tight ball, and threw it into the empty grate. He pushed his rucksack under the bed, and started to undress . . . And this day had begun so wonderfully! He'd been out of bed at six, waiting. There was a box of Terry's chocolates in his rucksack, hard-centres, the assortment she liked. He had meant them as a surprise. He wondered dully, what should he do with them now? Eat them himself, or give them away?

His whole life was turning into a sort of Odyssey, a painful search for a way of living. If only he could scrap his mind occasionally; if only he didn't choose so much. No one seemed to come up to scratch. His mother, Dave, Sam, Sarah; they all seemed to be going a different way. Maybe they were all right, and he the one who was wrong. That wasn't impossible. If two companions say 'drunk', the third should go to bed . . . Yes, he must be drunk, either drunk or mad. He'd go to bed and dream about the whole man, if he could, but he knew that the moment his head touched the pillow, he'd start weaving fresh pictures of Sarah, and acting imaginary little scenes in his brain of how they'd caressed each other in the bedroom of the village inn. He tried to shut her out of his mind, but her image persisted. He broke down and sobbed into his pillow miserably, like a hopelessly lost child.

CHAPTER XVIII

ALEC sat by himself at a table in a corner of the club-room at the Circle. There weren't many people about so early on Saturday evening; it usually filled up later on. Besides the bar attendant and the steward, only a couple of domino players, and two engrossed chess enthusiasts, Liff, and another man. He couldn't remember coming into the club-room and not finding Liff there playing chess. Either playing, or canvassing for opponents. If the Messiah came riding in suddenly on his white horse, Liff would be terribly upset, and with his last breath he'd most certainly beg him to put off the resurrection until he had finished the game.

Alec was at a loose end. All his Saturdays were like that lately, empty, ever since he'd lost Sarah. He couldn't work up enthusiasm for anything. He kept clear of women. He was constantly afraid of leaving himself open to another rebuff, he remembered the last one too well.

He sipped his lemon tea, and watched the door casually. One or two people came in, looked round, and went out again. Nodding acquaintances, no one he knew very well. He hoped someone would start up a political argument, then he could join in, and forget himself.

The door opened, and a group of three entered. Two men, and a youngish woman. He recognized one of them, a tall stooping young man of about his own age, with a sparse, gingery beard. He had been to school with Leopold Hartman, but hadn't seen him for years. The woman, also in the twenties, though slightly older than Leopold, wore a Donegal tweed costume, and suède shoes. Her black hair was parted in the centre, and coiled over her ears in plaits. She had dark eyes, and a keen, pleasant face.

The other man was also tall, but carried himself erect. His complexion was very pale, and he wore big, horn-rimmed spectacles. His sports jacket was in a hairy black and grey check. A dark shirt, green tie, green cable-stitch pullover, and flannel trousers, and of course suède shoes, the trade mark of the haute intelligentsia. He carried a pile of books and papers under his arm. All three looked as though they were hot from an I.L.P. conference.

Leopold caught Alec's eye. He came over at once, the others trailing behind, and shook hands with him. He introduced his companions, John Caplan, and Mary Summers, and they all sat at his table.

Leopold's accent was perfect Magdalen. Marvellous what a couple of years at Oxford did for a man! It wasn't the dirty little ruffian Leo he'd dared to run into the girls' lavatory when they were kids at the same elementary school. Churned out to pattern by the scholarship machine. Full of triple-firsts and God-knows-whats. He knew the old man Hartman pretty well, he'd worked with him, whenever Leopold spoke to his father now, he probably needed an interpreter.

'And what are you doing?' Leopold asked patronizingly.

'Oh, I'm in the clothing business in a big way,' Alec answered airily.

'Really! I'm glad to hear it!'

'Oh yes. I'm invaluable to my boss. I get one and three pence an hour, and six months' holiday in the year, without pay!'

It took some time for this to penetrate through Leopold's cranium.

'. . . Oh!' he said. 'You mean you're just an ordinary workman?'

Alec nodded. 'Yes. You've hit it friend, Just that. And what are you up to? Gone in for portrait painting?'

Leopold blushed. With his lean pimply face, fringed by the reddish down, he looked like an embarrassed goat. Caplan turned to Alec in surprise.

'Surely you've read some of Leopold's work?' he said. 'At least, you must have heard of him.'

Alec shook his head.

'Can't say I have . . . Why? Does he write?'

The girl looked indignant.

'Does he write!' she burst out. 'And you're a Jew! Didn't you read *The Voice of Israel*?

'No. I don't read much fiction. It's a novel, I suppose?'

John Caplan looked at him searchingly. He had an idea Alec was pulling his leg, but he seemed serious enough.

'A novel! – And what a novel!' he said. 'True, it didn't sell an awful lot, but that's to be expected from good books. Why the critics plump for him as the greatest modern Jewish writer since Israel Zangwill!'

Leopold lifted his hand in protest.

'Oh, I wouldn't say that!' he said in a low voice.

John Caplan turned on him.

'But the critics said that, didn't they?' he demanded fiercely.

'. . . Yes, they did say that.'

'Well then!'

John Caplan turned to Alec with a triumphant glare. He'd proved his point. Alec nodded feebly. He didn't want to say anything to hurt Leopold, but he didn't have an extra high opinion of Zangwill as a modern Jewish writer. And he was naturally suspicious of University geniuses. He was biased against Leopold right from the start, because of his beard, and his accent, and his clothes. He had a rough idea of the sort of stuff Leopold would write. Maybe there was something real in him. But genius could be the only justification for such a get-up.

Leopold sat modestly at the table. The others did all the talking. He was quite content to let his achievements (and John and Mary) speak for him. Anyway, what could an uncultured barbarian like Alec know of Literature or Art? But he felt distinctly uncomfortable, all the same. He hoped John or Mary would say something soon to impress him. After all, Leopold Hartman was somebody. He'd done something. They had both started level, and now he was a writer, and Alec was in the gutter. He shouldn't have come over to him like this, as if Alec were an equal. It was his own fault. Pearls before swine!

He noted uneasily that John was searching amongst

his books. That would be *Songs from the High Hills* he was looking for, John always carried a copy with him. And he would show the book to Alec, and Alec would glance through it casually, and say 'I don't care very much for poetry,' or something after that style, and just that sort of thing hurt him terribly. All those lofty thoughts and beautiful words, the product of a whole year's blood and sweat, dismissed with a shrug of the shoulders, as if it were of no account.

John put the slim, beautifully bound little volume on the table, and pushed it towards Alec. Alec picked it up, and looked at the title page.

'Yours?' he asked Leopold.

Leopold nodded, shrinking a little. His beautiful delicate child in that uneducated boor's hand. He shuddered inwardly. This was a rape! John should never have done it!

Alec read one poem in silence. About Jerusalem. He turned over the page, maybe the second would be better ... Confused images, twisting, rambling thoughts. A disciple of Ezra Pound and T. S. Eliot; echoes from the Palestinian waste land. The next step was utter incomprehensibility, and Gertrude Stein ... If this was modern poetry, he had to admit it didn't mean a thing to him. If you hadn't been through college, and didn't have a smattering of Greek, and French, and Italian, you were out of it. Perhaps Leopold did have something to say, but it looked as though he were trying his darndest to keep it to himself.

Alec put *Songs from the High Hills* back on the table

without a word. There was a moment's strained silence. They were all looking at him expectantly, waiting for the verdict. John couldn't contain himself.

'Well, what do you think of it?' he blurted out.

'It's difficult for me to say,' Alec answered. 'It's all a bit foggy. I don't pretend to understand this type of poetry, but what is it you're trying to get at?' He asked Leopold point blank.

Leopold shrugged his shoulders. He didn't see why he should have to explain such things to him; and besides, one shouldn't explain poetry. Alec obviously knew nothing of form, or rhythm, or dissonance, or plangency, or the theories of the Imagists. He, Leopold Hartman, had done his job. He had woven those magic words into a delicate gossamer pattern, and if the Philistines were without appreciation, so much the worse for the Philistines!

But John was not so easily satisfied. He was Leopold's self-appointed 'shamas', the faithful attendant who walked before the mystical rabbi when he went abroad, and carried his umbrella; the big-shot's personal bodyguard. He couldn't bear to hear any disparagement of the master. He leaned forward and shook his finger argumentatively in front of Alec's nose.

'Now let me tell you something,' he said. 'This tiny volume is one of the significant things in modern literature; especially to us Jews. These poems are the finest expression of twentieth-century Judaism. There are signs of a renaissance of Jewish culture, and Leopold's book is right in the van of the movement.

He sings of the glory of Judah, the miracle of the new Palestine. I ask you, as a Jew, have you never felt the urge, the desire, to go to Palestine, the home of our fathers?'

Alec shook his head. 'No!'

'But really, haven't you ever felt that Palestine was part of you, and that you'd like to live there, and help build the new Jewish culture?'

'Never,' said Alec. 'I've never had the least interest of that sort in Palestine!'

John was thunderstruck. He couldn't believe Alec meant it. He leaned still closer to him, a red flush glowing under his skin, looking like a feverish invalid.

'I put it to you,' he said weightily, like an amateur debating society's star orator, 'all the nations of the world have homes, countries, they can claim as their own, why should the Jew be the pariah amongst nations?'

Alec shook his head. He had heard all those arguments years ago, he had even used them himself while still at school, but the workshops and factories had taught him how much his nationalism was worth. He had scrapped that childishness for good, that part of his life was also way back, in the gone and forgotten.

'Look here,' he said. 'Whether the Jew is a pariah or not, I believe this nationalism talk is all bunk, whoever it comes from. I haven't the faintest desire to claim Palestine as my own. I believe that wherever a man lives, and does useful work, and brings up his children, is his country. As a worker, I won't be any better off in Palestine, maybe worse. I don't see why

I should change one set of exploiters for another because they happen to be Jewish. I don't see why I should sweat to make profits for rich Jews who've got pots of money invested there. — And as for Leopold's world-shattering poems, nobody'll even think of them in six months' time, and in six years, Leopold himself will wish to God he never wrote them!'

The girl, who had been listening intently, with her chin resting on her hands, leaning her elbows on the table, sat bolt upright, jerked back like a freed spring. This was really going too far! It was all very well to argue on the abstract plane, but when it came to personalities, it was time she put this workman in his place. Fancy talking this way about *Songs from the High Hills*! Why she remembered reading one long poem through eight times to get its inner significance, and going to bed with its music on her lips, and crying herself to sleep, because of the noble perfection of its unsullied beauty. And this ragamuffin, this soap-box screamer, dared to take Leopold's soul in his filthy hands, and scratch at it with his grimy finger nails!

'You have no right whatever to talk this way of Leopold's work,' she broke in tartly. 'What right have you to criticize poetry, or even prose if it comes to that. What do you know about these things? Why if you live to be a hundred, you'll never manage to understand the deep beauties of literature, let alone to produce a single line to compare with one of Leopold's! — Just listen to these words. Listen with your ears, and your eyes, and your whole mind!'

She picked up the book, and turned the pages, looking for 'Apotheosis'. She'd show him! Why even *he* would have to be humble before the sheer magnificence of its sweep.

Leopold stopped her, putting his slender white hand on her arm.

'Please don't,' he said gently. 'Please, let's have enough of this wrangling. It hurts me here!'

He spread one hand over his heart, and sighed. To Alec, he looked like a Christian martyr on the rack. Forgive them O Lord, for they know not what they do!

Alec got up. If he stayed much longer, he wouldn't be responsible for what he said. If this sort of thing hurt Leopold so much, what he really thought would certainly make him faint, or even pass away. He excused himself, and left the table.

He paid his bill, and went out into the street. Ugh! It made him seethe; all this posing and posturing. St. Leopold Sebastian, and his adoring disciples. And what made it worse was that Leopold himself didn't realize he was only a catspaw, a lackey to Big Business. It was very convenient for the rich industrialists to centre Jewish interest on Palestine. First class also, for the Anglo-Saxon imperialists to have some Jews there; to make Palestine a sort of buffer state in the East, cutting it off from other Mohammedan countries. To pit Jews against Arabs, whenever they seemed like making a common front. Divide, and conquer! Just as in India, egging on Hindus against Moslems. Perpetuating the old dog fights ... And now the pipe line ran through Haifa. Oil! Oil! ... Leopold was busy making Palestine safe for the Anglo-Dutch Oil Kings. But what did Leopold understand of these things? He had been a bright kid once with the makings of an intelligent man; now he was a lily, carried about on the arms of his admirers, securely wrapped in cotton wool, insulated from the harsh contaminating breath of the outside world.

CHAPTER XIX

It was always difficult to get into any popular West End show on Saturday night. Not that Alec wanted to see anything particularly, but the Hartman circus had upset him a little, and he wanted to forget himself, and go to some place where he'd have no need to think.

All the cheap seats were full up everywhere. He wandered about the West End like a lost soul. For the life of him he couldn't find what to do with himself this evening.

A young girl passed by. She was not unusually pretty, but what struck Alec about her was the complete lack of any make-up on her face, so strange here, in this street of artificial complexions. He turned automatically to look after her, and bumped up against a smartly dressed crowd, standing on the pavement outside the 'Contessa'. They were debating loudly, to go in, or not?

That gave Alec an idea. Why not the 'Contessa'? He hadn't been inside a dance hall for years, and it was as good a way as any of killing a lonesome evening. He decided on the spur of the moment, paid his half-crown, and descended the luxuriously carpeted stair to the dance floor.

The bustle, and excitement, and the warm mixture of sweat and perfume, came strangely to him. It was so long since he'd been inside one of these places. He had gone dancing quite a lot five or six years ago.

Went to places as far afield as Harrow and Surbiton. Even in those days groping for something different; a fresh, intelligent, unspoiled country girl.

And that time, he had thought he'd found her, at Farr's Academy in Harrow. He seemed to be the only stranger and she was easily the best dancer there. And he had treated her to a coffee, and they'd got to talking together. Then suddenly she'd asked if he were Jewish, and he had answered yes. Did he know another Jewish boy, Solly Goldberg, who lived in Whitechapel? He was an awfully nice chap, she said, she had been out with him several times. Alec had to admit he didn't know him, and besides, there must be dozens of Solly Goldbergs round where he lived. Then somehow, after that, he had lost all interest in her. She wasn't what he was looking for.

It seemed like a gala night. All the tables were occupied, and dozens of little groups stood around the dance floor, chatting gaily. He moved towards them, and leaned against a pillar, right on the edge of the sprung maple.

The band struck up a fox-trot. At once, a stream of flushed dancers trickled past him. He stood still by the pillar. He felt out of it somehow, a cold spot in a bubbling cauldron. Was it a good sign he couldn't get worked up any more about going to a dance? He shifted a little, he must be in the way. Couples pushed by him unceremoniously. Clark Gables, and Marlene Dietriches, and Tallulah Bankheads. . . .

In his day, the boys had all been Valentinos, with sleeked hair, and centre partings, and long sideburns.

There was an old photograph of himself somewhere at home, all dressed up like that. He looked like a little greener, just off the boat from Galicia . . . And that had been smart then. God! The tricks kids get up to! . . . And the songs had been jollier, more careless. Those were the prosperity days. Everybody had earned good money then . . . 'I love to see my baby do the Charleston . . . Charleston!' . . . 'When my sugar walks down the street' . . . 'When it's night time in Italy, it's Wednesday over here' . . . Even now, some lyrics were just as inane, but the tunes were like dirges.

No getting away from it anywhere; this was the end of an epoch. Everything linked up with economics; even in dance-halls, these swan songs of a decaying civilization. Sad wailings, cheap, vulgar sentiment. Last year it was 'spare a dime' then 'remember my forgotten man', Last round-ups, bread-line songs, steadily getting more and more doleful. Nothing for it, but to lie down and die. Trade is bad, exports have gone to hell, and we're all bankrupt, but there's nothing we can do about it, so let's dance, and cry our eyes out! . . .

More than half the crowd was Jewish. Alec recognized several of the dancers. Young boys and girls. Only yesterday they were playing nuts on the pavements; grown up overnight. Smartly dressed; too smartly dressed! Film stars, with padded he-man shoulders, and actresses to their plucked eyebrows, and bella-donna'd eyes. And none of them much over twenty. Thumbnail sketches ran through his head.

Katie Kreeger. The chap holding her round the

waist looked like a student from the careless looseness of his clothes. He was staring into her eyes, his mouth open, like a fish. He seemed very interested; interested in Katie! Katie, the stupid little dunce, always at the bottom of her class, half a cretin, whom the kids used to call 'Katie long-drawers'. Maybe she'd changed, but she had the hell of a way to make up. Not so long ago he had heard her talking to a friend in the street, her stupid ignorance had made him blush; but what did her student care about that? he was probably no better himself; all his interest was in the way she waggled her buttocks.

And Gertie 'snotty-mouth', because she was always slobbering. A queen, or at least a duchess, in a beautifully cut, black satin dress. Her whole poise, the way her slim body swayed, as if she'd had lessons in deportment from expensive teachers. And yet, on Monday, she'd be back at the machine, working like a horse for ten hours a day, waiting for next Saturday.

Two days, Saturday and Sunday, that they snatched from the dark, blind, overpowering maw of hard labour; when they put on the airs and accents that made them so much cheaper. Producers of wealth, rightful owners of the earth, yet they had to pretend to be ladies and gentlemen, to enjoy themselves at the 'Contessa'!

Three men came up behind him, and stopped, talking together. They made no attempt to lower their voices. Alec heard every word. One called Henry was speaking.

'... A flat in Maida Vale somewhere,' he said. 'We arranged about the price, and went to bed. In the middle of the night I felt terribly thirsty. I woke her up, and asked for a cup of tea, and what d'you think she did? — She turned her back to me and started snoring! Snoring!'

. . . 'So what did you do?'

'I'll tell you what I did. I was so disgusted, I dressed myself, and went out!'

'Without paying?'

'Oh no!' said Henry. 'She'd taken the money beforehand!'

'So you left her flat! That must have been tough on her!'

Alec smiled to himself. One of the three evidently had a sense of humour, but Henry took it seriously.

'Yes,' he answered, 'but I couldn't help it. I went to a coffee stall. I just had to have that cup of tea! . . .'

The encore ended, and the dancers streamed on to the carpeted lounges. One of the men said something, dropping his voice as the girls passed. Alec missed his words, but they all laughed, and from the shrill sound of the laughter, it was something obscene. They moved away, still laughing, and a young couple drifted beside him, conversing in monosyllables.

Someone gave him a hearty slap on the back. Alec turned round. He had to stare hard before he recognized Freddie Katz. He was fat, and sunburned, and looked very prosperous. A white diamond, the size of a pea, sparkled on his little finger.

'What you doing here?' Freddie asked.

'Why?'

'Well, this is the first time I've seen you, and I've been hanging round this gaff for years. Why the money I've spent here, I ought to own the damn place!'

Alec tried to shake him off, but Freddie was like a leech. It wasn't every day he met one of his old class-mates, and he had so much to tell, and enjoyed telling it. What he had crowded into his twenty-five years. How he'd started with his father in a little sewing machine repairing business, and worked his way up till they thought nothing now of buying complete factory plants.

... And he'd just come back from a tour of the Mediterranean countries. France, Italy, Greece, Turkey; even going so far as Palestine. Combining business with pleasure, having a holiday, and looking out for cheap machinery at the same time. There was tons of it about, too, but the duty was too high. Ten-pence a kilo. On weight, not on value. He could have wangled it if they'd have taxed the stuff on value, but there was no getting away from weight. You couldn't declare fifty kilos when there was two hundred and forty. The time he'd paid the tenpence, he could get it just as cheap in England. The trouble was, enough people weren't going broke.

Freddie rattled on. He was thoroughly enjoying himself. Greece was a lovely place. Spirits were two and nine a bottle in Palestine ... Nothing to touch Italian girls ... And only last week he'd bought a man out in Birmingham. Paid three thousand for the plant, and sold it the next day for five....

He offered Alec a cigar. A corona-corona. Alec took it, and Freddie lit it for him from a jewelled lighter. He patted Alec on the back patronizingly and walked off, strutting about as if he really did own the 'Contessa'.

Alec didn't believe half Freddie had told him. But the diamond was real, and he had seen his passport, that was genuine, too, complete with his photograph, and the stamps of the different consulates. Freddie and his father, become carrion, feeding on broken corpses. Travelling about the country, buying up plants, their one trouble enough people weren't going broke! Surely civilization was a joke, if such people could not only exist and grow fat, but wear big diamonds, and walk about boasting, as though they were doing something honourable! He spat the cigar on the floor, and crushed it beneath his heel. Unclean! Like Freddie. It left a bitter taste in his mouth.

He thought now he was inside, he might as well dance with someone. The evening was a flop all right, but he would have to make the best of it; it was too late now to go anywhere else. He looked round the floor. No use asking any of the good dancers because they'd be sure to refuse him. First, because he wasn't so nicely dressed, and second, because they hadn't any idea whether he could dance or no. And then, he wasn't one of their clique either. He remembered his dance-hall politics, how he had always resented it if a stranger tried to dance with one of his partners.

He noticed three girls sitting together in an alcove at the back of the lounge, near the band. He watched them for some time. They looked hungrily at the dancers, and shook their skinny shoulders with exaggerated gestures to the rhythm of the music.

From the suburbs, he guessed. Saved up the Lord knows how long for this night at the 'Contessa'. First, to get the frocks. Half a dozen yards apiece of silk tulle, with taffeta underslips. Then patterns from some women's fashion-book bureau. Excited discussions about what styles they should be, ankle length, or touching the floor. Then, when they were finished, the journey up town, and the heavenly moment of entering the 'Contessa'.

The thrill of feet sinking into the soft carpet of the stairs; the posh nickel fittings, and mirrors in the ladies cloakroom. The sudden bustle of bright lights, and bare shoulders, and swaying chattering bodies. Everybody miraculously at ease, except them ... Then excusing their way, a little frightened, to the alcove. Sitting there nervously, far back; as far back from the dance floor as possible, trying hard to look like regulars ... And then, when they got up to dance with each other, how tawdry their home-made frocks looked in comparison with the smart styles of the other girls. Luckily, they themselves didn't notice it!

They sat there, waiting for partners, and the only people to dance with them were gawky young boys, green like themselves, who ruined their new satin shoes, or else, shabby, bald-headed old gentlemen, whom none of the other girls would look at ... Well, Alec decided, he'd ask one of these for a dance. He was certain he wouldn't be turned down, and, he patted himself on the back, he'd be doing a fellow human being a good turn at the same time.

The girl seemed surprised when he came over to her. He had to ask her twice. Then, when it dawned on her, that he was really asking her to dance, she jumped up like a jack-in-the-box, almost upsetting the tea table in front of her. She smiled brightly at her friends, and followed Alec on to the dance floor.

He put one arm round her waist, and as he clasped her hand with the other, he felt her whole body quivering. Her small breasts were hard against his chest, he could feel the nipples pressing into him.

He tried to dance, but when her feet touched the floor, his partner lost all sense of rhythm. She failed completely to follow his steps, so he compromised on a sort of hop-skip-and-jump, that seemed to suit her. The waltz ended, and she stood still opposite him, clapping enthusiastically. The band weren't going to run away, they would play an encore in any case; he didn't see why she had to get so excited.

One thing he appreciated about her, she was quite dumb. He had tried talking to her during the dance, but she had only answered 'yes' or 'no', or shaken her head, concentrating on the tremendous business of hopping round the dance floor.

The encore finished. He led her, still trembling a little, to her seat, and left her safely with her friends. He thanked her, and walked off. This was an event! What poor stuff their lives must be made of, if this sort of thing could keep their minds, and their tongues busy for the next fortnight!

He bought a sixpenny ticket to dance with an instructress. He chose a pretty blonde in a close-fitting black lace dress, and she followed him nonchalantly on to the floor. Her arm rested lightly on his back, a resigned expression on her face. She chewed gum all the time. He could feel the regular up-down of her jaws against his shoulder. Apart from her closeness, it was like dancing with himself; she anticipated his movements, even when he made mistakes.

And the instructress wasn't the least bit interested in him. She had sized him up right away. She'd look blue if she took notice of every penniless little whipper-snapper that danced with her. She preferred them middle-aged and substantial, even if they did tread all over her toes!

When the dance ended, she took his ticket, gave him a hard, bright, mechanical little smile that stayed on her face for the fraction of a second, and walked off. Thank Heaven for that! she thought, but why must all the lousers pick on me? . . .

CHAPTER XX

On the way out Alec reckoned up. Half a crown to go in, coffee and sandwiches ninepence, sixpence the instructress. That was three and nine outlay, and in return he'd had two dances, without enjoying either one. He wasn't sorry; after six years, a dance hall was a novel experience, and it would probably remain so for another six.

It was quite early, half-past ten by the big clock at the corner. He was in no hurry; he'd mooch around for an hour or so, then walk home. He missed Sarah. More than ever when he compared her with the girls at the 'Contessa'. Still, it was no use being babyish about it; that was all over. If it couldn't be Sarah, it would have to be someone else, but it would be the hell of a job finding another anything like her.

He left the crowded fashionable streets, and walked through the darker side turnings. There must be some kink in his mind that always made him look for short-cuts this way. He'd always preferred side streets to the main roads; there seemed to be more character in the shabby little turnings, something about them that appealed to him. And they were quieter. He could think as he walked along, without being rushed off his feet, or diverted by tiddly little sideshows.

He stopped to get his bearings in Wardour Street, where three roads intersected. As he looked up at the street names, a man and a woman came round the corner talking excitedly, and collided with him. Alec apologized without looking at them, and walked off. The man ran after him, and caught him by the sleeve.

'What's the matter with you?' he asked. 'Don't you talk to poor people?'

It was Dave. Alec hadn't seen him since the wedding. Marriage seemed to agree with him, he looked like a well-fed duckling, soft, and pink, and plump.

Dave led him to the woman who was waiting at the corner. She looked very attractive. Alec didn't see what the hell Dave had to kick at. The way he had described his future wife that time, he'd expected to see a fifteen stoner at least . . . Legs like tree trunks! True, they weren't very slim, but he liked a leg to be a leg, something to stand on, and they were nicely shaped too . . . Grumbling for Luck! . . . She didn't look Jewish either, and he would never have taken her for a married woman . . . Maybe she wasn't! A quick suspicion shot through his mind. . . . 'The missus?' he whispered to Dave.

Dave laughed. This was funny!

'The missus? — Don't be an idiot!' He said out loud. 'D'you think I'd take MY old woman up West? — I don't if I can help it. I usually cart her where no one can see us!'

He laughed again. Alec ought to see his wife, then he'd understand. He was a hero to be able to stick her for one day a week, let alone all seven! . . . But it was funny running into Alec with this jane, and him thinking she was his wife.

'I won't introduce you,' he said. 'I believe you've met before.'

Alec shook his head.

'Not that I can remember.'

He was quite sure he hadn't seen her before. If he had, he wouldn't have forgotten her so quickly. He had always liked this quiet, reserved type, but where had Dave managed to pick her up? She wasn't his sort at all. Much too ladylike!

'So you've never met me before?' she said smiling. 'Sure? — Think again!'

Alec shook his head.

'Certain!'

He had never been so positive of anything in his life. He didn't have even a faint recollection of the voice, and that would change in a person least of all. He wracked his mind ... Concerts? ... No! ... Rambles? ... No! ... Dancing? ... Maybe; she was smart enough for that ... But that was so long ago, he'd altered enormously since then ... Where else? ... Where? ... He could not bring it back. He gave it up.

'No,' he said at last. 'I can't remember.'

'My name's Olive,' she told him in a low voice. 'You did me a good turn once. You let me sleep in your bed, when I hadn't any place to go ... Remember now?'

Alec nodded. But it couldn't be! It was impossible! Not this young woman! He had a memory of a big, untidy girl, with tousled hair, and dirty underclothes ... Someone who'd been in service ... And hadn't she worked for Dave's mother afterwards? ... Yes! ...

Yes, that was the one — and this smart young lady, the same girl! . . . Marvellous! Really first class! A better job than Shaw's Eliza Higgins . . . And to come across her again of all people, among the seven and a half millions of London!

They reached Shaftesbury Avenue, and stood on the pavement talking. Suddenly Dave bent his head, startled. His brother-in-law Joe was across the road. He hoped he hadn't been spotted. He looked up quickly, and saw him standing on the edge of the opposite pavement, waving.

Dave turned his head away. He'd behave as though he hadn't seen; perhaps Joe would move off. He looked out of the corner of his eye. Joe was already crossing the road. Dave groaned . . . Damn him! The fat idiot! Now there wasn't a chance of escape.

He waited, cursing beneath his breath, for a hard slap between the shoulder blades. If his back wasn't turned, he'd be punched in the belly. He had these playful ways, his brother-in-law, and he couldn't say a word of protest. Joe loved to greet people like that; a hard jab in the guts, and a roar of laughter. That was Joe's idea of a first class joke . . . Well one of these days, he'd get one back, only twice as hard, so that he doubled up. Then HE'D laugh! See how Joe liked his own medicine.

Plop! Dave felt the broad, hot hand, descend on his back. So he'd arrived! He turned round, and when he faced him, he tried to look surprised.

'. . . Oh! . . . Hello Joe! . . . Where did you spring from?'

'Across the way,' said Joe. 'I been waving about half an hour, only you were too busy jawing . . . Where's the missus?'

. . . 'Er . . . She's at home . . . I had to come this way on business.'

'Business? . . . Saturday night? . . . Who does business on Saturday night?'

'Oh' . . . said Dave lamely, feeling for a reasonable excuse . . . 'The chap I had to meet is a buyer in one of the big stores . . . This was the only way to get hold of him . . . Had to take him out to supper.'

'I see,' said Joe nodding. 'I see.'

But if Dave thought he was fooling Joey Brenner he'd made a big mistake. Joey wasn't born yesterday . . . Business! . . . Buyer in the stores! . . . He'd been buying a nice little tart, that was all the business he'd been doing. He couldn't blame him either; if HE got married, and to someone like his own sister, he would also go out looking for such business in the West End. Very attractive bit of business too . . . Still, he wouldn't let the cat out; he wouldn't say anything now, he'd play up to him, act sympathetic. One of these days Dave might be useful for an alibi — you couldn't tell.

'Well, did you do anything?' Joe asked.

'Nothing much,' said Dave. 'Trade's very duff at the moment.'

'You're telling me!' said Joe.

Suddenly Dave hit on an idea. He'd go off with Joe. Get him out of it. He could trust Alec to keep quiet, and Olive would understand. A nod was as good as a wink. He turned to Alec.

'Well, so long old man,' he said. 'I'll be seeing you.'

He touched his hat to Olive, and grabbed the astonished Joe by the arm and walked off. He turned after a few steps, and waved back cheerily, and the two of them were swallowed up amongst the shuffling backs of Shaftesbury Avenue.

For a few moments neither Alec nor the girl had anything to say. They looked at each other, and Alec turned red. Funny how two people like us knock up against each other, he was thinking, without any reason, like a couple of fag cards thrown separately in the gutter turning out two of a set, while millions ot dusty feet walk on without caring, without even knowing ... People, individuals, weren't anything like so important as they imagined. They were broken corks, tossed about on the sea of economic compulsion. Helpless, corks. That was the worst of their sort,but one of these days, they'd be the sea. The whole sea!

'... Well ... Here we are,' she was saying.

'... Yes ... We're here all right! ...'

That was all he could answer. He shifted from one leg to the other. He must be red as a beetroot. What could she be thinking of him? A grown man, and blushing like a schoolboy. After all, this wasn't so terrible, they were old friends. Why he had even seen her undressed! ... But what could he say? ... They couldn't keep on staring at each other like a couple of dumb baboons ... Say 'goodnight', and walk off like a gentleman, or what? ... Damn it all! He ought to open his mouth! ...

'... Well?' she asked again.

'. . . Well? . . .'

That wasn't much forrader. . . .

'How about coming some place?' she said. 'That is, if you want to.'

'I'd be only too glad,' he answered. 'Would you care for some tea, or something? . . .'

'That's right in my street,' she said, taking his arm. 'I never say "no" to tea.'

At the corner she stopped.

'Would you like to come up to my place?' she said. It isn't very far from here.'

He nodded.

'O.K.' with me.'

They walked on a little way.

'What are you doing now?' he asked.

She pretended not to hear.

'I said "What are you doing now?" '

'Oh, I make a living,' she said.

'You're lucky!'

'Not so very lucky,' she answered with a wry smile, 'but anyway it's better than being a skivvy. . . .'

'Where d'you live?'

'Jermyn Street.'

'That a posh street!' he said, half wondering if she weren't joking.

'Posh! – I'll say it's posh! The rent they charge for a couple of rooms, you'd think it was the Ritz Hotel. They don't half sting you, but it's convenient for business. When you pick up a chap in the West End you can't cart him half round London.'

'Oh! . . .'

She saw by the look on his face that he'd only just tumbled. She'd thought he had guessed before. It hadn't taken Dave that long to find out . . . But why was he so surprised? He must be very green. Where did he expect she'd picked up such expensive clothes? . . . They didn't grow on trees, not by a long chalk. . . .

'It's not so terrible,' she said. 'Really, I'm lots better off than I was before. When I was in service, the master would always be after me, or if it wasn't the master, there was sure to be a son . . . And they expected all that thrown in buckshee, with scrubbing the house, and clearing out the slops. And I couldn't say anything, or I'd lose my job. Now if I have to do that, I get paid for it, and at least I get SOME time for myself.'

They had to walk up several flights of stairs to the top floor of a big house. She shared a two-room flat with another girl. She hung up her hat and coat behind the door, and put the kettle on the little gas-ring. Alec walked round the room. It was a habit of his, he could never stay put. He could never sit still in a strange place; he had to walk round and take stock.

The room was simply furnished. A wide double-bed, a table, a comfortable plush sofa. The wallpaper was speckled beige, with a cubist border. There were two pictures on the wall, nudes, after Rubens. Reclining women, with big breasts and fat buttocks. They seemed out of place somehow, the room was otherwise so ordinary looking. What it wanted instead were a couple of pre-Raphaelite oleographs, just to add that finishing touch, to make it look exactly like a typical provincial bed-sitting room.

A brown curtain shut off a sort of open cupboard. The material was a heavy ottoman silk, very expensive, Alec judged, about fifteen bob a yard at least. He liked the strong, soft feel of it, like a good worsted; a pleasure to handle. As he moved away the rod shifted from the hooks, and the curtain fell on the floor. He stooped to pick it up, and turned to Olive.

'I'm sorry,' he said. 'This curtain came down. I must have pulled it.'

She went over to him. He straightened himself, and handed her the curtain.

'I'll put it back for you,' he said.

'It's all right,' she answered. 'I'll manage. Get me a chair.'

He brought over the chair, and she stood on it, holding on to him for support. He saw a queer collection of articles exposed in the cupboard, hanging from hooks. Manacles, whips, rods. Extraordinary high-heeled lace-up boots. A queer jumble of articles, like a corner of a junk shop.

She replaced the curtain, and got off the chair, and shifted it back to the table.

'Funny little museum you've got there,' he said.

'It isn't mine,' she answered. 'Those things belong to my friend. She's got some queer clients.'

. . . Manacles . . . Whips . . . It came back to him. He'd read about their use in Freud and Havelock Ellis, but he had never expected actually to come into contact with these things. It made him feel sick; a horrible business altogether! ... Some people had nothing better to do with themselves. They were not concerned with the fight for bread. Slaves existed to struggle for them, and they had nothing to think about other than the pleasures of the flesh ... But maybe some of those poor devils couldn't help themselves either. Perhaps the very same forces that drove these girls on the streets were responsible for twisting their desires. They needed mental specialists, not women with whips ... And there again, when he probed still further, even mental specialists were no solution. Back of everything, always, he came up with a bump against that solid wall, economics. What was the use of scratching on the surface? Take away the root cause of all the trouble, and most other difficulties would adjust themselves. There would be no more use for doctors, when a completely civilized state would prevent there being any patients, right from the beginning. ...

Olive brought him back from his wanderings.

'Tea's ready,' she said.

He sat down beside her at the table. The tea was very welcome. He helped himself to some biscuits. It was getting rather late. He wondered whether he hadn't better be going; her friend might be back soon, and it would be awkward if she had anyone with her. He finished his tea quickly.

'Another cup?' she asked, the teapot poised in her hand.

'... Well, I wouldn't mind ... But I don't want to be in the way, in case your friend comes back.'

Olive laughed as she emptied the slops and poured in the fresh tea.

'Oh, that needn't worry you,' she said. 'She won't be back to-night. She's gone away for the week-end; taking a very respectable married man to Brighton — God knows what high jinks they'll be up to there!'

He finished the second cup of tea, and got up. It was time he went. He felt so comfortable, he could stay here the whole night if she'd let him, chatting, and drinking tea.

She watched him buttoning up his jacket.

'Going?' she asked.

'Yes. It's getting rather late.'

She went up to him, and put her hand on his sleeve.

'Wouldn't you like to stay?' she said.

He turned red. He had forgotten her profession. He could kick himself for wasting her time like this; she might have been on the streets, and picked up someone really worth while . . . There was about tuppence in his pocket. He remembered now, he had left himself with just enough fare money to get home, and he'd had the cheek to invite her to have tea with him! Good job she'd refused . . . But he wasn't in such a very nice position now; he should have left her alone. He would have to tell her he was broke. He wondered, would she kick up rough like the woman that time when Dave went to Purley?

'I — I'm sorry,' he stammered. '. . . I'd like to stay — but I haven't any money.'

She seemed hurt.

'I wish you wouldn't talk like that,' she said. 'You're my friend. I wouldn't take any money from you.'

He sat down, the plush sofa yielding soft and springy

beneath him. What was going to happen now? . . . He was getting jumpy, the old fear was coming back. After all she WAS a prostitute. She had known dozens of men! . . . He was frightened. If she gave him half a chance, he'd excuse himself, and rush off.

She sat down next to him, and took his hand in hers, resting them on her lap.

'Why, you're burning!' she said.

She looked in his eyes. She could see something was wrong.

'Whatever's the matter with you, Alec?'

His lips were dry. He licked them nervously. God! He wished he were out of this! He'd never wanted it to happen this way.

'What's wrong?'

'. . . Nothing . . . Nothing . . . I'm all right,' he said. Olive felt she could put his head between her breasts, and rock him off like a little child. What was there to be frightened about? She wouldn't eat him! For all his clever talk, he was an ignorant boy after all.

'Haven't you been with a woman before?' she asked softly.

He hesitated for a moment, then shook his head. She'd thought so! Always those same symptoms. Poor chap! He must be having the hell of a time. She had never known what that torture was; she'd taken to men naturally and easily from the start, ever since she was thirteen; but some of those who'd come here, had told her the agonies they'd been through. Funny how they let themselves go to her, like to a priest at confessional. She'd heard some tales these past few months! . . . Maybe they thought that she wouldn't understand, but she understood all right, and it was always a wonder to her they didn't make themselves really ill through it . . . And Alec seemed so sensitive. He would have to be handled carefully. He'd babble all over her body, like someone in a fever, and probably bite lumps out of her. In the morning she'd tell him, but he wouldn't believe her. . . .

She got up, and switched off the light, and sat down again, close to him. He was trembling a little. She soothed him with her soft hands, stroking his moist palms.

'Don't be frightened,' she said gently. 'I've always looked after myself. You've nothing to worry about.'

He looked full at her. In the reflected light from the street she was more attractive than ever. He was glad she had told him that; he believed her, and wasn't frightened any more. A new excitement caught hold of him. He wanted to kiss her hands, to tell her how grateful he was. He felt like a mathematician wading through a confused mass of figures, then throwing the whole batch aside, and discovering the solution in a simple formula. He looked at her. He could only thank her with his eyes.

She got up from the sofa, and went over to the bed. His eyes never left her for a second. She could feel herself blushing in the dark. She had never dreamed she could blush any more over a little thing like undressing before a man; she couldn't understand it. She felt as though she had never had anyone else up here in her room, as though Alec were the very first one.

'... Turn around,' she said impulsively ... 'I want to undress.'

He got up, his blood tingling with excitement, and went to the window, and looked down into Jermyn Street. The street was just beginning to come to life. From a little way off came the rosy reflected glow of the Piccadilly neons, and the toy honking of the traffic.

He was lucky to have met Olive. Delicacy was the last thing he'd expected from a 'pro'. What a difference between her and that woman Jack had taken him to when they were kids....

... He remembered that day, when Jack had said he had to have a woman. Jack thought himself grown up. He was fifteen, he was a man. A man ought to have a woman, otherwise he wasn't, he couldn't be, a man. All the older boys said that; they wouldn't talk to you, you couldn't hang round their lamp-post, unless you could also tell smutty stories about the girls you'd taken out. Jack did his best; he lied so hard, he almost believed he had done the things he talked about, until he decided he must have a woman, a real woman. Then he'd tell them some yarns, he'd make their hair stand up!

Alec went everywhere with Jack, so he took him along to fat Clara. She opened the door to his knock, and they came into the kitchen straight from the street. Clara gave them a friendly nod, she asked no questions, although she had never seen them before, and went over to the gas-stove, where she was frying some liver and onions.

Another pale, pimply boy sat on a chair, waiting like

a mangy dog, his eyes fixed on the woman. He was also from their street. They called him 'Sore-face'; kids had an uncanny aptitude for nicknames. . . .

Clara waved to them to be seated, and went on with her frying. She was a stout, blowsy woman, about forty, or forty-five, with peroxide hair, stained with discoloured streaks of black. She wore a thin kimono, tied loosely round her belly, and carpet slippers. She looked as if she lived her whole life like this, half undressed, always ready to go to bed.

She prodded the liver with a fork, and when it was about done, she covered the frying-pan with a plate, and let it splutter gently over a small light. Then she leered at the boys, and climbed up the creaking stairs to her room.

'She's gonna get the bed ready,' said Sore-face with a snigger.

Jack giggled, and Alec tried hard to grin, but his heart was jumping like a steam hammer.

'I bring her all her stockings,' said Sore-face proudly.

He worked in the markets, helping at his father's hosiery stall. Whenever he could, he stole a pair of silk stockings, or O.S. knickers, French ones; Clara liked those especially, and she treated him as if he paid cash. And even when he hadn't got anything for her, she didn't mind; she knew she could trust him, and sure enough, next time he had scrounged two pairs of good quality silks. But he never gave her money. Never.

There was a whistle from the bedroom. Sore-face jumped up.

'That's for me,' he said.

He winked at the boys, and ran up the stairs.

Jack was excited.

'Listen!' he said to Alec in a high pitched whisper, 'Can you hear the mattress squeaking?'

Alec nodded. He'd heard all right, but he was sorry now he had come. It wasn't anything like what he had imagined it to be. He hoped Jack would hurry up, and get it over, and come home.

Sore-face came down the stairs. He looked paler than before, but his eyes were glittering, and the black-heads stuck out more prominently on his face. He grinned triumphantly, and sat down shakily on the chair next to Alec.

'Go on,' he said to Jack. 'You're next!'

Soon Jack returned to the kitchen, and Clara followed heavily on the stairs behind him, wiping her hands on a towel.

'Aren't YOU coming up now?' she said to Alec, peering into his eyes.

'... N—no ...' he answered. 'Not to-night. Some other night ... I promise you, I won't go anywhere else.'

'Well, don't forget,' she said. 'You'll enjoy yourself—and clean as gold!—clean as gold!—look!'

She picked up her kimono, and showed her huge legs, bare up to the thighs. Alec felt sick. He wanted to turn his head away. Clara dropped her kimono.

'You'll see more, next time,' she said with a leer, and turned away from the boys, transferring her attention to the gas-stove, bending solidly over the frying-pan.

. . . 'Alec!' . . .

Olive was calling him softly.

. . . 'Yes?'

'You can turn around now. I'm in bed.'

He went over to her. She stretched out a smooth shapely white arm from beneath the sheets, pointing to a chair.

'Leave your things on there,' she said with a smile.

CHAPTER XXI

He saw Olive pretty frequently after that. Her friend was nearly always away week-ends. Olive always managed to give him the tip whenever she expected to be alone, and he would come down to Jermyn Street Saturday evenings, and stay over Sunday.

It got so, that after a few weeks, he looked forward so much to these visits, that he missed her enormously when she sent word that he couldn't come.

He was feeling much better already. He slept well at night, a deep dreamless sleep. He ate better, his eyes sparkled, his head was clear as a bell. There was a new sort of buoyancy about him; he got up early in the morning without a grumble, and went off to work before time. And even in the factory, at Goldblatt's where he had been working for the past week or so, his mates noticed that something had happened to him.

For several weeks the thought of her acted as a tonic. He slogged away cheerfully in the factory, waiting for the week-ends. Then the novelty wore off. He looked round him once more. His position was still as unsatisfactory as ever. He had no home, no family, no proper meal times, or meals. And this was really a hole-in-the-corner affair with Olive. It always depended on her friend whether he could stay with her or not.

Olive was a fine girl, so sensible, that was what he liked about her especially. Just the sort of wife for a workman. A wife to come home to in the evenings, a companion. He wished he could afford to marry, he'd ask her like a shot, he was fed up with this sort of life anyway. But maybe she would live with him . . . The way she acted she seemed to like him. They could get a little flat together. He made up his mind to speak to her about it as soon as he got the chance. After all, she couldn't bite his head off; she could only say 'no'.

He had received a card from her that morning. Her friend would be away Saturday. He wrote back saying he would be down pretty early.

She was waiting for him. When he knocked she recognized his tap on the door.

'Come in, Alec', she called cheerfully.

The table was set for tea. He wished she wouldn't make such a fuss of him, he felt under an obligation to her as it was. He kept asking to take her out to tea, but she always refused. It was cheaper to stay in her rooms, and besides, it was quieter, they could talk together more comfortably about whatever they chose, and as loud as they pleased.

Alec had to admit she made him feel at home. They might be married already. All they were short of were a couple of kids rolling about the floor.

After tea she put on the gramophone. She hadn't many records, only cheap dance bands, and insipid vocalists. One of these days, thought Alec, I'll take her in hand, and teach her to appreciate real music . . . There he went, off again — always six jumps ahead! How did he know she wanted to learn about good music? and even if she wanted to, whether she would have the patience to stick it. Music wasn't everybody's meat; after all, Sam had tried, and given it best . . . And he hadn't even said anything to her yet about living together— maybe she'd just laugh at him. At least Sarah had taken him seriously. He'd sooner be turned down that way, than with a joke. He would go careful, feel his way. He'd fish around a bit first, and find out just where he stood with her.

Olive saw he wasn't interested in the gramophone, so she shut it up, and put the records away. He sat in a corner watching her clear away the tea things. It wasn't a bit of use asking to be allowed to help; he'd tried once before, and she was right to refuse, he would only be in the way.

He admired the quick precise way she moved about the room, her firm, capable fingers. These days you had to be quick. He remembered his father had always impressed that upon him. 'When you grow up, you'll go into the workshop,' he said. 'You must learn to be quick. Be quick and good if you can, but if you can't, be a botcher, but be quick. If you're a slow workman you might just as well go and throw yourself in the river. . . .'

When she had finished, she threw off her rubber apron, and sat down beside him on the sofa. She took his arm, and put it round her waist, and snuggled close to him, all set for the evening.

Alec sat still. At once she sensed the lack of response in his body. Goodness! He wasn't sick of her already! There came a sudden, flat, dull, almost painful emptiness in the pit of her stomach. She realized she had become very fond of him. She'd liked him ever since that first night he had stayed with her ... Now, he'd make some excuse, and go away, and she wouldn't see him any more ... Well, she had no right to expect anything else, but she had really thought he was different. She would miss him. He always spoke to her on level terms, as if being on the streets didn't matter ... Now he'd got what he wanted, and tried out his wings, he'd fly off somewhere to a pure, sentimental, snotty little virgin ... The girls were right after all. They always said 'They're all the same'; 'all tarred with the same brush.' It was hard to believe it of Alec, but she would let him go if he wanted to; she couldn't do anything else. No use breaking her heart over any man. She'd been a fool to let it go this far, the only thing now was to get it over and done with. She'd try her best to make it easy for him. Show him it didn't matter a fig to her, one way or the other.

'What's biting you, Alec?' she asked, twisting her body towards him a little.

... 'Nothing,' he said ... 'I was just thinking.'

... 'Thinking? ... about me?'

Her heart seemed to contract as she said it, to squeeze together painfully.

He got up from the sofa.

'Yes,' he said. 'About you — and about me too.'

He paced about the room. He always had to walk when he was excited, or thinking over something important. It sort of loosened up the thoughts in his mind, lubricated them. Now they were too well lubricated, they slipped from their grooves, all over the show. He'd started off wanting to say one thing, and the ideas got churned up in his brain, and worked over into something quite different. He had meant to talk to her now, in a detached sort of way, to speak in generalities, but it wouldn't come out right, the whole matter was too personal; a me and thee problem, if ever there was one.

'Aren't you fed up with this lousy racket?' he shot at her suddenly.

For a moment she couldn't catch what he meant. She had been expecting to hear something different . . . A lousy racket! — So it was, nobody had ever suggested it wasn't. He must be hedging or something, coming to the point in a roundabout way, didn't have the guts to come out with it straight from the shoulder. . . .

'Well, it's lousy all right,' she said puzzled. 'But what can I do about it? Go back into service? No thanks! I know when I'm well off!'

Alec looked at her. Her brow was puckered, she seemed a little bewildered, and worried. She was another who had never had a decent break from life. He sat down beside her. No use beating about the bush. He'd put all his cards on the table.

'Look here, Olive,' he said. 'Let's face up to things properly. We're both a couple of strays. Nobody cares two hoots where we go, or what we do. I'm fed up with the sort of life I'm leading, waiting all the week to come to you, then perhaps at the last minute, there's nothing doing. I'm lonely! — I mean it. I want some sort of home to go to every night, where I'm welcome, where there's a woman. It's my right as a man. I want my woman, and you're the woman for me!'

He leaned forward eagerly, his mouth wide open, holding her wrists with his two hands.

. . .'Well?' he asked.

She recognized the bitterness in his voice. She knew he was genuine, she'd often felt exactly like that herself; like an outcast, longing for someone to love, to depend on. An assured position in the world. To stay in one place with one man, not be constantly flicked around like a shuttlecock . . . To be a wife. Have kids. A home; furniture of one's own. A kitchen to potter about in; a new white enamel gas stove with all the latest gadgets, like she'd seen once at the Ideal Home Exhibition. All those things . . . Marvellous dreams, but what could she answer? he hadn't said anything concrete yet. What was he really getting at?

From her silence he thought she had doubts about the proposition. He got into a panic. She mustn't say no! He was properly done for if she turned him down! . . . He leaned closer to her, and his grip tightened on her wrists.

'Marry me!' he blurted out.

She looked at him, wide-eyed, in silence.

'Yes. Marry me, Olive. I want you to marry me — WILL you marry me?' he repeated.

She freed her hands gently, and got up and went to the window, and looked out into the street. He didn't mean that. He didn't really want to marry her, she could tell by the way he had repeated 'marry' —

'marry' — 'marry,' as if it were something poisonous, something to avoid like the plague . . . She supposed most young men were afraid of marriage, afraid to take up that terrific responsibility these hard times, especially a workman like Alec who earned barely enough to keep himself . . . It wouldn't be fair on him in another way too, if they got married. She was the first woman he'd known; maybe, when he knocked around a bit more he would be sorry, and she wouldn't want that to happen. It seemed to her that marrying meant taking him under false pretences.

He came up behind her, and put his arms round her waist. His hot, rough face pressed up against hers which felt soft, and cool, like velvet. The touch of her comforted him for a moment, then he sweated with the agony of losing her. Her coolness made him feel he wanted her more than ever. It was almost painful, he felt like groaning out loud.

. . . 'Well?' he asked half-heartedly.

Suddenly she made up her mind. She turned round to face him.

'I'll come and live with you,' she said. 'I don't want to get married — yet. I want to stay free.'

He looked at her. This was unbelievable good fortune . . . And her own suggestion too! — Oh boy! He'd got that break at last!

'All right!' he said eagerly. 'Have it your own way!'

He shook his head in delight, and his eyes danced. She saw how immensely relieved he was; she had been right again. She hoped it would be for the best.

Impulsively he stuck out his hand. He still couldn't believe it was true.

'Well, Olive, are you sure? . . . Is it a bet?'

She clasped his outstretched hand firmly, like a man, a comrade.

'It's a bet!' she said.

CHAPTER XXII

THEY moved into a bed-sitting room, on the top floor of a dirty three storied house in North-east London. It was an antiquated building, reminding Alec of a very old, very ugly, Victorian spinster. The room was quite large, stretching the full width of the house; it was in a bad state of repair, but it seemed watertight. The furniture looked usable, and the bed fairly comfortable. A stale musty smell hung about the place, as though the whole room and its contents had lain for years in storage. Altogether, it wasn't very marvellous, but beggars couldn't be choosers; it would do for the present, and anyway, they didn't intend to live there for the rest of their lives.

Olive had bought a wedding ring in Woolworth's, and though the landlady thought the couple looked rather suspicious, as long as they paid the rent regularly she asked no questions.

Olive found a job as a waitress in a café, through a friend of her's, Ettie, a woman from her home town. Every night for the first few weeks her legs ached so, she could hardly stand when she came home in the evenings. She had always been proud of her smooth, firm, shapely legs, now she knew it wouldn't be very long before the ugly blue knots of varicose veins started to bunch up under the skin.

She didn't tell Alec she found it so hard. She always

said she was getting along fine, but Alec guessed it wasn't all honey ... It was a damned shame about Olive. Out into the world at fourteen, and working away without a stop ever since. In service, on the streets, now the café; all the worst sort of jobs. But what made him feel so bad was that he couldn't do anything about it. He'd love her to give up the café, but there was nothing else for her to turn to, except the streets, unless she wanted to live on his wages, which would just about keep the two of them in cabbage-water.

It was the hell of a state to be in! Whichever way he crawled he found himself in a worse hole than the last, and now he had dragged this poor kid in with him, as if she hadn't gone through enough already.

When he grumbled, Olive tried to cheer him up. She kept assuring him that she preferred this way of living. After all, she wasn't a stranger to work. She'd sooner work with him than for some cheap pimp on the streets. But Alec saw her come home late in the evenings, and flop down on the musty armchair dog tired, and that made him miserable. He should never have done it. It had only been selfishness on his part ... If only there were some way of repaying her. Something he could give her or do for her, to make things a bit easier.

He would be waiting with hot water when she came home, then he would prepare the small tin bath for her feet, and fuss around her as if she were an invalid, making her tea, and buttering thin slices of bread. Then they would go for a little walk down the quiet back streets, talking of the things that had happened to them, and all they had wanted to be.

Strange, foolish, impossible wishes they dragged out from long-dead child minds. He had wanted to be a doctor, a musician; she, a trained nurse; an actor, an actress. Dreams of being rich, famous, admired. Travelling about the world, riding bronchos, dancing in ballets. All the things they hadn't a chance of doing, right from the beginning, but they hadn't known that then, and they had been happy with their dreams. Now, dreams weren't enough. The hard stuff of reality spun outwards from the subconscious even when they slept. Often she would wake up at night with a start, dreaming of some horrible episode in her life, and how could she think of dancing during the day, when her legs ached all the while, and throbbed like heated endless belts?

When they were very young, only the best in the world was good enough for what they were going to be, now, all they asked from life was a flat of their own and four pounds a week. Nothing more than that, even from their dreams!

CHAPTER XXIII

HER first whole Saturday off, they decided to spend at Southend. At the beginning, when he suggested it, she didn't want to go; she said it would cost too much; but when she saw how Alec was longing for a day by the sea, she gave up her original idea of a bus ride to Hadley Woods.

They started out early in the morning for the terminus at Fenchurch Street. Alec booked two cheap day tickets, and they waited for the train on the platform amongst a crowd of other excursionists. At last it steamed in, and even before it stopped the crowd made a rush for the carriages.

Alec secured two seats in a non-smoker, and they sat happily opposite each other. The train moved off grunting and squeaking till it cleared the station. It stopped at two or three more London stations, picking up passengers, who squeezed miraculously into the compartments until the train was chock full. Then it belched steadily towards the open country.

Alec glanced through his newspaper. There was nothing very interesting in it. He passed it to Olive, and looked out of the window.

. . . Dagenham, the drabbest part of Essex, a scraggy county at best; it seemed to be full of rubbish dumps. And this was where they'd shot those poor families from the Bethnal Green slum clearance. Still, dreary as it might be, it was ten thousand times healthier than their old disease-ridden homes in the stinking Bethnal Green back streets. The authorities had neglected only one thing, they had omitted to move the factories and workshops to Dagenham as well. Extra rents, and fare money getting up to town, took a good slice from the men's wages, and it meant also getting up an hour earlier in the morning, and coming home an hour later in the evening. Dagenham fresh air wasn't much of a compensation for the loss of two hours a day, and the liveliness, and friendliness of the East End, especially when the money needed for food had to go in fares.

... Laindon ... Stretches of mud ... Benfleet. Change for Canvey Island ... Tiny yachts sagging lazily on the water ... Leigh ... Southend at last. Southend!

Alec got up and stretched his legs. On the platform families were collecting their baggage. Excited kids with wooden shovels, and rubber pails, ran whooping up and down while harassed parents were turning out their pockets, searching for tickets. The porters waited patiently at the gates, joking with the sweating passengers.

Once over the railway bridge, and in the street leading down to the front, things looked different right away. Clean cut! This was the seaside, all right! Alec breathed in the keen salty air ... Ah! this was great! ... Take in a good stock, Alec, he said to himself, Lord knows when you'll be able to come here again!

He was silent for a few minutes, breathing deeply, beaming like a schoolboy. He hadn't felt so fit, and well, for a long time. He turned to Olive.

'Isn't this gorgeous?' he said.

She nodded, but she couldn't help thinking of the money they would spend. Seasides made you forget things, money went like water. She'd make him go easy, or they would be short next week.

They walked down the front a little way, then slowly along the pier, the full length to the pierhead. Olive wondered why people were so snobbish about Southend. Someone had once said to her, 'It isn't a seaside, it's a puddle,' but a couple of months back, a man had taken her to Le Touquet for a few days, and except for the sand, Southend was just as pretty, and twice as lively.

On the top deck they drew a couple of chairs to the rail, and sat down contentedly, staring across the sea to the liners anchored in the distance. A band played lazily somewhere below. Alec didn't even trouble to listen. The wind rushed pleasantly against their faces, the tingle of the salt pricking the skin. Olive felt she could sit there like that all day. Just sit there, and rest her feet. If there were a heaven, it must be a place something like this, where you could lounge about in deck-chairs, and do nothing, for hours, and hours, and hours.

They had dinner in a little Italian restaurant in the town. First, they each had a glass of beer in a pub. Alec said it would give them an appetite, but the way they both felt, they could have managed quite well without. They ordered double portions of eggs and chips, plenty of bread and butter, stewed apples and custard, and finished up with large mugs of coffee, made with milk.

Outside on the sidewalk, touts pestered them to go for runs in antiquated coaches. They stood for some time by the kiddies' boating pool, watching the children paddling their little canoes. It gave them both a marvellous warm feeling seeing kids enjoying themselves. In the whole world, there couldn't be anything fresher, or more delightful than a lot of children laughing ... Laugh! Laugh! Little ones, now's your time! You'll know soon enough what it means to struggle for a living! ...

They went for a ride on the little electric motors, both squeezing together in one car. Alec had one hand round her waist, the other on the steering wheel. They both laughed almost as happily as the children when they bumped into someone, or someone bumped into them.

Then they went for a cruise on the *Mary Ann*. Out to the ocean-going liners, and back, for sixpence!

A man in dirty white ducks, and a yachting cap, played a rickety piano with a couple of keys missing, singing in a tuneless voice ...

Oh I do like to be beside the seaside
Oh I do like to be beside the sea ...

The little boat chugged steadily towards the big ships. The captain bent over the engine, caressing the pistons with a dirty oil-rag, straightening himself, moving the wheel a fraction, bending over the engine again, with a dripping oilcan.

The big ship came nearer. They could see the Roman numerals plainly painted on its stern. The girl caught Alec's arm, and pointed out a couple of Lascar seamen, leaning over the side.

She waved to them. 'Ooh – Hooh!'

A glint of white teeth, and a tired salute came back. The sad-eyed seamen watched the little boat round the ship, and bent their heads to the water again.

'. . . Haven't you ever wanted to be a sailor?' asked Olive.

Alec shook his head.

'No.'

'. . . I think if I were a man, that's what I should go in for, to travel about. See the world. Strange countries, strange people. It must be a marvellous life!'

Her eyes were shining, glowing with the romance of the sea.

'It's work,' Alec broke in drily. 'Damn hard work at that, and lousy pay!'

He wondered if Olive had ever seen the crowds of coloured men down the Lane. Straight from the docks to Petticoat Lane, and going back to their hostels loaded with old frock coats, and ladies shoes, and Victorian Norfolk jackets. He'd often watched them when he was a youngster, with the other kids. It was a great game following them about the market. Every batch they would greet with a salute, and 'Salaam, Johnny! Salaam!'

And the lascars would gravely answer back, 'Salaam!'

Then the boys would say some filthy words in Yiddish, and the sailors would open their gentle, dark-flecked deers eyes, smile uncomprehendingly, show their beautiful teeth, shrug their shoulders and pass on.

Then they would call after them: 'Hey, Johnny! Jig-a-jig-a fourpence!' picked up from the Lord knows where, and run away. Nobody had any idea what jig-a-jig-a fourpence meant, if it meant anything at all, but they would always shout that after them, and run away.

And then, at some junk stall, a seaman would pick up a tattered mackintosh, and ask, ''Ow much?'

'Six shillings!' The stall keeper knew his customers.

The seaman would throw it down, pick it up again. ''Ow much . . .?'

'Four shillings!'

'Four pennies?'

He would spread his fingers in the air. 'Four-Pennies?'

'Four shillings!'

'Six pennies?'

'All right! – Three shillings!'

An excited consultation with the other lascars, huddled together like a rugby scrum. The spokesman would give his final offer.

'Ninepence . . .?'

'Go away!'

The stallholder would fling down the garment in disgust, and the lascars would move off. Suddenly he'd run after them, and pull them back to the stall, and wrap up the mackintosh in a sheet of newspaper.

'All right! – Give me your money. You got the biggest bargain in the market. – Anything else you want? – Shoes? Hats?'

More head shaking. No. Not now. Next stop the

cheap grocers. Sunlight soap. Bars and bars of Sunlight soap, almost half a case. What the hell did they do with all that soap? It was still a mystery, like jig-a-jig-a fourpence, but one thing he understood now, why they counted every farthing. Not because they were mean, but because they were so badly paid. It wasn't the sort of life to laugh at, or envy. A romantic, adventurous career, on tuppence-ha'penny a week!

Beside the seaside,
Beside the sea! . . .

The *Mary Ann* grated on the beach. The man in the white ducks reached them with the hat. Pennies clinked in it. Alec put in a sixpence. The man grinned from ear to ear, and saluted smartly.

'Thank you! Thank you, sir!'

Olive looked at Alec when he passed.

'. . . Why sixpence . . .?'

'Aw, the poor blighter's also got to live,' he said.

CHAPTER XXIV

THE new manager came to the firm with a big reputation. His last job had been to run a trousers floor. He had introduced there the conveyor belt system. The first week, nineteen girls turned out fifteen hundred pairs of trousers, the second week, two thousand pairs. Some of the girls became hysterical under the strain of watching the endless belt, others, nervous and jumpy, and a few fainted clean away, but after the first few weeks close on two thousand jobs were turned out regularly, sometimes a few more, sometimes a few less. Mostly more.

The average wage went down to thirty-two and six. One of the girls calculated that at ordinary piece rates. she would have earned four pounds for exactly the same amount of work. Four pounds! — and all she got was thirty-two and six!

That was the record of Mr. Harris. The boss, Mr. Goldblatt, felt he was just the man to speed things up in his factory.

The first day the new manager took a walk round the coat floor, smiling affably, talking to the hands, examining the work. Didn't seem such a bad fellow after all. In the evening, he reported to the boss, and they had a long chat in the office.

A couple of days later, an 'expert' with a stopwatch came round. He stood behind the workers, timing all the necessary movements. Stopping the watch when they dropped something, or hunted round for something else, or untangled threads, or took too long hitching their trousers, or pulling up their garters. He noted everything in a little stiff-covered book, and went away.

... Bedaux! ... Bedaux! ... Bedaux! ... The whisper went round. The Bedaux system. Bedaux! ... Bedaux! ... Those who had worked in Bedaux operated factories muttered about it to those who hadn't. For days after, at the luncheon breaks, knots of workers gathered a little way from the factory, and spoke together bitterly. They knew it was coming. The shadow of Bedaux hung over them, darkening their lives.

The pressers started it. They said they worked hard enough, they wouldn't stand any Bedaux. Alec was new to the job, but he spoke for the tailors. They resolved to see the shop steward. The steward said nothing could be done, and anyway it was best to wait and see what happened — maybe the new manager didn't want to start Bedaux at all.

'No!' said Alec. 'Of course not! — He's figuring out some way of giving us all a raise!'

And then, one Monday morning, the manager was waiting for them with a pile of blue cards. He explained the system. It was quite simple. Each operation became a unit. So much time was allowed for each unit, and there was a fixed price to be paid per unit, calculated from the old rates of wages. But for the faster workers, and the manager smiled benevolently, those who did say a unit and a quarter in a unit of time, there would be a bonus, and their wages would be higher accordingly. Simple, quite simple, a baby could understand it. He distributed the cards, one to each worker.

On the surface it seemed a good proposition, especially for the fast workers. But Alec had seen it in practice before. As soon as the fast ones earned too much, the rates were cut all round, and in the finish it boiled down to working twice as hard for the same money — turning out double the amount of work.

Morry, one of the baisters, leaned his elbows on the table, and puzzled over the blue card. So complicated; so damned hard to understand, especially if you hadn't been such a wonderful scholar at school.

... MINUTES ALLOWED FOR TEA. WAITING FOR WORK. MINS. MINS. MINS. TOTAL. ANY OTHER REASON FOR STOPPAGE OF WORK. MINS. MINS. MINS. TOTAL DELAY. . . ODD JOBS — SPECIALS. MINS. MINS. . . . ALTERATIONS ON ACCOUNT OF WRONG WORK. GIVE NAME. (Phew! That was a hot one. If it meant anything, it meant spying on the others, sneaking, toadying to the manager!) MINS. MINS. MINS. TOTAL TIME ON ALTERATIONS. TOTAL TEA — DELAYS — ODD JOBS — ALTERATIONS. CLOCKED ON TIME CARD. MINUTES ON BONUS. UNITS EARNED. BONUS UNITS. VALUE PER HUNDRED. BONUS IN PENCE . . . CALCULATED BY . . . INSPECTED BY . . .

Columns, and columns, and columns. Yes, simple enough, if you'd been to Oxford or Cambridge, but not so easy if you'd spent all your life in workshops. STANDARD/MINS. AND UNITS + 60/MINS. ON BONUS . . . Fancy checking up that sort of thing every night after a hard day's work! Suddenly the funny side of it struck him. He turned to the girls, scratching his head in perplexity.

'Hey! — Any of you ladies want a good job?' he shouted, 'I could do with a secretary — Full time!'

The girls laughed. A presser held up his card in the air.

'They've made a mistake with mine. They've left no space for mother's maiden name, or fingerprints!'

The laughter rolled round the workshop. The manager in his deal partitioned little room was surprised, and rather uneasy . . . Laughing! Well, let them have their little jokes. It would be first class if they kept on joking about it, and stayed in a good humour. Let them laugh now, the last laugh would go to Bedaux!

Then came a silence. The manager listened. The machines hadn't started. The Hoffmans were still. Something was up! He'd just walk through casually. He was expecting something like this to happen. He didn't know what to do about laughing, but he was used to little rebellions. He would fix that easily enough. His face set in a good-humoured smile, and he went into the workroom.

There was quite a crowd of men round the pressing tables. The girls were jabbering in another excited group. He went up to the pressers.

'Is there anything you don't understand?' he asked pleasantly. 'Let me help you.'

Marks, the eldest of the pressers, looked at the manager angrily. Marks was a tough Bessarabian, over sixty, but still strong as an ox, and active as a man half that age. He glared down angrily at Mr. Harris. The little worm! What was he smirking at? . . . What was so nice and cheerful? He felt like dropping a back-hander across his mouth. That would wipe off the grin, or a wallop in the guts . . . Don't understand! They understood too well! Marks was working himself into a rage. The manager would have to go careful, or he'd land out. His underlip stuck out, and he shook his huge head, so angry, he could hardly speak.

'. . . We don't want your help!' he blurted out thickly. 'We understand all right!'

'Very well,' said the manager, in a crisp, businesslike tone, 'then get on with your work.'

'And what shall I do with the card?' asked the presser.

'I told you what. Fill it up. You won't get paid otherwise!'

Very deliberately, Marks tore his card into little pieces, and with his strong fingers he forced open the manager's hand, and dropped the bits into his open palm.

'There! There's your card!' he said. 'You know what you can do with it!'

The manager went livid. He brushed the pieces on to the floor.

'Take your coat and clear out!' he shouted, stamping angrily with his foot. He pointed to the door. 'Outside! You're finished here!'

Marks turned very white. His under lip almost curled round completely, and a thin trickle of saliva started at the corner of his mouth. He clenched his horny hands till the nails bit into his palms. Fists like iron. Like iron . . . Gottenu! Allow me! Just one! Just one in the guts, that's all. A farewell present! Thirty-five years of misery, and sweat, packed into one swipe! He moved threateningly towards Mr. Harris.

But the other workers knew Marks when he lost his temper. They recognized the ominous curl of his lip, his white face, the thin drool from the side of his mouth. Two men stepped between him and the manager. They didn't mind so much Mr. Harris getting a hiding, it would do him good, but Marks didn't know when to stop. He could easily smash his face in, and finish up in the police court on a manslaughter charge.

Everybody crowded round, all shouting together. Marks shook himself free like a bear, and pushed his way to the rack for his coat. One of the pressers ran after him hanging on to his shirt sleeve, begging him to come back. Another argued volubly with the manager.

Mr. Harris was adamant. He refused to budge. Marks must go!

'All right then,' shouted the voluble little presser, 'if Marks goes, we all go!'

The presser tore up his card, and flung it in the manager's face, and rushed over to Marks.

Alec jumped on a table.

'We don't want any Bedaux here!' he shouted. 'No Bedaux!'

They all turned towards him. He was the pivot of their excitement.

'No Bedaux!' he repeated. 'And if the pressers don't work, we don't work either!'

He picked his hands above his head, and tore the blue card, and scattered the pieces in the air, and in a moment, the workroom was filled with fluttering blue flakes.

'Out! Out! All out against Bedaux!'

The manager stood calmly in the middle of it all. Bits of blue pasteboard stuck like confetti to his hair, and his shoulders. The workers surged hysterically round him, moving to the door. He stood looking on, his feet wide astride like Napoleon, smiling sarcastically.

'I warn you,' he said, speaking very deliberately. 'You're all walking out without notice. Your union'll have something to say about this. You're breaking the agreement with the firm. Not one of you will be entitled to a penn'orth of strike pay. Don't rush like lunatics! Think it over first! Think it over!'

But nobody listened to Mr. Harris. The hands swirled round him and past him, and he was left alone like a thin spur of rock when the tide goes out, covered with flotsam washed up by the sea.

He rushed down to the office. Not a very promising start, but the boss would see it wasn't his fault. And it only meant standing firm, and they would come back begging for their jobs. To keep firm! Not budge! In a couple of weeks, more likely days, they'd be crawling back on their hands and knees.

But Mr. Goldblatt didn't take it so philosophically.

Booked up with orders for two months ahead, and out of a blue sky a strike! A nice manager! Couldn't he wait until the slack time before he monkeyed about with the system? . . . No use sending the stuff out, not many factories did his class of work, and those that did, couldn't cope with their own . . . Disappointed shops! . . . Cancelled orders! . . . Maybe even summonses for breach of contract! . . . All the possibilities flashed like a murky nightmare across his brain . . . And all the fault of these damn workers! Workers! Workers, they had the cheek to call themselves! Blackmailers was a better name. Damned blackmailers! Nothing but blackmailers! . . .

He paced about the office angrily. The manager tried to efface himself. He stood silently in a corner, wondering what was going on in Mr. Goldblatt's mind. There was a tap on the door. It opened, and the shop steward came in. He stopped just inside the room, and glanced nervously at the floor, then up at the boss.

Mr. Goldblatt turned on him fiercely.

'Well — what d'you want?' he snapped, and before the other could reply, he loosed a torrent of words. — 'So you're trying to take advantage of me — eh? Well you can tell 'em it won't work! I'm still boss here . . . And what have I made agreements with the union for? Aren't you supposed to give me notice of a strike?— Go away! I don't want to hear you! I'd sooner close up the whole damned factory than be dictated to by a lot of unprincipled hooligans! . . . Get out!'

He pushed the shop steward out of the office. The

manager came from his corner. That was the spirit! He fawned on the boss, but Mr. Goldblatt turned on him in a towering rage. Those cancelled orders were still niggling back of his brain. The manager was getting too damned cocky. He also wanted taking down a peg or two. He glared at the manager spitefully, and Mr. Harris, sensing what was coming, turned very pale. Lord! Now he was in for it as well!

The steward reported to the workers. The boss wouldn't even listen. Pushed him out of the office! Well, they'd stay out till he would listen. They gathered at the street corner just facing the factory, directly opposite the office windows. Alec borrowed a box from a near-by house. He got on the box, and spread out his hands for silence.

The workers were in sullen groups. Knots of men talking together excitedly. Tailoresses, and finishers. Young people and older people; scattered, animated by different problems. Heterogeneous, diffused. The job was to weld them all into one, to get them to think and feel together; to unite, and agree on a common course of action. Once that was done, the strike was good as won. But how to do it? That was the problem.

'Fellow workers! . . .'

One or two looked up, but the majority of the hands took not the slightest notice of him.

'Fellow workers! . . .'

He had to shout to make himself heard above the tangled arguments. There were movements in the crowd; elbows, hands, a nudging, jostling, kaleidoscope. The groups split, spread out, knitting together into a more regular pattern. Faces lifted up to him. That was better. Something like! Now, to grab their attention, to make them feel, and respond as one. He leaned towards the bobbing heads.

'Comrades, you all know why we've come out. No need to go into that, but it reminds me of the bricklayer who had the same sort of job. He'd been working on a building, getting along pretty well, or as well as any worker can get along when he's got a job these days — which isn't saying very much — '

A couple of sniggers, and 'No it ain't!' — 'You're right!' from the body of the crowd.

'. . . Well, they changed the foreman, and one day this foreman comes up to him and says: "Hey, Bill, you ain't carrying up enough bricks in your hod. You've got to carry four more!"

'He stood by him while he put four more bricks in his hod and waited till he climbed the ladder. A little while later, the foreman passed by again, and Bill was climbing the ladder without the extra bricks. He called him down.

' "Now I thought I told you to take up four more! If I catch you doing that again, you're fired! Fired! Understand?"

'Bill said nothing, but put four more bricks in his hod, and the foreman went away. Then Bill peeled off his trousers and his pants, and started climbing the ladder. The foreman on the ground, looking up, saw a strange sight; a pair of big naked buttocks gleaming white in the sun, carrying up a hod of bricks. He turned purple with anger.

' "Hey! Hey!" he bawled. ' "Hey, you up there! Hey, Bill!"

'Bill looked down. "What d'you want now?"

' "Come on down! Down!" he yelled at the top of his voice.

'When Bill reached the ground, the foreman ran up to him in a cold sweat.

' "What's up with you, man!' he howled. "Gone up the bloody pole, or what?"

' "Up the pole?" said Bill—" 'Course not!—But you want me to work like a bloody horse, so why shouldn't I look like one?" '

There was a roar of laughter from the crowd. That got them! They were all listening attentively now. No more fidgeting. The faces blurred together, only one or two stood out here and there, the rest a blurry white cloud, with scooped out hollows and twinkling pin-point eyes. Nothing like a joke to start off with, but this was more than a joke, this was a prelude to serious business . . . Horses . . . Horses . . . He'd compare the workers under Bedaux with horses, except that horses were better off . . . Rationalization . . . Speeding-up and its inevitable sequel . . . Draw on America and Germany for examples . . . Link it all up. Bedaux . . . Rationalization . . . Unemployment . . . The Means Test . . . Fascism . . . War . . . Show how all these problems are bound indissolubly together, and must be faced as a whole, then back to immediate things and the best way to carry on the strike . . .

The boss heard them laughing. He looked cautiously from the window, at an angle, so that he should not be observed, and saw the crowd of workers, swelled by sympathetic passers-by, gathered at the opposite corner. He beckoned to the manager. Mr. Harris came over, and stood beside him.

'Who's that chap on the platform?' asked Mr. Goldblatt. 'Don't seem to remember his face.'

'Hasn't been here very long,' said the manager.

'Well he looks to me like one of those mischief-makers, paid to make trouble. They're lapping up every word he says. Swine! Fools and swine!'

He moved away from the window, and the manager followed, like Mary's little lamb, ready to bleat obediently. He wracked his brain, thinking of the right thing to say to pacify the boss, and stood holding on to the corner of the roll top desk, while Mr. Goldblatt paced up and down, cursing under his breath.

'What about the union?' asked the manager at last. 'The strike isn't official. If we get the secretary down, he might persuade them to go back.'

'Oh, all right,' said the boss resignedly, pushing over the telephone to him. 'Get me the union.' — 'No!' He suddenly changed his mind. He stretched out a hand, and pulled down the receiver. 'No need to ring up the Union this time. It isn't worth it over a little thing like this. Besides, we're too busy. Can't let any time at all slip by. This delay's costing me a small fortune. We'll let 'em have their own way this once, they've got us by the throats, but when the busy's over, I'll look to you to make some alterations, a few changes in the staff. Get 'em back! — Afterwards, you'll know what to do.'

He looked at the manager meaningly. Mr. Harris smiled.

'You leave it to me, Mr. Goldblatt,' he said.

CHAPTER XXV

THE summer flew by. They still lived in the same house, in the same musty room . . . 'We'll get something else next week!' 'Next week for certain!' . . . But it was already October, and they were still in the same place.

The leaves were brown, and continually falling, the luxurious mantles of the trees were wearing thin. Autumn always made Alec feel miserable. He thought of his father. His asthma always came on about this time. Twenty years of stuffy, over-heated workshops, fifteen hours daily of unremitting toil, had crippled the health of the lusty Ukrainian peasant. . . 'You see those leaves?' he would say to the little Alec. 'Well men are like those leaves. When the leaves begin to fall, we start falling too . . .'

Then he would shudder. He hated the English winter, the fogs, the smoke, the cold, drizzling rain. Everything was so different from the crisp clean air, and blue sky of his home, and the dark green water of the Black Sea. Every winter he expected to be his last. 'I'll never get over it!' he would say, but he survived to work hard for another year, another year, until at last it happened, as he'd expected, in the autumn.

One night, in the bus going home, Alec picked up a programme of the Promenade Concerts someone had dropped. It gave him a bit of a shock. Through the summer he hadn't missed music so very much, but now the bright days were drawing in, he felt a bit lost without going once in a way to a really good symphony concert . . . One of these days, when they moved, he'd save up for a decent radio set. That would be the very first thing. Now his portable gramophone was rusty and wouldn't work any more, there wasn't any music at all in the place.

Without music! Tough luck once you'd made it part of your life. No Beethoven! No Brahms! No Caesar Franck! No glorious Brandenburg Concerto! Only the Circle concerts on Sundays, and then he always had to leave early to meet Olive when she finished work.

He looked through the programme. Friday, that would be to-morrow night. The last Beethoven night. And Friday night is Amami night; Amami and Beethoven! — a good combination. The violin concerto, and the two romances, with Orea Pernel soloist, and of course Sir Henry Wood, and Woodhouse and Lauri Kennedy and ninety other disciplined musicians . . . Coriolanus. The seventh symphony . . . All first class stuff.

He could see it happening, so clearly, he might almost be there. Woodhouse coming in. Applause from the audience; the first violin bows gravely, stiff as a poker from the hips, then he sits, adjusting his pince-nez, and tucking his fiddle under his chin. Then the leader of the 'cellos, and the horn players. Then the old man himself, trotting over to his platform to a roaring audience, and the staccato rapping of bows on polished fiddle-backs . . . The baton swings up in the air. Down. A sweep of sound. Coriolanus! — Ah! Ah! Coriolanus! . . .

Two resounding chords, then the opening phrases ran through his head . . . Here the ground basses came in . . . Someone plucked at the bell. The bus stopped. Alec looked up. He had gone beyond his destination. He jumped to his feet. The bus was moving on again.

'Hey! Wait a minute!' he yelled at the conductor.

The conductor made a sour face, and pulled the bell.

'Why'nt you keep your eyes open?' he growled.

'I'm sorry,' said Alec sarcastically, 'my mistake, I'll recommend you to The Transport Board. They'll probably give you another quid a week for looking after their bus so well.'

'Aw! — Get off!' said the conductor.

Alec jumped to the ground, and the conductor gave two sharp tugs at the bell, and the bus moved off.

At home, he threw himself in the armchair, and went over the programme again. What wouldn't he give to be able to go to the Queens' Hall to-morrow night? . . . But with fares, and tea, and one thing and another, it would come to three or four shillings just for himself alone. It was criminal to spend all that money when the season was finishing. Soon, the Lord Mayor would ride by, and the work would pass away with him . . . All those slack winter months to look forward to. The others might be put on short time, but he knew he was marked down for the sack. They were only waiting for the chance. He'd get the bullet all right, he could see by the way his work was examined — He'd get the push, and no one would be able to lift a finger to save him. . . .

'Still up?' said Olive, throwing off her hat and coat. 'I thought you were going to bed early to-night.'

'I was,' he said. 'But I don't feel like it'.

He threw the programme over to her.

'Here Olive, look at this. Look at the stuff they're playing to-morrow night.'

She glanced through the programme, and gave it back to him without a word. Nothing to get excited about. — Beethoven! She'd sooner hear 'In a Persian Garden' any day!

'Well what d'you think of that?' he asked. ' "Coriolanus." " The seventh." "The concerto." "Two Romances." — All in one programme!'

She shrugged her shoulders.

'Is that so very wonderful?'

At once she realized she had made a mistake. There was a hurt, disappointed look on his face. But surely, he couldn't expect everyone to be so dotty about old Beethoven! The way he'd looked at her just now, she might have sinned against the Holy Ghost! . . . It would have been better to have said nothing at all. Now she must put it right somehow, get him in a good humour . . . Let him go? That was an idea! If it was so marvellous, why should he have to miss it?

'I'll tell you what,' she said. 'You're finished pretty early to-morrow night, why not go along?'

He looked up gratefully. He could see she really meant it. Good girl! Good old Olive! — But the money! She didn't know it would run to three bob at least . . . Tell her, or keep it quiet? . . . Aw! Keep it quiet! It's only once in a way! . . . No. No, he couldn't do that, that wouldn't be playing fair. Reluctantly, he decided to tell her.

'You know, it costs two bob to go in,' he said . . . 'Just to stand.'

'Stand?'

'That's right.'

'All the time? . . .'

He nodded. She shrugged her shoulders. Well, if he was lunatic enough to pay two shillings to stand for a couple of hours, listening to a lot of long-haired scrapers, that was HIS funeral — she wouldn't do it, not if they paid *her* two pounds! She stood quite enough all day . . . Some people had queer ways of enjoying themselves, if that sort of thing could really be called enjoyment. But he was desperately eager to go, she could see that. He wouldn't need much persuading . . . Maybe the night out would do him good. He was looking pretty seedy lately; anyway, it would be a change from those fat library books of his, give his eyes a rest.

'You go,' she said. 'You work hard enough. You deserve a little pleasure occasionally.'

'. . . But what about you?'

Why did he have to ask that? He didn't really want to know, he could only think of the concert, but he had to appear reluctant about it; it didn't seem decent to aquiesce without a show of hesitation. Olive helped him out. He expected she would.

'Don't worry about me,' she said. 'I'll have a night

out some other time. When Garbo's showing again, I'll go to the Empire, and book a seat for five-and-nine!'

He laughed. She was a real sport. She wanted him to go with an easy conscience. He could just about see her spending five-and-nine on pictures! At the best of times he had never paid more than half a crown, and those days were over now for both of them.

CHAPTER XXVI

At first, he was carried along with the excitement in the hall. Everything was as he had imagined it would be, only more intense, more vibrant. He was happy to stand there, sandwiched in the middle of the chattering crowd, listening to the high buzz of conversation all round him, punctuated by flicks from the violin tunings, and long reedy key notes from the oboes.

Just in front, a man was peering over a miniature score. He envied him. That was a double pleasure, to be able to enjoy the wonderful harmonies, and at the same time understand the technique, to appreciate the nuances, the why's and wherefore's. One of these days he'd join a music theory class, and learn the subject thoroughly . . . Yes . . . One of these days . . . Something more for the limbo of what was going to be, along with the new flat, and the new job, and the radio set . . .

Sweet, sweet, music! It seeped into him like water down a parched man's throat. Wonderful Beethoven! Greater than God Almighty! His senses whirled in a pleasant delirium of sound, then a split second's silence, and before he could adjust himself, a roar of applause.

'Bravo! Bravo!'

'Bravo! – O! – O! O! . . .'

He clapped and shouted with the rest. His face was flushed. He was drunk with the overpowering headiness of a wealth of unaccustomed beauty . . .The audience simmered down. The second item now. They were waiting for the soloist . . . Another delirious burst of clapping. The conductor led in the violinist. A handsome woman. If her technique was up to her looks, the concerto would be well worth hearing.

A comparative silence, like the wind quietening down after a violent storm, then complete silence except for an isolated cough. A last melodious tuning. A nod to the conductor. The baton swung up in the air. Now for the one and only concerto in D Major! . . .

During the interval, he pushed his way to the bar, and ordered a coffee; he needed it to freshen him up, it was so terribly stuffy inside. He felt like wet blotting paper. No wonder people fainted and had to be carried out, it wouldn't have taken very much more to get him off HIS feet.

He nodded to a couple he knew from the Circle, but didn't stay to speak to them. They would only ask awkward questions . . . Any work? . . . What are you doing now? . . . Where are you living? . . . You don't come up the Circle much, do you? . . . and so on, and so on, and so on . . . It would be uncomfortable telling them lies, and besides it wasn't worth it. He acknowledged their salutes, and passed into the corridor.

Walking round the promenade, he noticed a girl sitting by herself on one of the narrow ledges that jutted out over the hot water pipes, studying the programme. He recognized her at once; the girl from the Circle, the blonde. She was wearing a fawn satin jumper, and a tweed skirt. Round her neck, a red spotted crepe handkerchief, loosely knotted. Red sandals on bare feet, the polished toenails coloured crimson.

He went straight over to her.

'How are you?' he said.

She looked up.

'Pardon?'

'I said, "How are you?" – Don't you remember me? – I met you at one of the Circle concerts last season.'

'. . . Oh! . . .' she drawled.

She put out a hand languidly. The fingers were long and slender, with highly manicured nails.

'Oh – How are you?'

Alec shook her hand.

'Very well. And you?'

She nodded. She had a faint recollection of that concert, the heady, supercharged atmosphere. She'd been glad to run away out of it . . . And she had spoken to someone there, but who he was, and what he had looked like, she hadn't the faintest idea . . . She heard the strings tuning up on the platform. The musicians were returning. She stood up and collected her handbag.

'Going in?' . . .' he asked.

She nodded. He walked into the auditorium beside her. She said nothing, but she felt that really this young man was taking a lot for granted. What made him think she wanted his company? . . . Still, she couldn't very well tell him to go away. She'd slip out before the last item, then if he followed, she would find some pretext to get rid of him.

He spoke to her in between the items. She said very little, she seemed reluctant to make conversation, she contented herself mainly with nodding in agreement and one or two monosyllables. She was not entirely disinterested either, he seemed to know what he was talking about. A genuine music-lover. She began to thaw a little. Anyone who could talk intelligently about the things she loved, commanded her respect.

After the symphony, she looked at her wristwatch. There was only one more item. She had already decided not to stay. Alec saw at once she was preparing to leave.

'Going?' . . . ' he asked.

She nodded, and elbowed her way to the door. Alec followed close behind. He couldn't help himself. She'd got away from him once before, he wasn't going to let her give him the slip again without a struggle. He could think of nothing else, only to stay close to her. Just like that time at the Circle, she filled his mind. He would be content to say nothing, but sit still and stare at her for a whole evening.

Outside, the pavements were wet. A light rain had fallen a few minutes earlier, and the air was delightfully fresh. The big headlights from the waiting cars, shone on the black pavements. Fashionably dressed people overflowed from the vestibule, chatting animatedly. The girl nodded to several people, smart young men of about her own age, and turned around, quite surprised to find Alec still with her.

She had to admire his persistence. He wasn't the ordinary masher either; there was something likeable about him, something novel, too. She liked to hear him talk. His English was good, as good as hers, yet that half-foreign, half-cockney accent, made his words seem more piquant, different somehow, like old friends with their hair done a new way.

She looked more closely at him. He seemed quite presentable. He was not actually shabby, so she wouldn't be ashamed to walk beside him, and even if he were, he could always pass for an artist or something. They all knew of her artistic predilections, and secretly, she didn't at all mind someone inferior accompanying her, it only threw up to better advantage her beauty, figure and wit.

Alec watching her closely, detected immediately her change of attitude. There was an almost imperceptible softening of her face. Now's the time to step in, he thought.

'How about some tea?' he said.

She smiled.

'Not a bad idea . . .'

'Let's go into Lyon's – The big one.' He was so eager, like a schoolboy on holiday, but she shook her head with a little grimace.

'No. I don't like those huge, ornate eating stables. Too vulgar altogether . . . Come along to Perelli's – It's nice there.'

'Perelli's? – Where's that?'

'Don't worry,' she said. 'I'll show you.'

They walked along quietly. Alec felt rather uneasy. Perelli's sounded expensive.

'. . . Is it one of those posh places?' he ventured.

'. . . Perelli's?'

'Yes. You know, one of those gaffs where they charge you half a crown for a cup of tea.'

She laughed.

'Don't be alarmed, my friend. It's quite cheap. Nobody in Perelli's has ever got more than half a crown altogether. Besides, this is my party. You've treated me once before, now it's my turn!'

Alec protested. He hadn't meant anything like that, but she refused to listen, and he certainly wasn't going to let her pay. In the end, they compromised; they would each pay their own share, which seemed a quite reasonable arrangement.

CHAPTER XXVII

PERELLI'S was crowded. It was full of tobacco smoke, and chatter, and the clattering of plates. It was a long dark cellar. To get to it, they had to pass through a dimly lit passage, and down a flight of creaking wooden stairs. It was hidden away like a thieves' kitchen. Alec guessed that was what it must have been before it became fashionable with 'bohemians'.

The walls were distempered in light stone, and grotesque masks hung around like a frieze. Two or three framed modernist paintings were in the centre of one wall. In another corner, near the ceiling, someone had started a mural decoration, and probably got a regular job soon after, or else the proprietor had refused to buy more paint. From the look of it, the proprietor had been perfectly justified, but he might have completed his protest with a little more stone distemper.

Two people got up from a table, and Alec sat down with the girl on the vacated chairs. A slovenly waitress came up to them, and the girl ordered coffees. The coffee, she said, was first class. Alec didn't mind what he drank, so long as she was opposite him.

The waitress smiled familiarly. Evidently his companion was quite well known here, too. The girl looked round the room, smiling, raising her arm continually, and wiggling her fingers, saluting different people. Then she turned to Alec, and made an appraising gesture.

'... Well, what do you think of Perelli's?' she said.

'A bit stuffy,' he replied. 'I hope the coffee's as good as you say it is.'

He was quite unimpressed. It seemed a bit silly to stick yourself away in a dirty cellar, when you could be served just as cheaply in a bright, nicely ventilated café. Perhaps the place had other attractions, he would keep his eyes open, and maybe he'd find out.

The men were dressed either too smartly, or too carelessly. Either had beards, or powdered chins. The women had on far too much make-up; a wee bit more, and their faces could be hung up alongside the masks, without any further alteration. And two tables off, one perfectly turned out gentleman was making a big show of a *Daily Worker* to a very pale, red-lipped woman, smoking a turkish cigarette out of a long green holder. She lisped approvingly, showing her beautiful teeth, her caste mark.

Alec listened to their conversation for a few minutes. It was sickening! Some red's these two! Communism apparently was becoming fashionable. To them, carrying about a *Daily Worker*, was not a sharing of the bitter struggles of the proletariat, but a sign of the highest intellectualism. It meant being applauded for having the courage of their convictions, and admired as boldly unconventional spirits. Because there was no danger. He'd love to see just the flicker of a revolution. How these reds would scamper!

At another table, stuck away in a corner, he saw a long goaty head, a familiar sparse beard. It was Leopold, with his bodyguard, and two earnest looking women. Leopold looked towards him, and met Alec's glance. He nodded condescendingly, and turned his head away. He wasn't taking any more chances with Alec!

The girl noticed Leopold's greeting. She was surprised. He knew Hartman, the writer! Maybe he was a bit of a celebrity himself. Wrote, or painted, or sculpted, or something . . . She brightened considerably.

'So you know Leopold?' she asked.

'Who? – the poet of Zion?' he said disparagingly.

She missed the sarcasm, and nodded eagerly.

'Yes. Yes, I mean Hartman.'

'Of course I know him,' he said. 'I ought to. I used to go to school with him.'

'. . . He's awfully clever,' she said, a bit disappointed.

'I suppose he must be,' he answered drily.

'. . . You've read all his poems I expect?'

'No,' he said. 'I'm afraid I haven't. You see, I'm not very fond of poetry, and even if I were, that's not the sort of stuff I'd read.'

'But,' she persisted. 'I should have imagined, being a Jew and a friend of his, you'd have read some of his poems, or at least his novel. You've read THAT? haven't you?'

'No. I glanced through his masterpiece "Songs from the High Hills". That was enough for me. There really isn't anything Jewish about Hartman's work, or for that matter, the work of almost any Jewish writer, writing in English. They're fakers, exhibitionists, poseurs, almost to a man. None of them paints a truthful picture of the Jew as he really is. In England, at any rate, there aren't any more of their pet Jews left, with snotty beards, and greasy caftans. Their characters are horribly over-sentimentalized; the' 'vich's', and "vots", and "schadchans" are laid on with trowels. Their literary creations are as typical of average, hard-working Jews as Cab Calloway or Stepin Fetchit are of the negro dock workers of New Orleans. And if it comes to that, most of the novels written by Englishmen for Englishmen suffer from the same complaint. They may be easy to read, having a certain superficial smoothness, but they mean precisely nothing, because they might just as well be written about the man in the moon for all the connection they have with sober reality down here on this planet . . . People write books, and plays, as if there weren't any economic problems at all. As if workers, and unemployment never existed. As if it didn't matter that crops were burnt, coffee turned to manure and fish dumped back into the sea, while millions were starving! as if a third of Europe, and quite a decent slice of Asia weren't working for Socialism . . . With all these mighty developments shaking the world all round us, there are nitwits who are still busy ringing the changes on the old, worn-out themes. Still writing about a man falling in love with another man, or a woman, or two, or three; all moving against a background where the slightest whisper doesn't betray that everything isn't for the best in the best of all possible worlds. Where the worker's are docile menials, and completely ignored, or else idiotically misrepresented. And literature is supposed to be the mirror of contemporary life! – Life! What a joke! – and you expect me to read such stuff! . . .'

He gulped down his coffee. Phew! That was a mouthful!

For a moment, the girl was stumped for an answer. She hadn't expected anything like this torrent. She loved arguing about books, and had all the usual answers pat, but now, she couldn't find the exact words to counter with. If Laurie, or Una, or Myles were here, they would have known just what to say. They'd have laughed his head off. Of course he was wrong, his arguments were ridiculous! She felt it, her whole training rose up in opposition; but somehow, she wasn't articulate. She ought to say something about art, and propaganda, about the necessity for keeping them separate, but he'd already mentioned nitwits doing precisely that, and she couldn't very well put herself in that category. He'd said 'nitwits' with such conviction, as if there couldn't be two opinions on the matter. She changed the subject:

'. . . And plays?' she asked. 'Have you the same objections?'

He nodded.

'Even more so!' he said emphatically. 'Plays are worse than books. Further still from real life.'

'. . . Even Shaw?'

He was silent for a moment, thinking apparently. She felt she had him at a loss. She pressed her advantage.

'. . . Well, what d'you think of Shaw?'

'Which Shaw?' he asked.

She laughed. 'Don't hedge. You know which Shaw I mean, the one that writes plays. Aren't that Shaw's plays divorced from real life, and aren't they better because of that?'

'... Well, they are, and they aren't,' he answered, screwing up his eyebrows. 'It's difficult to explain how I do feel about Shaw. I've never missed a play of his, and those I haven't seen I've read, but I don't really believe his plays show him as being divorced from life. His people don't speak like any people we know, and they don't do things like anything we do, but he doesn't pretend his characters are photographic likenesses. He only uses them for his philosophical speculations, and as these are related to life, his plays have a very definite connection with reality. But of course,' he continued, 'the old man's been dead a long time, and we're talking about live, modern, writers.'

... Dead? ... She was puzzled. There was a catch in it somewhere ... Well, she'd buy it, she was getting the worst of the argument, anyhow.

'... Dead?' she asked.

'Of course!' he answered. 'Of course he's dead! Didn't you know? ... He died soon after *St. Joan*. It's easy to see he didn't write *On the Rocks*, or *Too True to be Good*. If you take the trouble to compare those two plays with Lionel Britton's *Brain*, or *Space-time Inn*, you're bound to see that they're written, all four, by the same verbose, muddled, amateur sociologist. Yes, the giant genius Shaw of *Androcles*, and *St. Joan*, and *Man and Superman*'s been dead a long, long, time.'

She smiled. Very good. She would remember that. Next time Una tried to get swanky about Shaw, the way she'd met him at a party, and shaken hands with him, and all that, she'd drop a little bombshell — It's impossible! You couldn't have met him. The man's dead — and watch her blush. And how the others would laugh when she popped in the denouement . . . Clever girl Elspeth! Knows what she's talking about! . . .

'So now you've disposed of Shaw,' she said with a smile, and a wide sweep of her hand. 'I don't suppose there exists the writer you couldn't annihilate without any trouble. I could do that sort of thing just as easily when I was fifteen, but I grew out of it. — You will too!'

He smiled. Maybe! But she hadn't answered his arguments.

'. . . But what *do* you like?' she went on, 'What DO you read?'

'Books on economics,' he said briefly. 'Sociology.'

'. . . Sociology? . . . That's interesting . . . You study Sociology?'

He nodded. 'Only in the evenings, at home. It's the only chance I have. I work all day in the factory.'

She shook her head. '. . . I see . . . In the evenings.'

So he was not even a University student; just an ordinary workman. She'd hoped he was something better than that. But he was mightily interesting, she had to admit she could learn a good deal from him, get a new angle on things. The old ways of looking at Life were stale; she could see herself putting new vigour into talks about Art, and Literature, making the blasé gang open their eyes. She'd be the life of every party. Beauty and brains . . . Decidedly, this was an intriguing tack; she must encourage the man . . .

He was talking to her. Her mind was a long way off, thinking of future conquests. She gathered her wits together, and smiled disarmingly.

'. . . Er . . . You were saying? . . .'

'I was saying we've been sitting here all this time, and I don't even know your name.'

'My name's Elspeth,' she said.

'Elizabeth?'

'No. Elspeth. I'm sorry, but I was christened that soon after I was born. – What's yours?'

'Alec.'

'. . . Alexander?'

'No. Not even Alec. I've got three Christian names, all Hebrew, and all untranslatable. Alec was the name I picked for myself when I grew up. – But Elspeth,' the name came strangely to him, had an unfamiliar ring, 'don't you think it time we went?'

'Why?' she asked. 'Are you tired?'

'I am a bit,' he said, 'but it isn't all that. It's the atmosphere in this place. I can't stick it!'

'All right,' she answered. 'I won't be long.'

He had finished his coffee some time now, hers was barely touched. He waited, while she drank slowly in delicate little sips. She seemed to be enjoying it, he wondered how; it must be stone cold by this time. He couldn't stay down here any longer, the place was getting on his nerves, what with the smoke and the heat, and the shrill giggles of the women, and the

Oxfordy drawling of the men. Perelli's seemed to him representative of a toppling culture. Everything was fake here. Fake intellectuals, fake communists, fake artists. All fake! It nauseated him, he wanted to get away from it. It stank of decadence, like a morgue. Communists in Bond Street suits, and artists, whose symbols of their craft were not hard work, and good pictures, but green beards, and corduroy trousers!

She finished her coffee. She had some good records at home she said, would he like to hear them? . . . Would he! He jumped at the offer. He shouldn't really be going with her, but he couldn't help himself. Nothing good could come of this, but he couldn't tear himself away from her.

At the door he thought of Olive . . . There was still time to turn back. He only had to say he was late . . . He was a dirty tyke for doing this; she must be waiting up, wondering what had become of him. He felt a twinge of conscience. There were a dozen reasons for his not going on with it, but he pushed them out of his mind. No use trying to reason with madness. He knew it was madness, but what then? An opium smoker knows that he is killing himself with the drug, yet he goes on taking it just the same . . . If this girl said 'Get a taxi!' he wouldn't argue, wouldn't think twice, he'd fetch one right away. He was delirious; call it love, like the old song writer:

'I did but see her passing by
Yet will I love her
Till I die! . . .'

CHAPTER XXVIII

SHE lived not very far from the café. They got there, ten minutes after leaving Perelli's. They walked down a long mews, illuminated by a single dim lamp, until, right at the end, they came to a newly varnished door, with a chromium knocker above a shining little name plate.

She opened the door with a yale key, and they went straight up a flight of carpeted stairs to her flat. Even in delirium, the first thing Alec did was to look round; the old habits were too strong.

There were four small rooms on the one floor, all leading into one another. A bathroom, a kitchenette, a lounge, and a bedroom, every room beautifully furnished. The lounge looked like an art plate from *Modern Homes*. A long divan, squat little tubular steel armchairs, heavy shaded curtains, a limed-oak radio-gram, limed-oak bookshelves, tinted walls, and two striking pictures. He wouldn't have the cheek even to dream about such a place for himself. It took his breath away. At last he said.

'This is a posh flat!'

'Yes, it is nice,' she answered, pleased.

'. . . Rent dear?'

A peculiar question to ask, she thought, yet she had half expected him to say something like that. He seemed to come from a different world. His whole mind worked differently. If he saw something especially beautiful, he would be sure to remark, not 'How lovely! but 'How much does it cost?'

'... Dear is it?' he repeated, turning to her.

'Two guineas a week,' she answered.

She felt half ashamed of herself when she said it, she hardly knew why.

Alec whistled. 'Phew! Two guineas! Last week I worked for thirty hours, and I didn't get that much as wages!'

'Your job doesn't seem to pay very well,' she retorted.

'That's true,' he said. 'I ought to tell that to my boss!'

He walked back to the pictures, looking closely at each one.

'These seem very good,' he said at length. 'What are they? Medici reprints?'

'No. They happen to be originals!'

She blushed. Goodness only knew why she was behaving like an imbecile. Every question he asked seemed to jolt her from her mental balance.

Alec sat down on the divan.

'Well I give up,' he said. 'I won't ask how much THEY run into. I can guess! – Now what about those records?'

She unlocked the cabinet of the radiogram, and threw open the door. The records were stacked in albums. She opened the lid of the radio, and switched on the current.

'What would you like to hear?' she said. 'Help yourself!'

He got up from the divan and crossed over to the radiogram. It was one of the latest automatic models, that could be adjusted to play up to a dozen records, continuously. It toned exactly with the rest of the furniture, looked as if it had been made to order. At a rough guess, he priced it at a hundred pounds, at the very least.

He took out an album at random from the cabinet. The Haydn Quartette in F Major, played by the Lener. He placed the album carefully on top of the cabinet, and took out another. The Mendelssohn violin concerto, with Fritz Kreisler, and the Berlin State Orchestra . . . Caruso . . . Yehudi Menuhin . . . Pablo Casals . . . Szigetti . . . Lotte Lehmann . . . Gigli . . . Cortot . . . Schnabel . . . Rubinstein . . . Backhaus . . . A bewildering selection of the best music, and the greatest artistes. She seemed to have something of everything there. All black and plum labels, no cheap stuff. And really, it would be sacrilege to play a shilling, or a one and sixpenny record on such a gorgeous instrument.

He felt a pang of jealousy. He loved music as much as she did, yet HE had nothing at all. He remembered, years ago, buying an old record, the second movement of Beethoven's fifth symphony, from a stall on the Mile-End waste. How he had treasured the dirty, scratched disc until it cracked, and he'd had to throw it away, and couldn't replace it. And she could listen at any time to any of the symphonies, in comfort, and if she didn't fancy Beethoven, she had only to turn a knob to get the Vienna Philharmonic, or Toscaninni, or the Scala Milan. Everything was on tap. Everything was made easy for her.

For him, and millions like him, music, like love, like everything else, was a fight, one continuous struggle. He had begged his father when he was a kid to buy him a fiddle, so that he could take the threepenny lessons in school, but he'd never been able to scrape together the few extra shillings; and besides, his father couldn't understand what a son of his should want with a fiddle. When he'd grow up, he'd become a tailor, so why waste his time on music? Far better to go to shop for a trousers-maker, or a waistcoat maker, in the evenings after school. He'd get experience of the workshop that way, and earn a few bob for boots at the same time.

'. . . Well?' she asked. 'What shall I put on?'

He turned to her.

'Really,' he said, 'you've got so much good stuff here, I don't know what to ask for first. If I could stay here for a month, it would just about suit me!'

She smiled. 'I'll put on this Bach Toccata, and Fugue. Stokowski and the Philadelphia Philharmonic – know it?'

He nodded.

'I've heard it on the organ,' he said. 'Didn't know it was arranged for full orchestra.'

She put the record on the turntable.

'Well here it is,' she said.

He sat on the divan, his head cocked slightly to one side, and closed his eyes, and the music swelled out from the machine. He suddenly felt as though he were very tiny, tucked away in a huge, dark cave somewhere, with a domed roof like a cathedral high above him, while the music filled the whole vast space, echoing, and re-echoing from the walls. He had a sense of exhilaration, of being lifted up with the long, measured surge of the strings. It worked up to a crescendo; a pause, the fiddles questioned again timorously, then swung along more surely, gathering the rest of the instruments into a glorious tutti . . .

The moment the record stopped, he felt lost. He had forgotten everything while the music filled his head; now, he felt sullen and angry, though at what, he couldn't for the moment determine.

'. . . Like it?' she asked.

'. . . It was marvellous!' he answered.

He got up, and went to the window, and looked down into the gloomy mews patched with darkness. He was full of a repressed hatred. It was all wrong! All wrong, that this, one of the most marvellous heritages of humanity, should be the preserve and privilege of one small section of society. That it could have the best the world could offer of everything, without having to fight for it, without having to struggle for every inch, every foot. He found it impossible to restrain his feelings. He turned to her with a gesture that embraced the whole room.

'Do you feel really comfortable, having all this?' he asked.

She looked at him in surprise. 'Whatever do you mean?'

'I mean, what right have you got to live in this

wonderful flat, to keep to yourself all this marvellous music?'

She flushed, up in arms at once.

'What do you mean "what right have I got?" – I haven't taken anything from anybody. Whatever I spend on these things is my own money – My own!'

'And where did you get all that money? – Two guineas a week for a flat! Do you work for it?'

She closed the lid of the gramophone sharply.

'I don't have to!' she said. 'I have an income from my father. Isn't that good enough?'

'No, it isn't!' he retorted. 'It isn't honest. That money comes from us, it's stolen from us, from the workers!'

She became very angry, but she controlled herself rigidly. After all, she was a lady. She drew herself up, and her nostrils dilated.

'I'm afraid you've made a mistake,' she said aloofly. 'My father is a landowner; our money comes from the earth, the English earth, my country. "Stolen from us!" – Why you should be the last to speak. You and your people are only guests here!'

Her words made him squirm. The cheek of the woman! He was a guest, while she calmly laid claim to the fields and valleys, the towns and the cities that were stolen from the workers. Her country! She didn't know what she was talking about!

'And why is it your country?' he asked.

She gave a little laugh. The question seemed so absurd. It was so obvious after all, it didn't need any explaining. Her people had lived on this land ever since William the Conqueror. Nobody had ever disputed that they belonged here, and now this little jew-boy wanted to know why she called it her country! – There wasn't any answer to such a foolish question.

'And we're guests!' he went on, his face flaming. 'Guests! My father was an emigrant, running away from the Czar's hell. He came here a pauper. For twenty years he slaved in the workshops and ruined his health, and died before he was fifty, in the prime of life, still a pauper. He started working when he was seven years old, and worked the whole of his life without a stop. I don't remember his ever having a single day's holiday, except when he was out of a job. That was my father's life. A guest! That's a nice way to treat a guest! . . . But I was born here. This is MY country. Much more mine than yours. I help to produce its wealth – when I'm allowed to do so – And you? What wealth have you ever created? Your country! It's MY country – because I work here – not yours!'

'Now you're talking like a Jew,' she answered icily. 'One who has no country.'

'But I don't need a country!' he exclaimed. 'The whole world is my country! Isn't it time they threw overboard the old barbaric superstitions? Up to this line it's my country, beyond this line it's yours. Away with all that mumbo-jumbo. Every country belongs to us! – To the workers. Only to us!'

She shrugged her shoulders. He would only be satisfied with the world; very well, he could have it. He would never be able to convince her, not if he argued for a hundred years. She was too firmly rooted here, she could afford to smile and say nothing. He must have an inferiority complex, that would explain his bombast; he was hard on the defensive, she understood that well enough, trying to justify himself—Well, let him keep on trying!

Alec talked on. He seemed to grow bigger as he spoke, more masculine, more powerful. She sat down on the divan, and he paced about in front of her, his eyes shining.

Suddenly he stopped. He had noticed the ghost of a sarcastic smile on her face; she was too much of a lady to display her feelings openly. He felt that roaring anger again, and a dull pain at his heart. He'd thought at least, she was listening with an open mind, but he might have saved his breath. All his arguments were wasted, thrown away. He was pouring his life before her, and she laughed! She was laughing at his sincerity. He didn't believe in hurting women, but she made him feel he'd like to strangle her . . . And she was so beautiful too, the bitch!

He sat down beside her, trembling. Suddenly he caught hold of her, and kissed her fiercely. He felt he must defeat her, maybe he could shake her this way, but her mouth was cool to his lips. He tried to infuse her with his warmth, but she stayed aloof, even her embrace seemed to be with reservations. He felt himself repulsed again. She was holding herself back, only allowing him part of her desire.

He bit her lips wildly, trying to get closer, closer; to swallow her up, dominate her, to make her feel him, and accept him; and she submitted, yet he felt that aloofness all the while. He hated her for enjoying him like some pampered mistress giving a menial a turn at loving her for the sake of a new thrill. Like a rich woman picking up a page boy at an hotel, taking him into her room, then dismissing him with half a crown . . .

He was glad to get out into the street once more. She had been very nice and polite and all that, and had asked him to come again, but he couldn't bear looking her in the face, and meeting her triumphant eyes. He had never felt so degraded before in all his life!

It was too late to get a bus, so he started to walk home. He felt much better in the cool night air. When he got close to where he lived, he was almost cheerful again. He'd been a fool to take so much notice of the woman. Maybe she was naturally frigid, or perhaps she'd had so many lovers, that another man more or less didn't amount to very much. Anyhow, he was glad to be going home. When he compared the two women, Olive was unquestionably the superior, for him, anyway. If he had to choose now between her and Elspeth, he'd plump for Olive every time. He realized she was part of his life. She understood him, they spoke the same language; there was no antagonism between their minds . . . Yes! There was only one woman for him — Olive!

He went up to their room quietly, and undressed in the dark, so as not to disturb her. He felt a sudden access of tenderness towards Olive. He was sorry no shops were open, or he'd have bought her some little present. He told himself that would have been for letting him go to the concert, but really he knew that it was a peace offering to his own conscience . . . He HAD behaved badly, there was no getting away from it. Still, it was all over. That sort of thing would never happen again.

He nestled up close to her, to feel her warmth. At once, she moved away.

'What's the time?' she asked in a small voice.

'. . . One o'clock, near enough . . .'

'. . . One o'clock? – it must be gone two! It was half-past one about an hour ago!'

'Past two?' he said. '. . . No. It can't be as late as all that. It might be half-past one, but it's no later.'

She was silent. He put his hand on her bare shoulder. She shook it off. Still, she said nothing.

'I'm sorry I'm so late,' he said apologetically, 'But I met a couple of pals, and we had a few coffees, and talking, and one thing and another, I missed the bus.

Missed the bus! She'd heard that before. She turned round on her side.

'Don't tell bloody lies!' she said angrily. 'You've been out with some tart. I can smell her perfume all over you!'

He lay quiet, feeling very hot, and flushed. He was glad she couldn't see him properly. She glared at him fiercely in the darkness, then abruptly, she turned her back. He put his hand on her shoulder again. He must explain himself. He'd tell her everything!

'. . . But listen Olive', he began . . .

'I don't want to listen!' she interrupted fiercely

without turning her head. 'You're a rotter! You're just like all the rest, a rotter!'

She pushed her face in the pillow, and he heard her snuffling. She was crying. Her shoulders shook with bitter sobs.

CHAPTER XXIX

In the morning he made her the usual cup of tea. She sat up in bed, red eyed, looked at him for a moment, then stretched herself back on the pillow. She looked tired too, as if she hadn't slept all night.

'Have your tea,' he urged. 'It's getting cold.'

'I don't fancy any this morning, thanks,' she answered in a flat voice, as though she were talking to herself. She turned on her side, and pulled the sheet over her head.

'... All right,' he said.

He poured the tea down the sink. So she was still sore about last night! She had something to be sore about too. He'd give her till the evening to get over it, she'd be in a better mood then, and they would be able to talk about it rationally. He said nothing more to her, but went straight off to work.

In the evening he waited for her at the usual place. She was a long time coming. He kept looking at his watch, wondering what was keeping her. At last, when she was half an hour overdue, he decided to go down to the café. He knew she didn't like him to go there, but he wanted to know what was detaining her. She had never been as late as this before.

Nick, the owner, was standing by the entrance, leaning against the doorpost. He was a stout Italian, with shiny white teeth, and dark, oiled, curly hair, just going grey at the sides. He grinned at Alec and stuck out his hand.

'How-a you do, my fren'?' he said.

'All right – You?'

'Mos'n gromble! Mos'n gromble!'

Nick always said that. However bad things were, or however good, he always answered in his atrocious English, 'mos'n gromble.'

Nick reminded Alec of his father. His father had lived in England for twenty years, and had never learned to speak the language properly. He had found no need for it. He never moved out of the East-end, and wherever he was, there was always a little bit of the Ukraine, and he was happiest when he could roar away 'Shto-te-koi?' and be sure of being answered in the same language. Nick too, had been in the country thirty years or more, and one of his sons was a doctor, and another at the University, and he still dressed, behaved, and spoke, as if he'd just come off the boat.

'What's the matter?' said Alec. 'Extra busy to-night?'

Nick grinned. Extra busy was right! He waved his hand towards the interior. Alec looked in. The café was empty.

'Ver-a busy,' said Nick. 'So busy, I mos' stan' by da door. No more room inside da place! No!'

He laughed loudly. Nick was always laughing.

'. . . Where's Olive?' Alec asked.

'Olive? . . .' Nick was surprised. 'She gone'a long 'a time! She go ver-a early to-night. Nobody in da place, so I say "Olive, go a-home to da ol'a boy". You see how I tink of you ma fren'! Me, I was'a young also — long'a time ago. Nick onderstan'. Si! Si!'

He winked, and poked Alec gently in the ribs with two podgy fingers.

'... Oh ...' Alec answered slowly. He turned to go. 'Thanks Nick. I must have missed her. I came home late from work — Good night!'

The Italian waved cheerily.

'Buono sera! Goo-ni'! Goo-ni'! — you tell her for not be late in da morn'!' he shouted after him.

At home, it was strange somehow without her. The room seemed empty. He tried to read, but it was difficult to force his mind to make sense of the jumbled sentences. He kept on thinking of Olive. The way she'd cried last night. All sorts of wild guesses flashed through his head ... Maybe she'd committed suicide. Easy enough to get a room in a hotel and turn on the gas. He could imagine her lying cold, and white, stretched out on the bed, with a gas tube in her hand ... No! It was ridiculous! She was too sensible, she wouldn't do a thing like that! ... But somehow the gruesome thought kept returning. He could see the exact position of her body, with her white arms outstretched, and her legs dangling over the side of the bed ... And if anything like that happened, it would be HIS fault! ...

He undressed and got into bed, lying there with his eyes open, waiting for any creak on the stairs. Once or twice he dozed off, but woke up with a start at some slight sound, straining his ears for the sharp clop of her heels ...

When she did come in, he was asleep. He didn't hear her undress. The first intimation he had that she was back was the sudden tug on the bedclothes. He opened his eyes, and saw her lying on the other side of the bed, with her back to him. He lay quietly, relieved. Thank heaven she was home again!... The clock ticked away on the mantelshelf...

'Alec!'

She was calling him. He closed his eyes and kept silent. Now he felt stubborn about it. Last night, HE'd had to do the pleading, now, she'd have to come to him.

'...Alec!...'

'...Yes?' His voice sounded cold.

'Turn around,' she said.

He turned on his side without a word.

'Put your arms round me!'

He smiled to himself, and put his arms round her, and she snuggled close to him. She could feel his embrace was cold. There was no love in his arms; now HE was angry.

'...You don't love me any more!' she whispered piteously.

Alec was silent; he was still piqued about last night. She could think what she liked! He held her closely, breathing into her hair, wide awake, feeling strangely calm, and aloof. Suddenly something seemed to snap inside her, she broke down, and he felt her hot tears on his neck. At once he was sorry. He had a genius for doing the wrong thing! He clasped her more tightly, and kissed her eyes. He was warm now, he meant this embrace.

'Don't cry dear,' he said soothingly, kissing all over her face, hot and sticky from her tears – 'Don't cry!'

The paroxysm passed at length, and she lay quietly in his arms, panting. He heard the muffled thudding of her heart as her bosom pressed against his . . . He thought she was asleep. It was uncomfortable lying like this; gently, he tried to disengage his arms. She stirred.

'. . . Alec!'

'Yes?'

'Don't leave me,' she said softly, half asleep. 'Do what you like, but don't leave me alone!'

He kissed her tenderly, as if she were a child, stroking her shoulder reassuringly.

'. . . Don't be a little idiot,' he murmured.

She kissed his hand, fondling it with her soft palms, then she turned, pressing one of his arms round her waist, and went to sleep.

CHAPTER XXX

Olive whisked away the crumbs from the tablecloth, put down the customer's egg and chips, and went back to the kitchen for his tea. She had a splitting headache. Nine o'clock, she thought gratefully, another hour, and she'd be done . . . Seemed as if the day would never end!

Ettie had to force the tray on her. What could be the matter with the girl? . . . Must be ill! . . . She was never like this, standing there, like an imbecile.

'. . . Here, Olive. The pot of tea!' Ettie said for the third time.

'Oh — thanks!' Olive answered.

She passed one hand across her forehead. All this was like a bad dream . . . She pushed the kitchen door open with her knee, and went into the café. Suddenly the chairs and tables tilted up to one side, then they whirled round and round in a confused mass. She caught hold of the counter to steady herself, and the tray dropped with a crash.

The next thing she knew she was sitting on a chair in the yard, and Ettie and Nick were standing over her, watching her anxiously.

Nick put away an empty glass on the window ledge.

'. . . Dat's 'a betta!' he said, relieved.

'. . . Feel all right, now, duckie?' asked Ettie.

Olive nodded feebly.

'Yes, thanks!'

She tried to stand, but her legs were weak, as if she had been bedridden for a long time. She sat down again. She felt damp and sticky. Her dress was open at the neck, and her hair was wet. She tried to tidy herself up a bit as she sat, her hair looked terrible when it was wet, like dank hen's feathers – she must look a sight!'

'Lend me your comb Ettie,' she said.

Nick, after another anxious look at her, went inside. She'd be all right now; he couldn't keep the customer waiting any longer, he wanted to pay his bill.

Ettie ran into the kitchen, rummaging in her bag for a comb. She found one at last, and rushed out quickly, in case Olive went off again. She was all right; still sitting up . . . Must be the heat. Miles too stuffy for this time of the year!

'Take it easy now,' she said.

Olive nodded. Ettie stood over the girl, her big bosom heaving excitedly. Her large, gentle cow's-eyes, looked at Olive compassionately. She wasn't so much older than her, but she felt like her mother. They came from the same town, and she it was who'd got her this job. She felt sort of responsible for her.

'. . . Better?' Ettie asked.

'Yes thanks . . . The headache's gone off, but I still feel a bit sickish.'

'. . . Sickish!'

Ettie's big eyes opened wider. She leaned over Olive.

'. . . And you told me you were sick yesterday morning as well . . .'

'So I was . . .'

'Any idea what it could be?'

Olive shook her head.

'No . . . Unless it's something I've eaten.'

Ettie bent down still lower.

'. . . Sure you haven't clicked?' she whispered in her ear.

Olive smiled, and shook her head. No it couldn't be that. She reckoned up quickly . . . Yes. She WAS a few days late! . . . God! She hadn't thought of that. She wasn't so certain now . . . A baby! All she was short of! . . . She felt bad again, and reached up for Ettie's big red hand.

'. . . I am a couple of days late . . .' she whispered.

'A couple of days?' said Ettie reassuringly. 'That's nothing! Might turn out to be something you've eaten after all!' She turned round quickly. 'Sh! — Here comes Nick!'

'. . . Well, all-a ri'?'

'O.K. boss,' said Olive with a wan smile.

'Now you put-a on you' coat and go a-home,' said Nick.

'Thanks boss. You're a sport!' she whispered.

Her strength seemed to desert her as she thought of what Ettie had put in her mind. She got up shakily, and went into the kitchen leaning on her friend, and tidied herself a little. She said good night to Ettie and the other waitress, put on her coat and left the café.

A few steps from the door Nick came up behind her. He tapped her on the shoulder. For once his face was serious.

'Wassa matta?' he said. 'You not-a looking too well lately. You gotta da blues – You hard-a up, eh?'

She shook her head. Nick gestured impatiently.

'. . . But I gotta plenta mon' – You say how much you wan'. You pay me back, tree, four, months, when-a you like – huh?'

She shook her head again.

'No thanks, Nick. It's not that. On my word!'

He shrugged his shoulders, and looked after her as she passed down the street, then he went back to the shop . . . Plenta mon' was right! He owed his son, the doctor, fifteen pounds now, for his last rates bill, but if the girl was short of a few shillings, he'd scrape it up somehow . . . Caramba! Good times! In business over twenty-five years, and couldn't even pay the rates! He'd worked his way up! Lucky he'd insured himself; he had a son a doctor!

CHAPTER XXXI

THE days that followed were convincing enough. One or two mornings she missed the sickness, and she was happy and light-hearted all day long. Her eyes grew brighter. She didn't care a damn about anything else now, about her aching legs, or the long weary hours; her whole mind was turned in upon this one thing. Until she knew for certain one way or the other, she kept the dread of a child in a tenacious grip, uppermost in all her thoughts.

. . . Maybe it was a false alarm after all! She had stray flashes of optimism in the darkness. She grew almost cheerful. Really, she hadn't known when she was well off; she promised herself, once she got over this, she wouldn't grumble any more. But the nausea came on, again, and again. She was sick as a dog. She dreaded the mornings, knowing that she would only have to touch her food, to bring it all up again, soon after.

Luckily, Alec noticed nothing. He went off to work before she got up, and in the evenings she was her normal self. She only confided in her friend, Ettie.

Ettie had had some experience of these things. She was married, but her husband, a sailor, had only lived with her for a year. She never saw him now, except when he wanted money. Then he would come and stay with her for the week-end. He would get drunk, and beat her up, and make her give him the few shillings she had hidden away. But she still loved him, and he always left behind memento's of his visits. Twice Ettie had children, born dead, both of them, and even if they had lived, they'd never have amounted to much because of the disease their father had handed on to them. So after Ettie had buried the second red, wrinkled little body, she swore 'never again!', and she was doubly careful whenever her husband was around.

Now, even Ettie was worried about Olive's condition. Every morning when the girl came into the kitchen, Ettie would lift her thick, expressive, eyebrows . . . Well? . . . And Olive would most often shake her head in reply. She had no need to speak, her face was eloquent . . . Sick again. Sick again. I'm for it all right! . . .

She went to the public baths, and had a hot plunge every morning, as hot as she could bear. She walked to work, ran up and down stairs, lifted heavy weights, dosed herself with Epsom salts, but nothing helped. The seed still flourished in her womb.

'Look here, Ettie,' she said one day, she felt desperate. 'I've GOT to get rid of it somehow!'

'Well,' Ettie replied. '. . . I know a woman . . .'

She stopped. She was troubled for more than one reason. An illegal operation was dangerous. If anything happened to the girl, she'd get into hot water, too. But apart from that, there was the pain. The horrible pain! She had been through it herself, it was worse than having half a dozen babies. Olive didn't know what she was in for, talking about abortions so lightly. Didn't know she'd be at the mercy of a cruel tight-lipped old woman, and a clumsy, probing instrument. No. She wouldn't do it. Better for Olive to take a chance, and have the baby.

She wished she were in Olive's condition. She'd change places with her, any day. To be able to mother a clean, healthy child! How she'd cherish it! How she'd bring it up! . . . Still, that was the way of life; those that wanted kids, couldn't have them, and those that could, didn't want them!

Ettie tried her best to persuade Olive to see things her way, but the girl's mind was definitely made up. She didn't care how painful it was, so long as she got it over. In her position, living as she did, she didn't dare have a baby. The kid wouldn't have a chance. She'd seen too many dragged up that way, old, half-starved men and women, before they could talk properly. No thanks! Not for her! She loved babies, but she couldn't think about them till she was properly settled. It would drive her mad to have a child crying for milk, when she didn't have any, when she wasn't sure of anything from one day to another. No! That wouldn't be fair on a fresh, innocent, little life. Best to get rid of it now, and done with; avoid those heaped up years of curses that would certainly fall on her head if she dragged another soul into this filthy world.

Ettie arranged for a friend of hers to take her place for the day, and took the time off to go with Olive. The girl was silent on the journey, but Ettie could guess from her drawn features what was going on in her mind.

The woman lived in a big house, near Forest Gate.

Walking through the long front garden, Olive shivered. It was the first outward sign she had given of the fear that possessed her. She felt as though she were delivering herself into the hands of a vicious maniac of a dentist, who was going to tear all her teeth out without an anaesthetic.

The woman took her money first, asked her a few questions and made her undress. Ettie came into the room with her, and Olive held her soft arm tightly with both hands, while the woman began.

. . . . . .

For three days she stayed in bed, at home. Ettie came to see her every morning, and every night after work. Nick sent with her a big bunch of hot-house grapes, and some flowers.

Alec was alarmed. Olive looked so pale and fragile lying there, her face, drained of blood, looking like yellow wax. He wanted to get a doctor, but she kept putting him off. It was nothing, she said, the doctor would only laugh. Women had this same trouble every month, only some times, it came on worse than others . . .

But Alec was not satisfied with her explanation. He felt she was keeping something back. She looked so terrible, as if she were dying. He threw himself on his knees before the bed, and begged her with tears in his eyes, to let him go for a doctor. He was afraid she would die. He wouldn't know what to do without her. The world would be empty again for him, there was little enough in it as it was . . . She must have some medical advice. He'd make her see a doctor.

But for once, Olive was obstinate. She stayed firm; she absolutely refused to see a doctor. She was so weak, he couldn't argue with her too much. She turned her head away from him wearily, even listening was an effort, and let him talk over her. In the face of her silence, there was nothing, nothing at all he could do.

She lay like that for three whole days. On the fourth she felt a little better. She got up, dressed herself, and went to work.

CHAPTER XXXII

GREY days. November days. The Lord Mayor rode by in a drizzling rain. The Lord Mayor's fat, red-faced coachman was featured in all the morning papers. Every year they ran the same photograph of his wife putting the finishing touches to his costume. The evening papers had double page spreads of mace-bearers, and sheriffs, and tableaux, and the gilded, lumbering, cinderella monstrosity, the ceremonial coach itself... Pompous speeches at the banquet, relayed on the radio... MY LORDS LADIES AND GENTLEMEN PRAY SILENCE FOR HIS EXCELLENCY THE PRIME MINISTER. THE RIGHT HONOURABLE BLAH! BLAH! BLAH! ... Sprats were in season. The blue blooded Sunday paper gossips were sharpening their noble pencils for the busiest time of the year.

That same week, the manager enclosed a little white slip in Alec's pay docket. Alec and ten others had notice to quit.

Unemployed... What was he going to do now? How about that new flat, and the radio set?... Aw hell! Radio sets!... Flat's! He could forget about such luxuries, he'd be glad to have a roof above his head this winter, and enough to eat; though that last part shouldn't be difficult. He couldn't go short of food; he'd have seventeen shillings, and the British Medical Association had worked out that he only needed five and threepence a week to get all the necessary vitamins

. . . Very nice of them! The cost of living had gone down they said, yet specialists still charged ten guineas a visit. He'd think twice about calling them in, in future.

He'd rub along somehow, till after Christmas. Then it should be fairly easy to get another job. One thing about his trade, he did have a few months work every year, not like some poor devils who stayed unemployed for years at a stretch. And it was safe employment too. He went to work in the morning, and came home safe and sound, every night. The only accidents that could happen to him, were a festered finger from a needle prick, or a pair of shears dropped accidentally on his foot. But a miner took his life in his hands every time he went down the pit, and when a mine closed down, a whole village could become destitute, from the first to the last, without any alternative.

Comparatively then, he was well off . . . Well off! This was cock-eyed reasoning. Out of work, and he'd discovered he was comparatively well off! . . . But compared with whom? He could always be well off if he were prepared to reason that way. When in work, he got lousy wages, but he was well off compared with the German worker, or the Japanese worker, or the Pole, or the Italian. On the dole, he was better off than a pauper. A pauper was better off than someone who couldn't get charity, the one who couldn't get charity, was better off than a chronic invalid, and even a chronic invalid thought himself well off because he wasn't dead!

He despised himself for thinking this way. It wasn't like him at all. It showed how, when the horrible disease of Unemployment gripped a man, even at the beginning, his mind started to go, as well as his body. He had never been unemployed for long before, he'd always managed to scramble from one job into another. He had never troubled to sign on, but it was different now, he couldn't afford to take any chances. He felt himself responsible before Olive; he had no right to expect her to keep him . . . Well off! He was developing the mind of a slave.

He put off telling her until the very last day. On the Saturday night, he walked home from work with Olive, and seemed strangely silent. She could see he was upset about something, but she waited until he would tell her of his own accord.

She was not affected greatly by the news. She could not understand yet, what unemployment meant to a man who had always been in work. She could not foresee the steady disintegration of his character. She tried to console him, tried to make a joke of it, but he was depressed all night, and hardly said a word.

On the Monday he went to the Labour Exchange. He hated having to do it. They made things so hard for you here, as though you were coming for charity. They forgot about all the years you'd been paying for insurance stamps without claiming a penny. They looked at you as though you were a swindler, an impostor, when all you came for wasn't a quarter of what was rightfully yours.

The first week there was no money for him. He signed on, Monday, Wednesday, and Friday. As an able bodied, adult male, he was allowed two and tenpence per day. The following Friday he went to the Labour Exchange to collect his money; he had only eight and six coming, they reckoned the week to start from Wednesday, and always kept a balance of three days pay in hand.

He started out early, but there was already a long queue before him, and a few minutes later, a good number of men tagged on behind. The long grey line shifted slowly, shuffling like men who'd lost all the dignity of human movement. Mostly tired, pale faces, stooping shoulders, green threadbare overcoats. The younger men still had something hopeful about them. Their faces were bright and open, and challenging, they looked as if, given the chance, they would know how to take it. They could even make jokes about coming to draw the dole. They asked a newcomer not, 'Who's your clerk?' but 'What's your trap?' The pay clerks had big cards in front of them, and the men were graded like dogs, according to trade, or surname. The A's went to clerk one, trap one, the B's to trap two, and three, and so on, like greyhounds at the White City.

The older men, the grey stubble-beards, didn't even have the heart to joke. They were defeated. There was no fire or defiance about their bodies, only a shroud of dull apathy, they were crushed.

Alec reflected, he was one of the lucky ones. He had only himself to worry about. Some of these had wives and children dependent on the paltry few shillings of dole money . . . Children! He shuddered. He loved kids, but he couldn't bear to see them suffer. For a worker to have children these days, was to condemn them to semi-starvation, and stunted growth. He'd seen any amount of kids where he lived, existing on fish and chips, or chips without fish, and on Saturday nights, festival nights, a sausage, and a fistful of greasy mash, hot from the butcher's shop. Ugh! Hearts as pure and fair, may beat in Mayfair, as in the lowly air of Seven Dials! . . .

There was a disturbance in the roadway. He became conscious of a loud voice. A man was addressing the queue from a soap box in the centre of the road. For a few moments he listened closely, then his attention wandered off. He shifted a pace and a half, pushed on by the pressure behind, without being conscious that he had moved. Suddenly there was a ripple in the line. The man's voice had stopped.

Alec looked into the roadway. A policeman, materialized from nowhere, was arguing with the man on the box. He was a good looking young constable, tall, blond, and well built, with a complexion that showed he hadn't long left the country.

'You can't stay here!' insisted the policeman.

'But this is a free country, ain't it?' said the man on the box.

He was a small dark man, shabbily dressed, wearing an old cloth cap.

'. . . Look here,' said the constable in a slightly aggrieved tone, ignoring the other's question. 'I've got my orders. You know meetings are not allowed outside the Exchange. Now if you'll be sensible, you'll get down off of there.'

The man on the box turned to the waiting line, presenting his back to the policeman.

'... Comrades,' he shouted. 'This is what we're up against all the time. This is ...'

He broke off. The policeman had pulled him roughly from his platform.

'Hey!' bawled a young man from the back of the line. 'Hey you! Leave him alone!'

The speaker argued angrily; a crowd gathered almost at once. Several men left the queue, standing on their toes at the edge of the crowd, to get a look-in. Suddenly, there was a little scuffle. The crowd tightened to a swaying knot, and the speaker got up again on the box. He was red, but triumphant, and he had lost his cap. He stuck out one fist aggressively in front of him.

'Comrades! – Com ...'

He swayed unsteadily, and was down again. The constable had charged like a rugby footballer with a body tackle. Angry cries came from the men around. The speaker bobbed up again for a second, then disappeared. The policeman's helmet gave a lurch over his eyes. His blue-striped arm wriggled free, and there was a glint of white metal chain, then his whistle sounded shrilly three times.

Two more policemen came hurrying down the road. The three of them surrounded the speaker, their tall helmets towering over the little man, then the two newcomers marched him off to the station, still shouting defiantly.

The box stood forlornly in the centre of the road. Alec knew that he ought to get on it and take the other's place, but something kept him back. What the hell was the use? . . . Like banging your head against a brick wall. The way he felt now, he didn't much care what happened, one way or the other. If he got on the box and started to speak, he'd get pinched, before he'd said half a dozen words. Let the others have a go! He'd done enough sacrificing. If he hadn't started that strike at Goldblatt's, he wouldn't be standing here now!

The young policeman straightened his uniform. His face was very red. He was conscious of the hostile glances from the queue. His heart was beating very fast, but he was pleased with himself. In his book, there would be a little note describing how his prompt action had prevented an ugly situation from developing. And the inspector would probably compliment him. One up! But he didn't exactly like having to do this sort of thing; he wished they would stick someone else on this beat.

He walked up slowly to the soap box, and shifted it with his foot into the gutter. Then he stood on the opposite pavement with feet astride, his thumbs tucked in his leather belt. — Lor-an-order!

Everything was quiet now. The queue shifted steadily to the entrance. Up the stairs now to his trap. Alec held his money slip in his hand.

'. . . 864 Pay fifteen shillings . . .'

'. . . 231 Pay seventeen shillings . . .'

It was his turn now to go to the desk. The cashier took his slip, and looked at him with the arrogance of the superior white-collar worker.

'. . . 779 Pay eight and six?'

'. . . Eight and six' came the reply from the checking clerk.

The cashier gave Alec his money '. . . Come along now!' to the next man.

Alec hurried down the stairs. He felt like hitting the cashier on the jaw for the brusque way he spoke. Who the hell did he think he was talking to? — They might all be galley slaves! . . . Slaves . . . Maybe he was right at that. They could be no better than slaves to stand all this so docilely . . . Pay? . . . Pay! . . . Pay? . . . Pay! . . . Some bread for you! . . . Some marge for you! . . . For thine is the kingdom, the power and the glory! . . .

CHAPTER XXXIII

THE weeks dragged on. He was resigned now to being out of work, for a few months at least. He didn't trouble any more to rush to the library reading-room, and crane his neck over the shoulders of job-hunters cramming the situation-vacant ads. in the newspapers. When they gave him an address to go to at the Exchange, he went there apathetically, knowing it was useless, and always came back with his card endorsed 'Vacancy filled.'

Unemployed! Completely without work! Before, he had ached for more leisure; there were so many things he wanted to do if only he'd had the time. Study the theory of music, polish up his economics, maybe learn a foreign language or two. Now he had all leisure, and did nothing with it. He read less than before, he had no head for books now, the problem of living took up all his time, and worrying about the future; the terrible, uncertain, ever darkening future.

Now, he snatched at any sort of excitement. The first items he read in the newspapers were the crime reports, and divorce cases, things he had hardly ever troubled about before. He knew now why men went to dog races. They had to have some opiate to take their minds off the overwhelming burdens of life. It was cowardly, it was running away, but he couldn't blame them for it, he felt just like that himself.

The unaccustomed idleness began to make a different man of Alec. He altered a great deal. Olive noticed the change working on him, almost from day to day. She had never known him to lose his temper before but now he was irascible all the time, susceptible to any petty irritation. He walked about like an ogre with the toothache. Olive had to be on her guard continually because the slightest thing upset him.

'I don't know what to do,' she said to Ettie. 'He's worrying me. He sits about the place, and mopes all the time. He won't read, or go to pictures, or do anything. Mostly, he stares out of the window, and grouses. — I don't know what to do!'

'Oh, he'll get over it,' said Ettie, wiping her hands on a tea towel. 'But if I were you, I'd get him interested in something.'

'Yes . . . But what?'

Ettie shrugged her shoulders. 'That's for you to find out. He's your chap, not mine.'

Olive put on her coat. It was her half-day off. She twisted the elastic of her garters, tightening them, and smoothed her silk stockings. As she drew her hands up one leg, she felt a ladder. There was a sudden tug of dismay at her heart. More expense! Those were her last pair of stockings, and they'd been darned and patched till there was as much cotton on them as silk. But this ladder was too bad! It stretched from the heel up to the reinforced top. She sighed. No use putting it off any longer. She would have to replenish her wardrobe.

On her way home, she made a slight detour to pass through the market. She usually bought her stockings from one of the stalls. A cold drizzle started to fall, and it grew darker, as if night were approaching. She shivered, and pulled her coat about her. She'd have to be thinking about a heavy velour or something soon, for the winter, the wind cut through her thin tweed as though it were paper. But it was December already; another couple of months and the weather would be getting warmer. Perhaps she could manage with the coat she was wearing if she dressed up extra warm underneath. Even then, she needed a couple of pairs of woollen vests and knickers, and one or two jumpers. That would run into nearly as much as a coat; it was about as broad as it was long.

The rain came down more heavily, with a sudden gush, the cold and damp seeped into her bones. Ugh! She twisted her face into an expression of disgust. Raining, for a change, and always on her half-day too! This weather gave her the pip!

She looked in several shop windows. For thirty shillings she could get the very garment she wanted. A green ripple-velour, with a beige fox collar. — Thirty bob! God knows how they manage to turn 'em out so cheap! — She glanced at the names over the shops. All Jews. And most of the stallholders were Jews too. Suddenly Alec came into her mind. Why hadn't she thought of it before? Jews were supposed to be good business men, why couldn't he have a shot at markets? If so many people made a living that way, why not Alec?

She bought her stockings, and hurried home, bubbling with the idea. This would be sure to pick him up, give him something to look forward to. No more slaving in the workshops, he'd be his own boss. Independent. He'd become himself again.

She was surprised to see a light in their room. She hurried up the stairs and opened the door quietly. Alec was sitting at the table, bending over a book, so absorbed, he failed to notice her entrance. She hung up her coat and came behind him softly so as not to disturb him. She was glad to see him reading, that could only be a good sign. At last, he looked up.

'Hullo!' he said. 'When did you arrive?'

'Only a few minutes back. Carry on with your reading, Alec, I won't get in your way.'

'Oh, that's all right,' he replied.

She glanced over his shoulder at the book. The pages were yellowy, and the print worn faint from constant handling. She made out one heading, 'History of the Jews in Europe'. It was too dilapidated to be a library book, probably one of his own.

'Is it a good book?' she asked.

'Depends on how you look at it,' he answered. 'It's a history of the Jews. It just about dovetails with the mood I'm in now.'

She looked at him. There was something strange about his face, a look of intense suffering, and intense exaltation.

'What do you mean by that?' she asked.

'Well,' he said. 'I'm in rather a bad way now, I feel pretty rotten about everything; but when I read of what my people have gone through, I get sort of lifted up, you know, the way you feel after a good cry.'

She nodded. Now she noticed his eyes were red, as if he had been weeping. She was surprised. She had thought only women cried over books. One day, when she had a bit more time, she would read it too, and find out what there was to cry about.

That night Alec dreamed he was a kid again. The reading of the *History of the Jews* had kindled a long dormant religious spark in his blood. It all came out in a succession of flickering, incoherent dreams, like a highbrow expressionist drama, about the time when he had been washed in the Blood of the Lamb and become a True Believer.

He could hear the missionaries singing in the big hall of the 'Nazareth Medical Mission to the Jews'. Above all the other voices, resounded Mr. Baumer's deep bass.

> 'All by nature are doomed to die
> So saith the Ho-ly Wo-ord
> Welcome therefore the joyful cry
> There's Life in the risen Lo-ord' . . .

Then the scene changed, and Mr. Plover, the travelling Evangelist, was talking to them from the platform.

'These were your sins,' he was saying, pointing to a crimson cardboard devil. 'Red! Red as blood! Red as sin! Red as iniquity and hell fire, but washed in the precious Blood, they shall become whiter than snow!' He held out a spotless cardboard heart in front of his chest. 'Whiter than driven snow!'

'Praise God!' . . . 'Glory Hallelujah!' . . . Ecstatic cries came from the entranced missionaries.

'. . . I got to have a Bible,' said Lou. 'The master says we all got to have Bibles for the scripture lesson. That's the worst of these blooming high schools! They always want something else. The scholarship money's supposed to pay for everything, but I ain't never got enough! . . .'

The painstaking efforts to write a suitable letter to Mr. Plover. Two boys bending over a table, and an open exercise book.

Dear sir,

Ever since your last prayer meeting, me and my friend Alec have become True Believers. We believe in Jesus, but we have not got any bibles to study the word of God. Please try to help us. Yours in Christ . . .

Then the reply from Mr. Plover. The interview with him in the mission hall, and the promise to join Daniel's Band. The unctuous interminable speech as the boys receive his blessing and a Bible apiece. Then Lou dropping out of the picture, and Alec coming to the mission by himself. Mr. Baumer's voice again.

'Dare to be a Daniel
Dare to stand alone
Dare to have a purpose firm
Dare to make it known.'

In a small room this time. About ten or twelve other little Jewish boys and girls, meeting secretly, in the mission like conspirators, Daniel's Band of True Believers. A sign from Mr. Baumer. Down on the floor, kneeling on praying cushions, eyes shut. . . . 'Please

God, forgive me for cheating at sums in school. I promise in the name of the Lord Jesus Christ never to do it no more.'

'Amen!' from the rest of Daniel's Band.

'... I answered mother back.'

'... I stole blotting paper and a pen from the post office.'

'Amen! Amen! Amen!'

Lewd gestures, a pulling of tongues and a thumbing of noses behind Mr. Baumer's back. His loud bass throbbing to the Almighty.

'Lord God, look down on these little Jewish children. Make them see the Way, the Truth, and the Light. In the name of Our Heavenly Father ... Amen! ... Amen! ... Amen! ...'

In the morning Olive looked at Alec curiously.

'What's wrong with you?' she said. 'Got religion?'

'Religion?' He was puzzled. 'Me? ... Why?'

'Well,' she answered, 'you were singing hymns all night. Christian hymns, like they used to teach us in Sunday School.'

Alec laughed. 'I used to be religious once, when I was about ten years old. There was a mission near where I lived, I believe it's still there, but I don't know whether they've had any luck yet. They used to run a Bible class, and they'd give us fountain pens, knives, paint-boxes, all sorts of gadgets if we learned off bits of the New Testament and repeated them by heart. "For God so loved the world, that He gave His only begotten Son, that whosoever believeth in Him, shall not perish, but have everlasting life. John. Three. Sixteen." — I got a painting book for that. Anyway, after a bit, I began to take it seriously, and joined a class called Daniel's Band . . .'

Olive smiled, 'Yes, I know. I heard you.'

'. . . Heard me?'

She nodded. 'Last night. Dare to be a Daniel, Dare to stand alone . . .' she mocked in a deep voice.

Alec grinned. 'Oh! — Of course,' he went on, 'when I was about twelve, I grew out of it, but they still remembered me in Daniel's Band, and sent me lovely picture postcards every birthday. Well, when I reached seventeen, I thought I'd give them a look-up again. They welcomed me back like the prodigal son, and introduced me to the Young Men's Bible Class. There were a lot of chaps about my own age, and a bit younger, listening to Mr. Baumer, the head man. After a while he asked for questions, so I put a few that he couldn't seem to answer. The other kids were enjoying themselves, and I wouldn't stay quiet, so in the end they had to call the porter to throw me out. Every since then I didn't get any more postcards on my birthday from Daniel's Band.'

Olive laughed and finished her tea. She stretched herself. Time to go to work!

'Another cup?' asked Alec.

'No thanks.'

Alec walked over to the window. Another day. Life on the street was in full cry. The coalman with his slow moving cart, costers with fresh vegetables, housewives going to market, children frisking on the pavement, a woman banging dirty mats on her window ledge. Another day! It was foolish to look down on all these busy people and make himself miserable, but there was nothing else to do. Now, when he could lay-in as long as he pleased, he got up earlier than ever in the morning. Something pulled him out of bed. It seemed to mock him. Everybody had tasks; work to do; everybody, except him.

Olive came up behind him.

'Have you ever thought of going to markets?' she said.

He turned round. 'What?'

'Markets. A lot of your people make a living that way. Maybe you could get a stall somewhere.'

'I dare say I could,' he answered. 'But what am I going to sell? — And if I do know what to sell, where am I going to get the money to buy the stuff?'

'You don't need much money for that sort of thing,' she said, 'it isn't like a shop, you don't have to have a lot of stock. You buy only a small parcel at a time, and when you sell it, you can get some more.'

Her voice was brimful of optimism. It hurled against his morose dejection, struggling hopefully to pierce him.

'. . . Well? . . .' she persisted.

He shook himself. He really ought to pull himself together; like this, he was a nuisance to himself, to Olive, and to everyone else, walking about with a perpetual grouch. He might be ninety the way he was behaving, dead to everything that mattered, like those old wrecks at the Labour Exchange. He moved away from the window to the opposite side of the room. There was something in what she said; it was a wonder he hadn't thought of anything like that before. After all, there was nothing to lose. He turned it over in his mind. The oppression that had hung over him seemed to grow lighter. Maybe she'd hit the nail on the head . . . Yes. He'd have a go! It was a chance; perhaps this was for him, that tide in the affairs of men . . .

He opened the wardrobe. In one of the sliding drawers there should be Olive's post office savings account book. Yes. There it was. He opened it eagerly, totting up the withdrawals against the deposits. Eight pounds. Surely there was more than that! He had an idea that there ought to be ten pounds there at the very least. He added it up again. No, he couldn't make it more than eight. He noticed a recent withdrawal of three pounds. What was that for? Olive had been talking about a new coat, but so far as he knew, she hadn't bought one yet. Three pounds; there was something he didn't understand about that. He turned to Olive.

'Is that right, we've only got eight pounds left in the bank?'

She nodded. 'That's right. Eight pounds.'

'But I thought there was more than that,' he said. 'About ten, or eleven.'

'There was eleven,' she answered. 'But I had to take three out.'

'What for?'

He was puzzled. Any other time he wouldn't even have asked; he supposed she needed the money for something or other, but just now, that represented their entire capital, and if he was going to markets he had to know just how much he had to fall back on. The girl was silent.

'Do you have to know?' she said at length.

'Well, if you'd rather not tell me . . . Is it a surprise?'

Olive laughed, she couldn't help it. 'Yes. But not the sort of surprise you think. I was going to have a baby.'

'What!'

He was astounded. His mouth was open, so that he looked almost comical.

'Yes. That time when I was ill. The money was to pay for an operation.'

'Oh! . . .' he said. '. . . I'm sorry. But if I'd have known, I'd never have let you do it.'

'And what would you have done instead?'

'Well . . .' he said slowly, after a pause. 'We could have got married.'

That wouldn't have made any difference,' she said firmly. 'I'd have had to get rid of it just the same.'

'But why?'

'Ask yourself.'

He considered for a moment. Of course she was right, but it must have taken enormous will power to do what she had done. He lowered his head; he felt ashamed before her, she was so strong and resolute. He'd been out of work a few weeks, and walked about as if it were only left for the heavens to fall any minute, while she had gone through all that torture without a murmur. He was thoroughly ashamed of himself. She came over to him and hugged him, looking into his eyes tenderly.

'You're not angry, are you?' she asked anxiously.

'. . . No,' he said. 'It's you who should be angry with me.'

She gave him a little squeeze. 'Don't be a goose!' she said cheerfully. 'Good morning!'

The door slammed, and he heard the sharp patter of her feet running down the stairs.

CHAPTER XXXIV

NEXT day he started out to find Nat. Nat had been working markets for years, he was just the fellow to help him. Alec felt different already, as if all he had to do was to get hold of Nat, and then everything would work out all right. At Nat's house his wife told Alec he was working. She recognized him although he had changed a good deal She told him exactly how to get to the market, and where to find the stall.

On the bus, he was almost cheerful. He had a feeling that something was bound to happen. Olive was right, if so many people made a living that way, he should be able to as well; after all, trading was in his blood. He hummed to himself an old folk tune his mother used to croon when he was a kid, a lullaby to send him off to sleep.

> Sweet dreams little son
> Of raisins and almonds
> Sleep well little Jew
> Get bigger and stronger
> And when you grow up
> You'll deal in sweet perfumes
> And almonds and raisins. Almonds and raisins . . .

A policeman directed him to the market. It was a long, narrow street, the end of which twisted out of sight behind a block of dirty buildings. The stalls ranged in both gutters, piled high with every variety of merchandise. Very few people were about; he walked slowly in the centre of the road, keeping a sharp eye open for Nat. The stallholders regarded him suspiciously, he could sense hostility in their glances. A strange Jew looking round in that part of London meant, nine times out of ten, a new stallholder, and a new stall meant fresh opposition; it was hard enough to share what little trade there was amongst those already there, without somebody else coming along and making matters worse. Alec turned red, and walked more quickly. They made him feel he was doing something mean and sneaking, but after all, he wasn't out to make a fortune, he only wanted to live.

At last Alec saw him. He almost passed Nat by, but a second glance told him he'd found his man. He had always been used to seeing Nat in a smart suit or overcoat; it was a bit of a surprise to find him wearing an old leather coat, with a dirty felt hat stuck at the back of his head. Nat always wore some sort of headgear; he had been bald ever since he was twenty, but by some sort of malicious compensation the rest of his body was as hirsute as Esau's. His torso, arms, and legs, were covered with dark matted tufts, he used to complain comically that he had hair everywhere, except on his head.

Nat looked up when Alec came over to the stall.

'Hullo!' he said surprised. 'What are you doing here?'

He shook Alec's hand without waiting for a reply. He seemed pleased to see him.

'What are you doing round this end of the world?' he repeated. 'Aren't you working?'

Alec shook his head.

'No. I'm out of a job,' he said. 'I came here to see if I could get a couple of tips from you.'

'Tips? – About what?'

'Markets.'

'Oh,' said Nat thoughtfully. 'So you want to try markets.' He turned to a neighbouring stallholder. 'Give eye, Alf,' he said. The man nodded. 'Come on,' Nat said to Alec. 'Come with me.' Alec followed him into a coffee shop a little way down.

'But there's no one at your stall,' Alec protested by the door.

'That's all right,' said Nat, sitting at a table. 'Nobody'll run away with it. Now what are you going to have?'

'Nothing, thanks. I had something to eat before I came out.'

'Have a ham sandwich,' Nat pressed.

'No, thanks. No, really not. I'm not hungry.'

'A cup of tea then; at least I expect you to have a cup of tea with me.'

'All right. If you insist, just a cup of tea.'

Nat turned to the man at the counter.

'Two teas, Jock, and two ham sandwiches.'

Jock nodded. 'O.K.'

'... So you want to try markets,' Nat said again. 'What sort of gear have you got?'

'I haven't got anything yet,' said Alec. 'That's what I wanted to talk to you about.'

'Well, I'll tell *you* something; if I knew of anything good, I'd go in for it myself. My game's properly washed out. Haven't you got any idea at all of what you want to sell?'

'. . . Silk stockings?' said Alec tentatively.

Nat shook his head. 'No good. Too many at it.'

'. . . Underclothes?'

'No good either. Whatever line you think of, for any market, you'll find a dozen there before you. And everything's cut to pieces. Now take my swag, curtains, fancy goods, and linens. I used to make a ton of money at it years ago, but now, it isn't worth a light. You stay here with me to-day, and you'll see for yourself. It's only a couple of weeks to Christmas, I should be tearing busy, but all I've taken this morning is eight bob, from one customer. That was four yards of curtain net at two bob a yard. It costs me one and nine, so all I earned out of that sale was a shilling; a morning's work! Just enough to keep me in cigarettes. It's all right to work on such profits if you can sell enough, but you can't. Sell enough! Why, some days, you can't even give the damn stuff away!'

Jock brought over the teas and a plate of ham sandwiches, and went away silently.

'Yes,' Nat went on. 'That's the way thing's are today. The only people I know who are making money are the croakers, the quack doctors. If you can sell a tube of coloured sawdust shavings for sixpence, and guarantee it to cure anything from cancer to housemaid's knees, you can be certain of a good, steady income. I've often thought of doing that sort of thing myself, it's easy enough if you can talk, but I can't bring myself to robbing poor people. I believe in legitimate graft. I may sell something for two and nine that perhaps only costs me a shilling, but it will be worth two and nine, otherwise I wouldn't sell it. That's why I'm in the gutter, and likely to stay there!'

The man called Alf popped his head inside the coffee shop.

'Customer for you, Nat!' he bawled.

Nat bit a large segment out of his ham sandwich and stood up.

'There you are,' he grumbled with his mouth full, 'As if it isn't bad enough, you don't get a bloody minute to yourself!' He swallowed hastily. 'Won't be a tick,' he said to Alec.

He slouched out of the shop. Alec finished his tea. The cadaverous taciturn Jock came over silently and removed the cup and saucer without a word and went back behind the counter. Alec wondered whether, if someone stuck a pin up him, he would jump in the air and actually say 'Oh!'

Nat returned a few minutes later. He sat down again opposite Alec and picked up the remnants of his ham sandwich.

'False alarm,' he said resignedly. 'The bloody woman knows I haven't got the stuff she wants, and that I'm not likely to have any, but she's been worrying me for the past three weeks – and always when I'm having something to eat!'

He held his breath for a moment, then belched loudly.

'Excuse me,' he said apologetically. 'Gastric trouble. We all get it in the markets. It comes from never sitting down to a proper meal. You have to jump up every five minutes, and see what somebody wants.'

Alec nodded sympathetically. Nat bolted the second sandwich, and gulped down his tea as if someone were chasing him. No wonder he had indigestion, Alec thought, but he said nothing.

'In the old days,' Nat said, 'we used to get up at five in the morning, while it was still dark, take a barrow from the stable, and rush off to the market. It was tough going, too, carting a barrow load of stuff all the way here from Whitechapel. Well, when we arrived, we waited round the corner till eight o'clock. Then the policeman gave the signal, and we dashed for our pitches and planted our trestles in the gutter, like pioneers staking claims in a goldfield. But all that was years ago. Nowadays there's no need to rush. The pitches are licensed, and even if they weren't, men wouldn't split each other's heads over them. Markets aren't goldfields any longer, more like graveyards, and people don't scrimmage for plots in a cemetery. Market men are the biggest liars in the world, but when you ask them, "How's the game?" and they answer, "No bloody good!" or "On the ribs!" then you can be sure that for once they're telling the truth. Only an incorrigible optimist can say "Not too bad", and if someone does happen to answer, "Pretty Good", you can be certain he's wearing borrowed socks, and owes the landlord ten weeks rent. And it's not only here, that trade's bad. I work five different markets a week, in Bermondsey, Acton, King's Cross, Poplar, and Aldgate; I travel from one end of London to the other, and come into contact with thousands of people, and it's the same tale everywhere, there's no money about.'

Nat stood up, brushed the crumbs from his trousers, and buttoned up his leather coat.

'Now we'll get back to work,' he said with a comical grimace. 'Perhaps I'll take some money this afternoon. Maybe you'll bring me luck.'

'I hope so,' said Alec, following him into the street.

Nat busied himself at the stall, arranging the materials so that they showed to the best advantage. Draping a roll of silk curtaining so that it hung over the board in golden flounces, heaping up a gaily coloured cascade of cushion covers, stacking the rolls of casement so that they were easy to handle. He stood a little way back, his head cocked on one side, regarding his handiwork like an artist. The arrangement seemed to satisfy him. He came back to Alec's side, a pleased expression on his face.

'Looks nice doesn't it?' he said.

'Very nice indeed,' Alec answered.

'Two hundred quid!' said Nat waving an expressive hand at the rolls of material.

'How much?'

Alec had heard the first time, but it gave him a queer sinking feeling, so that the words came out involuntarily. His eight pounds shrank to insignificant small change, he made up his mind to say fifty if Nat asked how much money he had to start with. Nat on the other hand, thought that Alec doubted his word; after all, he'd said himself that market men were the world's champion liars. He hastened to justify himself.

'Yes, there's two hundred quid's worth of stuff there,' he said, 'maybe more. But I haven't paid for it all, my credit's good; too damn good! If I go into a firm to buy stuff, they say to me "Take", and they don't ask any questions about when I'll be able to pay them back, consequently I'm tempted to buy more than I need'. He grinned. 'That's just the trouble. I wish I had the money I owe!'

Gradually people started to come into the market. At first, a thin trickle of stragglers, the advance guard, then shifting islands, then a solid block of slow-moving shoppers occupying the whole width of the road from gutter to gutter. Nat got up on a box, and started shouting. At once, a semi-circle of curious faces collected round the stall. He cracked one or two jokes, the stock jokes of the market cheapjack, and the people laughed although they'd heard them dozens of times before; then he sold some oddments of lace in tuppeny bundles. These were snapped up, and when he judged his audience to be in a buying mood, he started work on the cushion covers. After a good deal of cajoling, he managed to sell three of them. The crowd started to drift away, there were much more exciting things to be seen in the market. Nat had to hold them somehow. He tore off the wrappings from a roll of fancy panelled curtaining.

'Hey! Hey!' he shouted, thumping the roll on the stall. 'Sixpence a yard!'

One woman felt the material sceptically. She thought for a moment. 'Give me six yards,' she said, convinced.

The others followed like sheep, and in a few minutes the whole roll vanished into different market baskets. Nat opened a second roll, and that too was swallowed up. Then he tried the more expensive curtaining, bellowing its virtues till the sweat rolled down his cheeks, but he only succeeded in selling a few yards. He wiped his face with a handkerchief, and got off the box. He'd finished shouting. If anyone wanted some stuff they'd have to come up and ask him, he'd save his lungs.

The market emptied almost as quickly as it had become crowded. Only a couple of eddies were left of the dark stream that had rolled between the gutters.

'Well, any good?' asked Alec.

'Not much,' said Nat. 'About fifty bob.'

'Why didn't you sell some more of that cheap curtaining?' Alec asked. 'You've got another couple of rolls, you could have shifted the whole lot easily enough.'

'I dare say I could,' said Nat with a wry smile. 'But that stuff costs me sixpence a yard.'

'And you sell it for sixpence?'

'That's just a call bird, a bit of psychology. Throwing a sprat to catch a mackerel; but nowadays these women are cleverer than I am, they snap up the bargains, but won't even bite at the stuff I can earn a penny on — I'm the mackerel!'

Alec looked round. The market seemed deserted.

'Where have they all gone to?' he asked.

'Tea, I suppose,' said Nat. 'In an hour or so, they'll all be coming out again.'

A woman passed by the stall, wheeling a pram in front of her. A pale, dirty little boy lay in it, fast asleep, one tiny grubby hand hanging over the side, clutching a filthy dummy. She smiled at Nat as she went by, a pathetic little smile from a face that looked as if it never did anything but cry.

'See that woman?' said Nat.

'Well?'

'How old d'you think she is?'

Alec looked after her. From the back she could be any age. A dark tight-fitting hat covered her head. Her black coat hung down loosely, the shoes were down at heel, and her stockings wrinkled over the thin legs in unsightly folds.

'About thirty?' Alec hazarded.

Nat laughed — 'She's eighteen!'

'Eighteen? — No! Surely, she's older than that.'

'She's not. As a matter of fact I don't think she's eighteen yet. — You saw she was wearin black?'

'Yes. I noticed that.'

'It's for her husband. She's a widow, her husband died a few weeks ago. Pernicious anaemia. I've sort of watched her grow up. I've been following her life. I can tell you I see and hear some queer things around my stall. Her mother used to buy a lot of stuff from me a couple of years ago. One day, the mother comes up to the stall and asks me prices of one thing and another, and I keep telling her how much this is, and how much that is, and all the time I can see she isn't taking a blind bit of notice.

' "You're looking worried," I said.

'She looked at me. "So I ought to be," she answered. "You know my little May what comes round to your stall with me sometimes?"

' "May? May?" Then I remembered. A shy, pasty-faced, skinny little girl who used to hide herself behind the old woman's skirt whenever she came round. "Oh yes," I said. "I know, nice little kid". I had to say something like that, she was a customer after all.

' "Well she's got into trouble," said the old woman. "She's been hanging about with a feller what worked down the docks, a feller about ten year older'n what she is, and she's gonna have a baby. Pore kid! She's only 16, she's a baby herself!"

'Sixteen! From the size of her, I'd thought she was twelve, or thirteen at the most, but I didn't say anything about that. What I did ask was what she intended doing about it.

' "Christ knows!" she answered. "He ought ter marry the pore kid, only he's done a bunk, and we don't know where to find him, mate!"

'She fiddled about a little longer at the stall, and then she went off, as if she didn't have any idea where she was going. A few months later I saw her again.

' "Well, what's happened?" I said to her. "Found the chap?"

"Yerse. We found him all right," she answered. 'We put the police on to him. He says he wants ter marry her. I don't want him to marry the pore kid; after all, the damage is done now, but she keeps crying, and carrying on, and saying she loves him and she'll die without him, so what can I do? – She'll have ter marry the blasted swine!"

'Then the kid was born, a little rat; it weighed about three pounds, premature I think. The old woman brought it round to me proud as anything, to show me her grandson, young Jackie. Of course I had to say he was a marvellous little thing, and she kept cooing "Ain't he lovely, bless his little heart", and in the same breath cursing the father. She'd never forgive that bloody swine, never! Then the mother moved out of the district, and that was the last I ever saw of her, but the girl, May, started coming to my stall, looking as though she'd put on ten years. Every time she came round, she had another hard-luck story for me. Her husband knocked her about; he hated her for having had him arrested; he hated the kid; he was out of work again. Then he fell ill, and they found out he had this anaemia bad. They sent him down to a sanatorium, and May used to visit him once a week regular. She'd come back and tell me that every time she went to see him, he made her feel ill too. All he wanted to know was how his little nephew Ronnie was getting on. She kept talking about his son Jackie, but he wouldn't listen. Only Ronnie. He made her promise to send him a photograph of Ronnie. She said she would, but she didn't, and she never went to visit him again. Then I saw her in black, and I knew he'd died, so I said to her "He's dead, eh?"

' "Bloody good job too!" she answered, but there wasn't anything vindictive in the way she spoke.

' "What are you going to do now?" I asked.

' "I'll get something,' she said. "I'll move over to mother's. She'll look after Jackie while I go out to work".

'That was a week ago. She's still here. I suppose she's having a job getting rid of the furniture.'

Nat dismissed her with a shrug of his shoulders, he had his own troubles to worry about just now, and started on his stall again, trying to make it look respectable. Yards and yards of crumpled curtaining lay as he had undone it, tangled amongst cushion covers, and linen table centres. He rolled the curtaining back smoothly, and sorted out the fancy goods, piling them in a gleaming shot-silk heap. Alec watched Nat hopping about agilely from one side of the stall to the other. All this sweating, this rolling and unrolling, arranging and re-arranging, and for what? — to sell a lousy few yards of curtaining at an infinitesimal profit! Alec had enough of markets for one day, he decided to go home. He could see by the way an old hand like Nat ate his heart out, that this sort of life wasn't for him.

'Well Nat,' he said. 'I've got to be going now'.

'So soon? — Anyway, look me up if there's anything you want to know. I'll be glad to help. The missus'll always tell you where to find me.'

'Thanks a lot,' Alec replied. 'It's very good of you. So-long Nat!'

He turned to go, but only managed to take a couple of steps before Nat called him back.

'Well,' said Nat. 'You've had a half-day in the market. Got any idea yet of what you can sell?'

Alec shook his head slowly. 'No. No idea at all. What is there left to sell? All I can think of are almonds and raisins.'

Nat grinned. 'Even they're no good. Smith's, the crisp people, sell them in tuppenny celophane packets, all nicely wrapped up, untouched by hand. Can't compete with Smith's. No. Us poor Jews haven't got a chance. We'll have to sing our kids to sleep to some other tune.'

'You're right,' said Alec.

He turned away again, walking off swiftly in case Nat wanted to call him back once more. At the stopping place, he had to run for a bus. Boarding it, he climbed to the top deck and slumped back on the seat like a sagging balloon. He felt very tired, but somehow not very disappointed, only bitter, and rebellious. All his hunches ended this way, pricked flat. Nat might have given him some more good advice while he was about it. He might have said, 'The best game today is a regular job,' then he'd have answered, 'So it is, but where do they grow?' — Then they'd both have laughed. Hell! And where would it get them? He'd still be signing on at the Labour Exchange, and Nat sweating his skin off, making manufacturers rich. This was Olive's idea of freedom and independence; of being your own boss. Your own boss! Well, well, this wouldn't be the worst. The conductor came up, and he took his ticket mechanically. Raisins and almonds! . . . Born to the business! Huh! What was going to happen next?

CHAPTER XXXV

WHEN he met her in the evening, Olive was eager for news. She could hardly wait to greet him, but asked as they walked down the street, how he'd got on. He mumbled replies under his breath, half ashamed to admit that the first tiny rebuff had upset him so much. He didn't tell Olive all that had transpired in the market. When he thought of those hard, hostile stares that had followed him, he felt again an uncomfortable pricking under his skin; he couldn't even talk about it, all she could get out of him was that he didn't think there was anything much doing in that line.

The girl knew him well enough not to argue. She supposed something had happened to turn him from the idea. If he was satisfied to let it drop, so was she; but it was a pity, she'd certainly thought he'd have managed to do something about it.

The following morning when Olive left for work, he took a book to read, but gave it up as hopeless after a quarter of an hour. Then he returned to his regular job, staring out of the window. He was getting fed up with this room, with his surroundings, with everything. The same grey walls facing him every morning, the same kids in the gutters, the same woman banging her mats on the window ledge. All these things seemed suddenly alien to him, as though he had no connection with them, nor they with him.

He looked about the room with distaste. It had never

lost the first musty smell, and the ugly cretonne covered furniture became more hateful the closer he looked at it. The hideous, scrawly pattern grated on his nerves, although he should have been used to it by this time; aesthetic nerves were a luxury no poor man could afford. This was his home, yet nothing about it was tied to him. If he never saw this room again, there would not be a single regret in his memory. Maybe that was because he was a nomad, a roof and four walls could never be a home for him. He was a tent-dweller. For centuries his people had carried their homes strapped on their backs or on camels. He felt it more and more clearly, he didn't belong here, never had done . . . A tent-dweller! . . . A tent-dweller! . . . Hell! He was getting some idiotic notions into his head. He'd never felt this way before. A tent-dweller! – He'd be wanting to go to Palestine next!

He went down to the reference library. He hadn't felt any particular desire to go there, but any place would do, so long as he got out of the room. He felt he must go mad if he stuck up there much longer. All the life seemed to be crushed out of him, like the juice from a grape. In the south of France they gathered the big juicy grapes, and heaped them in the huge wine-presses, and peasants trod them down with their dirty bare feet to give the bouquet for the connoisseur. And the residue was thrown to the pigs, or used for manure. That was about all he was fit for just now.

An old tramp sitting next to him snored loudly. He had come into the library out of the cold for a rest. An open periodical lay on the table before him. At first he had made some pretence of reading, but gradually his head had nodded, and now he was fast asleep. The assistant librarian came over as soon as he noticed the old man, and shook him roughly by the shoulder. At once the tramp's eyes opened wide. The librarian gave him a sharp little lecture, and walked back to his desk like a virtuous watch-dog. The old man sat up stiffly in his chair, his eyes glued on the print before him; he scarcely moved, but he was three parts asleep. So long as he kept his eyes open they couldn't shift him.

Alec got up wearily, and left the library. He walked aimlessly until he found himself in Commercial Street, bearing towards Aldgate. There, the shops were brightly illuminated. Only Three Weeks To Christmas! Shop Early This Year! People were staring at the hosiers, and in the windows of the bag and stocking shops, worrying about presents for uncle John, and aunt Martha. The butchers were already displaying plucked turkeys, and shining corpses of scalded hogs with red rosettes stuck ludicrously in their snouts, and snared rabbits, their intestines pried open showing the frozen grey fat, the tiny legs spreadeagled, bound, and kept in position by sticks decorated with frosted tinsel. Only three weeks to Christmas; the Santa Claus racket was in full swing.

In one of the side streets a strong smell of cooking reached him as he passed a little shop. He looked at the steaming windows and deciphered 'Odessa Restaurant' written in Yiddish across the top pane. Odessa! How often had his father talked about that Paris of the Black Sea; his eyes would shine as he spoke of the broad boulevards, and beautiful white buildings – 'They live like God in Odessa!' ...

Alec felt in his pockets, he was never without a few shillings, but apart from cigarettes, he spent very little. A man came out of the restaurant, bringing with him through the open door an almost overpowering gust of appetizing smells. That decided Alec. He went inside, and sat at a table.

A fat woman, middle-aged, with dark fuzzy hair, greeted him with a good natured smile.

'Yes?' she asked.

'Something to eat,' said Alec in Yiddish.

The woman's smile became wider. She drew up a chair next to Alec and sat down beside him, and placed a friendly hand on his arm.

'Now what do you fancy?' she asked, speaking softly like a mother to a child.

She was interested in this boy. He spoke like a 'landsman', he might even be from her home town. Every time she heard a fresh voice with that fleshy Ukrainian brogue, her heart jumped in the air. Like a little bit of home!

... 'Well, what?'

'I leave that to you,' he said.

Ah! That was a real South Russian. She'd find out what town he came from, perhaps she knew his people; he could even be a relation, stranger things had happened in her restaurant. She sketched out a meal rapidly. First, chopped liver or chopped herring. Cabbage soup, sweet or sour, roast veal chops with kasha, stewed prunes, and lemon tea. Alec nodded to everything. He felt comfortable, at home. It might be his father talking at his elbow.

'You're from Odessa?' said the woman, getting to her feet.

'No. I was born here. My people came from that way.'

'What town?'

'I can't remember the name of the town, the province was Kamenetz Podolsk.'

'Ah!' exclaimed the woman, delighted. 'A landsman! I thought so. I also come from Kamenetz Podolsk Gubernia.' She shook his hand warmly, and bustled off to the kitchen to prepare the meal.

The bill came to two-and-nine. Not a lot considering the amount he'd had, and the quality of the food. He sat back sated, and lit a cigarette. The woman came and sat down beside him once more, and asked him how he'd enjoyed the meal. He told her he hadn't tasted anything so good for a long time, and promised to come again.

In the street, he found himself walking towards his mother's house. He felt an irresistible longing to see her. He hadn't been anywhere near his old home for months and months, it seemed like years. The long winter night was falling, spreading a dark blue haze over the roof-tops. He walked up and down Gurnham Street several times. He could see his mother's house clearly each time he passed the turning, but it was quite dark when he finally plucked up the courage to approach the door.

A woman poked her head from a window as he went

by and smiled at him. He smiled back and nodded. She'd known him since he was so-high; not a bad sort, but an awful gossip. He could imagine her turning round now and whispering to someone behind her — 'Look! — That's Mrs. Benjamin's son' . . .

He stopped in front of the door. He could feel his heart thumping excitedly, as if it were trying to rush through his throat. His hand rested for a moment on the knocker. It wasn't too late even now, he could still go away, but in the midst of his debating he heard the knocker bang twice.

He waited. In a moment there were heavy footsteps down the passage and the door opened. It was the cossack, in his shirt-sleeves, his braces hanging loosely down his back. He looked at Alec suspiciously.

'Yes?'

'Is my mother at home?'

'No,' said the cossack gruffly.

'Oh! . . . I'm sorry. How is she?'

'Oll right.'

'And how are you?'

'I'm oll right too.'

The cossack seemed reluctant to answer. He felt there was a catch in this somewhere. Alec turned to go.

'Joost one minute!' the cossack called after him.

'Yes?'

'Come inside if you like. She's gone to de market. She won't be long.'

'No thanks,' said Alec. 'Tell her I've called. I'll come some other time — Good night!'

'Good night!' said the cossack in a slightly gentler tone.

He stood watching Alec for a while. He didn't understand that boy altogether, something queer about him. He shrugged his huge shoulders and pushed the door to.

Alec got away from the house as quickly as possible. That hadn't been a very pretty sight, the cossack with his braces dangling over his backside. So his mother had done it at last! It must have taken some courage to install him in the house in spite of the malicious tongues of neighbours. The street was like a country village. Every woman knew what was cooking in the other's pots. Well, good luck to her! She deserved it. He made up his mind never to bother her again.

He came out opposite the Great Assembly Hall in Mile End, 'One of the sights of London,' where the hungry lines of ragged men were waiting for their free tea and slice of Gospel. Always something doing at the Assembly Hall, prayer meetings going on now for the umpteen thousandth night in succession; ex-detective preachers, and ex-convicts, and ex-chorus girls.

He walked along Whitechapel, the broadest pavement in London. He'd often promenaded there as a kid, dressed in his smartest clothes, chasing young girls, and snatching kisses. It was the same Whitechapel, the same irresponsible boys and girls, the same seedy orators at the corner of Vallance Road. Only the shops had blossomed out in new fronts, and even they had the seasonal tags in the windows, decorated with holly and pink Father Christmasses. The Jews had also adopted Saint Nicholas.

Every two steps there was an amusement arcade, or a pin-parlour saloon. Another sign of the times. Cut-price amusements. Pay your penny and take your choice. And what amusements! What a choice! Catapulting balls into numbered holes! When he was about ten those games had been very popular with youngsters, now full grown men stooped over the slot machines, and busily added up the thousands.

Outside 'Luna Park' there stood a big man with a tray hanging round his neck, selling peanuts. He lowered his head as Alec looked at him, as though he were ashamed of being recognized. An able-bodied man selling peanuts, one obviously unused to that sort of thing. A worker, the skilled craftsman type, having to stoop to this for a living! There was not more than a shilling's worth of peanuts on the tray altogether, how much could he earn if he sold the whole lot? This was horrible! A degrading spectacle! A cold shiver oozed down his back. Sooner than do anything like this, he'd starve, or steal. Take from those that had too much!

A group of taxi-drivers were lounging about near the cab rank at Gardiner's. One detached himself from the knot, and hailed Alec as he passed. It was Johnny Cohen, an old schoolmate.

'Hullo Alec! — How're you going?' he shouted. 'Haven't seen you for donkeys years.'

Alec crossed over to him and shook his outstretched hand.

'I don't live down this way,' he said.

'Working?'

'No. Resting at the moment.'

Johnny grinned. 'Maybe you're better off.'

'Maybe. But I'd sooner be working,' said Alec. 'Have you been at this job long?' he added as an afterthought.

'A few years,' said Johnny. 'But it's like everything else, played out. There are too many at it. According to official figures, and you know how far you can trust them, there's been an increase of six hundred drivers, and a decrease of two hundred cabs in the past three years. Why, there are five chaps in my street who used to be tailors, now they're cabbies too. Some days, when we're all at home together, the street looks like a taxi rank.

'How long does it take to learn?'

'What? – How to drive a cab?'

'Yes.'

'Oh, you can pick that up in a couple of lessons. What takes time is knowledge of London. That can take from nine months to three years, or longer. Unless you've got enough dough behind you to stick it out that long, I don't advise you to go in for it. It's a hard life anyhow. You've got to be out in all weathers, from eight in the morning to six at night, or from about six at night to three or four in the morning. You either work on the clock, that is, you get thirty-three and-a-third of what the clock shows, or else you can hire the cab for ten bob a night, buy your own juice, and have what you can get. Then there are the cops. It seems as if they're all born with a special grudge against cabbies. They're always ready to haul us up under the Hackney Carriage Act of eighteen hundred and something . . . Yes. Take it from me, it's a tough life!'

'So you can't even make a decent living out of taxi-driving,' said Alec.

'Oh no!' Johnny answered. 'I wouldn't say that. One of my mates does quite well at it. He's the only one I know who does, but that's because his wife goes out to work, and she earns four pounds a week.'

Alec laughed. 'So it can be done! The idea is to get hold of a rich wife first.'

Johnny grinned, and slapped him on the back. Somebody whistled, and he hurried off to his cab to pick up a fare. He turned at the wheel and waved cheerily.

'So-long, Alec!'

'So-long!'

. . . Played out! . . . Played out! . . . Everything was played out, and yet life seemed to go on in the same old way, there still seemed to be plenty of money about. Smart cars were drawn up at the kerbs. Wealthy gown manufacturers, the new rich, sleek pod-bellied men with their mink-coated wives. Their factories were here in Whitechapel, but they themselves lived far away, in Hampstead, Golders Green, or Hendon. Thousands of young girls slaved for them in their workrooms, machining dresses all day at three and six a dozen, while they drove about in luxurious limousines. These were the people who found it easy to make a living, coining money, rolling in the shekels hand over fist, while his sort had to fight hard to exist. Work was played out!

His father had been fond of quoting from the Talmud 'The man who has not taught his son a trade, has taught him to become a thief,' and he'd thought he had done his duty by taking him into the workshop. How wrong he'd been! Neither his father nor the Talmud had ever foreseen such a world, a world in which only thieves could exist, big thieves and little thieves, where honest hard graft only landed you in the gutter — selling peanuts!

No! He couldn't find a place here either, not even in Whitechapel where he was born. He felt like O'Neill's Hairy Ape, without moorings, he just didn't belong. Elspeth's words cut through his mind. 'You and your people are only guests here.' That was true too. She, or Olive, could walk straight down any street with her head in the air, without any fear, but he had always to keep his eyes skinned in case someone was waiting round the corner to throw bricks. It wasn't so very long ago he'd played cricket with other schoolboys in Victoria Park; then, they had to go home in batches because there would always be a mob of youngsters from Bethnal Green, waiting for them at the cinder path. The cry would go up 'Here come the Jew-boys!' and they'd be pelted with stones, gravel, and other rubbish, and have to fight their way clear to the gates with bats, stumps, and whatever was handy. . . .

Played out! . . . Played out! . . . It was a pretty lousy situation, but he had one consolation, this sort of life couldn't last much longer anyhow. These were the last death-kicks. He felt like the prophet looking down on Sodom and Gomorrah. Doomed! Doomed! Amusement parlours, and streamlined cars, and eight-story factories. All doomed! All heading for the deluge that would sweep everything to splinters, him along with the rest of the flotsam! . . .

CHAPTER XXXVI

GOING home with Olive he appeared to be more dejected than usual. She tried to cheer him up, telling him of some comic incidents that had occurred at the café, but he didn't smile once, he didn't even seem to be listening. She sighed, he had one of his moods on again. They walked the rest of the way in silence.

He slept very badly. All through the night he kept tossing from side to side, and his body burned as if he had the fever. His brain was active all the time. Little disjointed pictures kept forming in his head, and disappearing before he could grasp them. Snatches of conversation, long, meaningless speeches, droning on and on. His head felt swollen and heavy, like a hive with a host of disconnected ideas buzzing inside, trying to force their way out all together.

Olive spoke to him once, when she thought he was awake, but all she heard in reply was an incoherent mumble. In the morning when she left for work, he was sleeping peacefully, like a child.

The sun, shining powerfully through the window, woke him. He sat up, rubbing his eyes, and looked at the alarm clock. Half-past ten! He'd be late! He jumped out of bed hurriedly, and started to dress. Then he remembered. Late! — Late for what?

After he'd performed the ritual, signed his name in the golden book at the Labour Exchange, he was free for the day. The sun was still shining in a cloudless sky, the air was mild, more like early autumn than December. He decided to walk to Hyde Park.

He sat for a while on a form by the Serpentine. Hungry little ducklings touted for crumbs at the edge of the lake, while the gulls cawed shrilly, wheeling and hovering over the water. Tall soldiers walked by briskly, slapping their flanks with their canes, and tittering nursemaids strolling along, pushed expensive prams before them. Alec wore no overcoat, and after a time it began to feel chilly. He got up and set off sharply towards Marble Arch.

The forum was in the throes of its late afternoon session. The Catholic Evidence Guild, the Open Air Mission, the Salvation Army, the Latter-Day Saints, all were busily pointing out the one true road to Heaven. Itinerant preachers without platforms were dotted about, holding impromptu discussions, while another double ring of people were singing hymns, training for an orgy of carols at Christmas, and one forlorn figure threaded in and out of the crowds like a somnambulist, speaking to nobody, but carrying in front of him a banner, with 'God is Love' on one side, and 'Repent saith the Lord' on the other.

Alec sampled each of the platforms in turn. None of the speakers was particularly inspired, not even one good laugh amongst the lot of them. He moved round the bend to the political department. Business was brisker here, better talkers, more listeners, more hecklers. A black hatted comedian, king-pin of the Hyde Park messiahs, was surrounded by a laughing crowd. This brand of crazy anarchism had made Alec laugh too, years ago, but he'd grown up since then. He skirted the edge of the crowd and came upon the 'Newists', propagandists of a new world philosophy. Alec found the speaker quite incomprehensible. He was a very young man, and several other young men stood around listening politely as though they understood what he was talking about. Alec moved on. Newism had all the appearances of having been evolved in school, between visits to the tuck-shop.

A negro caught his attention next. A large red flag fluttered from a pole beside him, and on the breast of the platform was chalked in white crayon 'National Unemployed Workers Movement'. Alec listened attentively. Yes, the negro was quite in order, but he'd heard all that before, he'd even said these things himself, only in much better English, and got the sack for his pains.

The negro was just concluding his speech. He thanked the audience for having given him such a kind hearing, and descended the platform to a few desultory handclaps. The chairman got up to announce the next speaker. Alec, for no reason, took a dislike to him at once. He decided he'd had enough of meetings. He elbowed his way through the crowd, and crossed the road to the gates. The sky was overhung with low dark clouds, and the air had suddenly become heavy, as though it were going to rain. That would mean riding home. He wasn't very flush after yesterday's outing, he hoped the soup would keep off for another couple of hours at least.

He went into the small Lyons' and ordered a cup of

tea and some currant cake. Unobtrusively, while he was glancing round, a man slipped into the seat opposite him. It was the negro. He fiddled about with the cruet, and kept turning his head as if he were looking for something. Alec picked up the menu from the floor and passed it over to him.

'The menu, comrade?' Alec asked.

The negro grinned, showing broken, discoloured teeth behind his thick lips.

'No thanks, friend,' he replied in a hoarse voice. 'Ah knows what ah wants. Ah was jest seein' if dey was somebody heah.'

The waitress came over, and the negro ordered a pot of tea.

'Nothing to eat?' asked the waitress.

'No thanks,' said the negro. 'Ah never eats an' drinks togedder.'

He looked across to Alec and grinned again. Alec was drinking his tea, he had finished his cake.

'Dey got a couple of good customers heah,' he said. 'Lyons' would make a lot more profit if dey all spent like us.'

Alec smiled. 'You're right!'

The waitress brought over his pot. The negro poured himself a cup of tea and swallowed it at one tilt. He cleared his throat.

'Ah! Dat's bettah!' he said.

'Thirsty work, talking,' Alec remarked.

'You' right dere', said the negro. 'But it's got to be done comrade, it's got to be done.'

He tossed the dregs into the slop basin, and poured

out a fresh cup. He looked up, and his swimming purple-flecked irises held Alec's eyes so close they might be rubbing faces.

'You a party membah?' he asked.

Alec shook his head. 'No. I don't belong to any party.'

'Ah!' said the negro. 'Dat's a pity!'

They both left the restaurant together. Alec offered the negro a cigarette, and he accepted it gratefully.

'Well,' said Alec, handing him a match. 'I'm off for home now.'

'Me too,' answered the negro. 'Which way you goin' comrade?'

'Through Islington.'

'Me too!' said the negro. 'Wahkin?'

'Sure!'

'Dat's good . . . What's yoh name?'

'Alec.'

'Mine's John Thomas King, but in de movement dey calls me Jo-Jo.'

'Pleased to meet you, Jo-Jo.'

They walked on a little way without speaking.

. . . 'You know,' Alec said, 'we Jews, and negroes, have a lot in common.'

'Dat's so,' Jo-Jo answered, nodding gravely. 'It's hard to be a black man.'

'Harder still to be a Jew.'

'Oh you Jews ain't got so much to kick about,' said Jo-Jo.

'No? — When in all the history of the world there's never been a people so persecuted as ours?'

'Dat's open to question,' Jo-Jo answered. 'De Jews have been in Europe most of de time, but nobody's written a history yet of de way black men have been exploited in Africa. You Jews are a funny lot. All de workers are suffering in Germany, but de whole East-End turns out 'cause de Jews are in trouble as well.'

'Nothing funny about that,' said Alec. 'That's only the expression of feeling, brother for brother.'

'All men are brudders!' Jo-Jo answered.

'I believe that too.'

'Den why didn't dey demonstrate when de Japanese t'rows bombs on Chapei, and murders t'ousands of innocent Chinese men, women, an' child'en? Ain't de yellow men brudders? An' why don't dey demonstrate about de way negroes is treated in Africa. Ain't de black men brudders? Dis Hitler is a gentleman compared wid some of de white bosses in Africa. Dey had concentration camps years an' years ago dere, dey still got dem, de compound system. Dey beats negroes to death wid bullock's harness, an' nobody demonstrates about it, dey shoots negro boys when dey's drunk, an' gets away wid it altogedder, or else gets sent to jail foh' a couple of years. But dey ain't no jail foh' white men in Africa. No sah! Only de poor whites, and communists gets it in de neck, but de rich planters — dey ain't no jail foh' dem! Deys rest-cures. If we ate every day what dey gets in dem rich men's jails, we'd get fat like pigs in no time!'

Alec was silent. He had no answer to all that; Jo-Jo was right, he knew it.

'Dey refuses a Rothschild a meal in a road-house,' the

negro went on, an' all de Jews in England kicks about it. Dey makes protests in de papers, dey shouts, dey feels indignant, but ah knows of places in anudder civilized country, America, where dey don't only refuse to serve a black man, but won't even let him step in de place. Ah've seen a young negro come out of a smart car, buy a soft drink at a wayside joint, and have the glass smashed in front of his face so's no white man's lips will be polluted. Ah've travelled in Jim-Crow cars on de railroads down South, in cattle trucks, not good enough foh' cattle, but too dem good foh' us dirty niggers. Ah remembers in New Yo'hk when dey showed de first negro talkie "Hallelujah", dey refused to admit cullud people to de white man's theatre, but ran a special first night foh' blacks, down town in Haarlem. Dey ain't a week goes by, but what anudder black man isn't lynched. Dey takes a negro foh' a ride, an' strings him up a tree, an' shoots him full of holes 'cause a white woman said he smiled at her. Dey empties petrol tins over pregnant women, an' ties 'em to stakes, an' burns 'em to cinders . . . Yes sah! When it comes to persecution, we negroes shuah knows somet'ing about it! An' dat's jest de trouble comrade, dat t'rows us right into de arms of de nationalists. We ain't jest Jews, and jest Negroes, we's workers too. We got to know all dese t'ings an' stick to our class at de same time.'

Jo-Jo looked inquiringly at his companion as if he expected him to say something in his turn, but Alec was still silent. After all, there was nothing in what the negro said with which he could disagree. Not so many months ago, he had spoken this way himself, but he'd felt different then, he'd been working; now Jo-Jo's words seemed to strike with a fresh truth, as if he were hearing a new doctrine for the first time. The past few weeks he had been walking around with his mind in blinkers.

'Ah bin to Russia comrade!' Jo-Jo continued enthusiastically. His eyes lit up, as if a flame had suddenly crackled into life. 'Yes sah! Ah bin to Russia! Ah was delegated from de N.U.W.M. Dere, a black man, a yellow man, a Jew, it don't make no difference at all. Ah seen Langston Hughes, de American negro poet, no place in Moscow he couldn't go in an' not be a welcome guest. Ah seen anudder negro writer, Claude McKay, photographed on de old czar's t'rone. Where-ever ah went, dey treated me like a comrade like an equal. Dey don't t'ink of demselves as jest Tatar's, Kalmuks, or Khirgises; first an' foh'most, dey's workers, den Tatars, Khirghise's or whatever dey happen to be. Yes sah! Dat's de way to look at it. Ah knows. Ah bin to Russia!'

Alec's tongue loosened under the fire of the negro's enthusiasm. He began to tell Jo-Jo about himself, about his life with Olive, about the jobs he'd worked at, and the strike at Goldblatt's. The negro listened intently, and when he had finished, he shook his head reprovingly.

'A man like you should be in de movement,' he said. 'You got no right to stay outside, wedder you workin' or not. If you t'ink de way you do, yoh place is beside us in de ranks!'

They stopped outside a tall, dark grey block of tenements. Squawling kids could be seen through the dismal iron bars playing on the upper landings, their games illuminated by naked fan-shaped gas flares.

'Dis is where ah lives,' said Jo-Jo. 'Meadows Buildings. De fourth floor.'

Alec shook the negro's hand.

'Well I'll be leaving you here,' he said. 'I've still got a good way to go.'

'Wait a minute.' Jo-Jo held his hand in a firm grip. 'Yoh can't leave me flat like dis. Come on upstairs, have a cup of tea and a bit of a rest. Ah wants you to meet de missus an' de kids.'

'All right,' said Alec. 'Thanks. It'll be a pleasure. And I wouldn't mind another cup of tea.'

They climbed up the stairs to the fourth floor. The kids on the landings greeted Jo-Jo familiarly as he passed, he was evidently a favourite with them. The negro stopped outside a door marked 6B, and tapped gently.

'Come on in,' sung a cheery female voice.

Jo-Jo stuck his head inside the room.

'Yoh dressed, Mog?' he asked. 'Ah got visitors.'

''Course I'm dressed, stupid!' the woman answered with a giggle. 'Someone would think I always walk about in my bloomers. Come on in!'

Alec followed Jo-Jo into the room. In the yellow gaslight it looked chock-full, cluttered up with objects like a wardrobe dealer's shop. Tiny garments hung from lines stretched taut across the room near the ceiling, and there seemed to be sticks of furniture in every square foot of space. A crimson light glowed from the fireplace the opposite end of the room, but the fire itself was obscured by the broad back of a negress sitting on a low stool in front of it, and dripping pieces of washing hanging over the guard to dry. A vapour arose from the wet garments merging into the faintly ammoniac smell of baby clothes, that was the predominant odour of the room.

A little black boy sat on the floor reading, near a tin Woolworth tub half filled with soapy water. He looked up, glanced disinterestedly at Alec, smiled to his father, and returned to the book. The woman turned her head, revealing behind her, like an aura framing her coiled black hair, a sparkling, heaped-up coke fire. Her face was like a black sun, radiating warmth and life. She smiled at Alec first, showing two strings of perfect teeth, then fixed Jo-Jo with a reproachful stare.

'Time you knew there's a draught blowing from the landing, Jo-Jo,' she said.

Alec closed the door immediately. 'It's my fault,' he apologized. 'I left it open.'

The negress turned completely on her stool with her back to the fire, and Alec saw a chubby piccaninny wriggling between the folds of a huge white bath towel spread on her lap.

'Dis is Mog', said Jo-Jo, pointing to his wife.

The negress grinned and inclined her head. 'Pleased to meet you comrade.'

'Alec's de name,' said Jo-Jo.

'Pleased to meet you, Alec,' she repeated after him.

Jo-Jo indicated the boy on the floor. 'John Thomas Junior. One day he's gonna write fat books. Ain't yoh sonny?'

The boy nodded gravely. 'Sure I will pa.'

"Dere,' said Jo-Jo. 'Dat settles it. He's gonna write books, and dis —' he pointed to the baby, 'is Eric. Eleven months. De latest addition to de family. He ought to get on fine wid a good Nordic name like dat.'

The baby looked up and opened its mouth, showing two tiny front teeth glistening in the aperture. 'Dada!' it called wriggling its little arms free from the towel. 'Dada! Dada!'

Jo-Jo became a different man. It seemed as though he had left his bitterness and rebellion in the street. All tenderness, he leaned over his wife and picked up the naked baby, and flung him in the air between the clothes lines, caught him, and flung him to the ceiling, again and again. The child rested in his arms with a sort of triumphant grin, gurgling happily, while Mog looked on tolerantly, beaming on both of them. She rose slowly from the stool, filled the kettle at the sink, and put it at the side of the fire, then she sat down again.

'Dere,' said Jo-Jo seriously, holding the baby before him in his arms, like a sacrifice. 'Dis is what Ah'm fightin' foh'. Ah don't want him to grow up an' go t'rough all Ah've suffered. He's gotta come to a bettah world. Yes sah! Ah'm fightin' so's mah little sonny will have a chance to grow up a man 'mongst udder men.'

He looked at the infant, his moist eyes passing like

a caress over the child's warm body, then he hoisted the baby in the air again and held him at arms length, admiring him. His manner changed once more, his voice bubbling over with pride.

'Ain't he one grand kid?' he said enthusiastically.

Alec nodded, but he couldn't help feeling a cut above all this parental sentiment. Suddenly Jo-Jo flattened his face against the boy's little rump, and baring his teeth, pretended to bite him. The baby screamed with delight, and waved his hands in the air. Jo-Jo turned to Alec.

'Dere. Jest you hold him,' he said.

Alec took the piccaninny in his arms. The strong spine, with its little knobbly joints, pressed against his fingers. The skin had the touch of soft velvet, and a soft glow seemed to come from it. The boy wriggled in his arms with the supple grace of an eel, he seemed to be full and bursting with rosy life. Alec was afraid to hold him for long, the little beggar twisted so, he might slip right out of his hands. He revised his views on parental sentiment; regretfully he gave the child back to Jo-Jo. He'd certainly got a kick out of holding that little lump of black mischief.

Mog came over and retrieved her child. She sat down on the stool again, and laid the baby across her lap, dusting some powder between its thighs. It lay contentedly, kicking its fat legs, looking like a cherub from some Negro Heaven.

Going home, Jo-Jo's 'Ah bin to Russia' echoed in his mind recurring like a well-plugged theme song . . . Russia! . . . Surely that was the solution to all his problems? He wondered why it had never occurred to him before. The more he thought of it the more certain he felt that that was his one chance of salvation. A rejuvenated country trying out a huge experiment, needed men, needed workers. He was a worker, his credentials were clear, his father's occupation 'Journeyman Tailor' was written across his birth certificate. And in a sense he wouldn't be beginning there anew, but rather reforging the links his father had snapped. His father had belonged to Russia, his grandfather and generations of forbears before him had all been chained to the Russian soil. He felt now he belonged there too. This was a strong and clear orientation. Russia! He'd take to the life like a duck to water.

He made up his mind to find out all the details immediately. He was itching to do something about it, he felt that every day he stayed in England was wasted, thrown away. He stopped at a telephone booth, and hunted up the address of the Russian consulate in the directory. Then he walked home, whistling cheerfully . . . 'Ah bin to Russia' . . . Soon he'd be able to say 'I'm GOING to Russia!' . . . That would be the day!

The letter to the consul was not so easy to write as he had imagined it would be. He wrestled with the wording for hours, and when Olive came home she found him hard at it. At last, he finished the missive to his satisfaction, and rushed out to catch the last post.

When he came back from the street, Olive had cleared the table, and was throwing the spoiled sheets of paper into the fire.

'What's all the excitement about?' she asked him 'Trying to write a book or something?'

'No!' He crossed over to her and hugged her tightly, lifting her off her feet. 'No! We're going to Russia!' he said enthusiastically.

. . . 'Russia?'

She released herself from his grip, looking at him as if he'd suddenly gone off his head. He wondered why she was staring at him so curiously. Then it struck him. Of course! He hadn't said anything to her about it, he had taken her acquiescence for granted.

'Russia!' he said eagerly. 'There's a chance for us there Olive, they're short of workers. I'll get a job in Moscow or Leningrad, and you won't have to slave any more the way you do. There's nothing for us to look forward to here. To hell with it all! Will you come to Russia with me?'

She nodded her head slowly in assent, carried away by his enthusiasm. To her there seemed to be only one objection, that they couldn't talk Russian, but she supposed they'd soon get over that. He kissed her again. That was one thing settled. Only left now to hear from the consul . . . Roll on Russia!

CHAPTER XXXVII

THE following Saturday Alec waited indoors all the early part of the afternoon. There was to be a big anti-Fascist demonstration to Hyde Park, and after the meeting a deputation would march to the German Embassy and lodge a protest there. Jo-Jo was to call for him at two o'clock, and they were to go to the rallying point together.

At half-past two there was no sign of Jo-Jo. Alec waited another quarter of an hour, then he decided to go without him. He put on his hat and mackintosh, and went downstairs.

The landlady's parlour was on the ground floor, opening on to the passage that led to the street. She usually sat in there on an armchair, knitting by the window, with the curtains drawn, eyeing the passers-by. Alec stopped outside her door, maybe she'd seen something of Jo-Jo. Timidly he knocked, the first time he'd ever approached her holy of holies apart from paying the rent, and waited.

There was a rustling movement, as of somebody pushing something out of the way, then the landlady's firm step came towards the door. It opened wide, and she stood framed between the doorposts looking at him, folding her arms aggressively across her huge corsetted bosom.

'Yes?' she said, eyeing him severely, as though he

wanted to borrow some money, or complain about the state of the roof.

'Er — er . . .' Alec faltered. He looked right past her into the room. Staring at him disconcertingly from the opposite wall was a coloured head and shoulders enlargement of her late husband, wearing his uniform of sergeant, Royal Engineers. He gazed down sternly, a typical regular army martinet, his straw-coloured coif sleeked over his forehead, his small eyes set wide apart, with a huge Kaiser Wilhelm moustache spreading luxuriantly across his face. Just below his portrait rose the topmost pinnacle of an Albert Memorial sideboard, overloaded with pictures of departed relatives, and clusters of consumptive wax fruit.

'Yes?' the landlady repeated coldly, without changing her expression. She was certain now he was after something or other.

'Er — I was expecting a friend,' Alec said. 'Has anyone called for me, Mrs. Carter?'

The landlady shook her head.

'No.'

'Nobody at all?'

She hesitated for a moment . . . 'Well, I was standing by the door,' she said slowly, 'when some black man come round, but I couldn't make out just what 'e was talking about.'

'— But didn't he ask for me?'

''E wanted to walk straight upstairs!' she said indignantly.

'Surely you could have let him in!' Alec protested.

Mrs. Carter stiffened. 'A black? — No fear! Not a

black! This is a respectable 'ouse. They talks about me and my lodgers quite enough as it is. I won't 'ave no blacks in my place. That's flat!'

The moustachios of the late Mr. Carter that had bleached for twenty years under the Indian sun seemed to stick up approvingly. That's the ticket missus! Alec turned away in disgust. He could think of no words to dent the ignorance of this massive monument of flesh. Thank heaven he wouldn't have to stick her for very much longer. Still, it was a damned cheek on her part to turn Jo-Jo away like that.

... 'At least, you could have called me down,' he threw over his shoulder.

'I didn't know you was in,' she replied, without the slightest sign of contrition. 'In fact, I told 'im you'd gone out.'

'That was very good of you!' he said sarcastically, fumbling with the lock. This was a real home from home, and no mistake!

'Just a minute!' Her voice called him back from the door.

'Yes?'

'There's a letter 'ere for you. It came last night. I forgot to give it to you, and I didn't see your wife — if she *is* your wife,' she added maliciously.

Alec snatched the letter from her hand, and went out into the street, slamming the door behind him with such force that the ground floor windows rattled. He was bursting with anger. The cheek of the woman! To turn his friends away, to hold up his mail! He should have banged harder still; it would have served her right if a couple of loose panes had smashed over her head!

He opened the typewritten letter on the doorstep. A hammer and sickle impressed on the top of the thick official notepaper caught his eye immediately. From the consulate! He began to read it, his whole body trembling with a feverish excitement, the words running together under his eyes, swimming in a black trickle across the page.

He read it through twice, at first slowly, a couple of words at a time, then right off without a stop. It was like stepping under an unexpected douche of cold water. The letter told him baldly, that reviewing all the circumstances, the consul had been unable to consider his application. He stood on the doorstep, staring at the signature, quite bewildered, then looking up he caught the landlady's face peering at him suspiciously from the window. He rammed the letter into his pocket, turned sharply on his heel, and walked off.

As soon as he reached the next turning he stopped, and read the letter again. It seemed final enough, they had taken all the circumstances into consideration. But surely they hadn't! — not all! There were so many things he could tell them that he couldn't put into an ordinary letter. If he couldn't go to Russia he would only decay. There was no future for him here, he'd just rot away! There must be some court of appeal. If he went up to the consulate he'd make them understand, or better still, to the Embassy. It was an idea! He'd go and see the Ambassador himself!

At Barker's he got off the bus, and inquired the way

to Kensington Palace Gardens. There, a top-hatted porter, with a string of medals on his chest, pointed out the Soviet Embassy.

'That's it,' he said. 'Harrington House. The first house over the hill.'

The sight of the Embassy sobered him a little. It was a huge sedate mansion, set well back from the road. Going to the Ambassador didn't seem such a simple easy thing at all, now he was here in cold fact. Something like panic caught hold of him as he crunched up the gravel of the drive. The house seemed to grow enormous as he approached it, the big green plants in the conservatory arched like a miniature tropical jungle through the windows to his right. It would probably be overrun with flunkeys too, who'd want to know who, and what, and when, and he hadn't the faintest idea of what to say. He felt he was going to make a prize chump of himself, but now, there was no retreating.

He walked up the steps to the massive oak doors, and knocked boldly. After a slight interval they opened, and a young man in a dark suit inquired his business.

'I want to see the Ambassador,' said Alec.

'Have you got an appointment?'

'No. But . . .'

'I'm sorry,' said the young man firmly. 'The Ambassador is not at home.'

Alec put his foot against the door. He could see a lofty dim hall, and a man seated at a desk bending over some papers just a little way inside.

'I say comrade!' Alec shouted.

The man looked up. At that moment a second man entered the hall and walked towards the desk. Alec recognized the newcomer as the Ambassador; he couldn't be wrong, he'd seen his photograph often enough. Now was his chance!

'Comrade Ambassador! Comrade Ambassador!' he shouted.

The Ambassador turned towards him, rather surprised. The door-keeper meanwhile was trying hard to push Alec outside, but he held on grimly.

'Comrade Ambassador! Just one word with you comrade!'

The Ambassador looked at him for a moment, then nodded to the attendant.

'Let him in.'

The young man stepped back, and Alec passed into the hall. His heart beat faster. This was Russian territory!

. . . 'Yes?' said the Ambassador kindly.

Alec told him briefly of the reason for his visit. The Ambassador listened thoughtfully, one hand in his pocket, the other on his chin, smoothing his trim black beard.

. . . 'Well,' he said at last. 'What do you expect me to do?'

Alec's heart gave a little leap. The Ambassador's query seemed sympathetic, as if he wanted to help him. Alec opened his mouth, but before he could reply, the Ambassador walked towards an off-room and beckoned to him to follow. He opened the door, and spoke a few words in Russian to someone inside, then he turned to Alec.

'Go in,' he said. 'My attaché will explain everything to you.'

The attaché stood up as Alec entered the room. He was a tall man, broad shouldered, with keen grey eyes, and close cropped fair hair. He waved Alec to a chair and sat down opposite him, a table strewn with documents between them. He smiled good-naturedly, and passed a flat white box to Alec.

'Cigarette?' he asked – 'Soviet Cigarettes.'

'Thanks!'

Alec helped himself to a cigarette, and the Russian took one too, and they both lit up. The attaché leaned back in his chair and blew out a puff of blue smoke.

'Now. What is the tr-ouble?' he asked, speaking slowly, as if he still had difficulty with the language.

Alec leaned towards him, and repeated his story. As he spoke he grew more and more confident, he felt things were going swimmingly. The attaché smoked quietly, listening patiently without interjecting a word. Occasionally he nodded, as though to emphasize that he understood very well. When Alec had quite finished the attaché snubbed his cigarette on an ash-tray, and cleared his throat.

'What is your work?' he asked.

'Tailoring.'

'What is it, you are a cutter or something?'

With his fingers he imitated the motion of a pair of shears. Alec shook his head.

'No. Just an ordinary workman.'

'Hmmm! The position my friend is this,' said the

attaché. 'We are not so short of semi-skilled workmen in Russia, especially in trades like tailoring. The men our country needs are technicians, engineers, mechanics, surveyors; highly qualified craftsmen, and even those are finding it difficult to get into Russia. A few years ago they used to come across on a temporary visa, get a job, and stay there permanently. Now, that sort of thing has been stopped. No one is allowed to come to work in Russia unless he or she can produce an invitation issued direct from the Soviet Government.'

'. . . Oh!'

Alec's face fell. It was hopeless. He had no idea it was hedged around with so many restrictions. He didn't want to hear any more.

'You can't do shorthand, or type in Russian can you?' the attaché asked jocularly, and continued without waiting for a reply, 'You see we are very short of typists in Moscow. All our girls want to study engineering. No!' he concluded, serious again, 'I'm afraid you haven't a chance.'

Alec got to his feet. There was no longer any point in his staying there. He'd heard his sentence, now it was straight from the dock to the jail. The attaché noticed his woebegone expression, he hadn't thought he would take it so hard. He crossed to Alec, and placed a sympathetic hand on his shoulder.

'I am very sor-ry,' he said.

The patient eyes of a painted moujik with a ragged beard, and a sack on his back, followed Alec from the room. He had a dim impression of the man at the desk looking up curiously from his papers, the doors opening as if they worked automatically, and walking down steps, steps, any number of them. Then he was amongst crowds again, in the High Street of the Royal Borough of Kensington. Well, that was another nice little trick he'd pulled. Now he thought it over rationally, there was hardly anything else they could have done. It was an insane thing to have imagined that he only had to write to the consul to be snapped up as an acquisition, and another act of lunacy to crash in on the Ambassador. He looked at his watch. Half-past five. He might still catch Jo-Jo in Hyde Park.

When he reached the park the meeting was over, and the demonstrators were reforming their ranks. He had no difficulty in picking out Jo-Jo under the big N.U.W.M. banner, and fell into step beside him.

'Where yoh bin all de afternoon?' Jo-Jo asked.

'I waited indoors till nearly three,' he replied.

'Ah went round foh' you, an' yoh landlady wouldn't let me in. She told me you was gone.'

'Yes I know,' said Alec. 'She told me when I asked her if she'd seen you.'

'Dere!' said Jo-Jo. 'Don't dat prove Ah'm right when Ah says de blacks get more kicks dan anybody? — Anyways, ah'm used to dat. But surely, it didn't take all DAT long to get to de park. Where yoh bin?'

'I went to the Russian Embassy.'

'What foh'?'

'To try and get a job in Russia.'

'An' what dey say?'

Alec shook his head disconsolately. Jo-Jo laughed out loud.

'Yoh silly!' he said. 'What dey want you foh' in Russia? Besides, deys plenty work foh' you to do heah. Dis is where you belongs. If it was so easy to go to Russia, what sane workin' man would stay in any of dese capitalist countries? Dey'd be goin' across so fast all de British fleet couldn't carry dem, not if all de boats was ten times bigger dan de 534. No sah! We gotta stay heah. We don't scuttle from de hold like rats cause de ship is sinkin'. We'se de crew, we'se got responsible jobs. We'se got to chuck de officers overboard an' save de ship. De ship is got to be saved, 'cause it's ours, it belongs to us. Yes sah! It's our ship!'

Alec walked beside him in silence, thinking over what the negro had said. It was all true enough, but giving up the idea of ever going to live in Russia was a bitter pill to swallow.

Suddenly the demonstration stopped. A forest of hands shot up in the air, giving the signal to those behind to cease marching. Alec was jolted out of his reverie by sullen, excited cries. He looked ahead and saw a cordon of mounted police blocking the road. An inspector was bending over the side of his horse, arguing with the leaders of the demonstration.

'What's wrong?' Alec asked.

'Nutting much,' said Jo-Jo. 'Dey had a week's notice dat we was sending a deputation to de Embassy, an' dis mornin' dey writes back and says dey can't see us.'

'Well?'

'Well, we decides at de meetin' dat dey *is* goin' to see us, an' dat's where we's goin'.'

The parley apparently over, the inspector straightened himself, and sat bolt upright on his horse, like a cavalry officer. One hand gripped the reins tightly, while the magnificent roan animal pawed the ground nervously with its hooves. The leaders went back to the demonstration. One of them lifted his hands for silence.

'Comrades!' he yelled in a hoarse voice. 'The police say they've got orders not to let us go any further. They say we must turn back. What shall we do comrades? — Go back?'

Angry murmurs ran the length of the line, and shouts of 'No!' 'No!' 'March on!' Jo-Jo's face set in a grim line. He gripped the pole of the banner tightly, and his head stuck up like a shiny black bullet. Alec felt the pressure of the men behind, and with one impulse the demonstrators moved forward.

The inspector raised his hand. Shrill whistles rent the air, and foot police poured into the road from a concealed turning. Alec trod on something soft, a man had fallen. Curses. Cries, savage oaths; the police laying about them with their truncheons. He saw Jo-Jo fall to the ground, and a policeman bend over him and wrench the pole from his hand. Then he himself was violently brushed into the gutter by the powerful impact of a horse. As he fell he curled up instinctively, and covered his head with his hands, and heard the sharp clop of hooves stepping over him daintily like a ballet dancer.

When he looked up, the road was almost clear. Two policemen were dragging Jo-Jo away. He got to his feet boiling with rage, surely it was no crime to carry a banner! With a wild cry he started towards his friend, but two hands gripped him from behind and pulled him on to the pavement, and a voice whispered harshly in his ear, 'Don't be a bloody fool!'

Suddenly there came a triumphant roar. The demonstration had broken through lower down. The inspector gave a curt command and the mounted police wheeled round and galloped off to meet the new menace. Nothing could stop Alec now. He shook himself free and rushed after them, a crowd of workers racing at his heels. . . .

That Saturday was Olive's late night. When she left the café at half-past eleven, she was surprised to find Alec waiting for her at the corner. She noticed a strip of plaster on his forehead, but refrained from questioning him about it. She guessed he'd got hurt in the rumpus outside the Embassy; the papers were full of it. A cut forehead wasn't so bad, better than a broken arm, or leg, or bashed-in ribs. She was thankful for small mercies; as it was, she had been worried about him all day, half expecting a telephone call any minute from the station, with a request for bail.

Alec was still silent on the bus, and Olive, after a gruelling day, was only too thankful to be left alone. She was half dozing already, counting the minutes until she would be able to throw herself into bed, and sleep. Alec opened the street door for her, and following behind, let it swing-to with a crash. Olive gave a little jump and turned round, startled.

'Quiet!' she whispered, white-faced. 'You'll wake up the whole house!'

She tip-toed up the stairs, and Alec climbed after her without attempting to soften his footsteps. Olive turned again, her finger on her lips.

'Shush! Be quiet for Heaven's sake! Mrs. Carter'll be down on us like a ton of bricks!'

'Let her!' said Alec. 'I expect she'll give us notice Monday in any case.'

'Oh? . . . Why should she give us notice?'

'Well . . . We had a bit of a row . . . I'm not sorry. I'm fed up with this dump anyhow!'

Before even the door of their room was properly shut behind them, Olive threw off her outdoor clothes, and started to undress. She put on her pyjamas gratefully, and flopped into bed.

'. . . It's a pity!' she said, yawning. 'Now we'll have another moving job. I thought we'd stick on here till we went to Russia. Maybe you'll hear from the consul this week.'

Alec shook his head. 'I've heard.'

'Well?'

He gestured with his hands, and shook his head once more.

'Forget about Russia,' he said.

She yawned again. Oh well, Russia or no Russia, it was all one to her. She was only sorry for him. Poor Alec! She stretched herself out in the bed, keeping sleep off a few seconds longer, as an extra luxury, and lay still, so still it seemed that the only part of her that moved were the varicose veins throbbing in her tired legs . . . When would all this struggle end? World without end, work without end. Ham and eggs and tea for two, for ever and ever and ever. . . .

Alec paced about the room restlessly. He had no desire for sleep, so many things had happened to him to-day, and the events were still playing themselves out in his head, like bits from a newsreel. He crossed to the window, and looked out into the street. Now, in the dark, it seemed quite habitable, as if human beings could flourish there. He looked at the black wall opposite, with its curtained rectangular peep-holes, and glimmers of light like shrouded candles. Behind that wall whole families were dying, they thought it was living, herded together, a dozen people to a couple of verminous rooms. But beyond, there *had* to be something better. In his ears resounded again the rhythmic tread of the demonstrators, and in his mind the negro's face stood out, strong and confident, shining as if a fire were burning beneath his skin. Surely if a black man belonged here, he did too? Of course! Of course he belonged! He'd known it all the time. The past few weeks didn't count, they had been like a bad dream; it had needed Jo-Jo's broken English to wake him up. Everything led irrevocably to this. He had shirked the issue too long, now it had been decided for him. His place was in the ranks, it was criminal to stay out any longer. He marched again, step for step by Jo-Jo.

All over the world men must be marching. Black men, white men, yellow men, all with the same cries, the same slogans. Freedom for the oppressed! They were the new life force, the new blood stream, and he was part of it, one of that world-wide fellowship. His pulse quickened. This was something to live for, even here! The red banner fluttered in the wind, and the tramp of the marchers echoed once more down the quiet West-End streets, a sombre threat and a hammered warning. The Christmas decorations suddenly looked hollow and unreal, like paint on a dying clown. The new reality swept on with its grim challenge. Goodwill towards all working men, and for the rest, no Peace. No Peace until the disinherited regain the Earth!